A Hidden
Sicilian History

A Hidden Sicilian History

Second Edition

Ettore Grillo

Strategic Book Publishing and Rights Co.

Strategic Book Publishing and Rights Co., LLC
USA | Singapore
www.sbpra.net

For information about special discounts for bulk purchases, please contact Strategic Book Publishing and Rights Co., LLC. Special Sales, at bookorder@sbpra.net.

ISBN: 978-1-68235-406-3

To Sebastiano Cannizzo

ACKNOWLEDGMENTS

I thank the SBPRA publishing house and all its staff.

In particular, I thank Vice President Bruce Martin, a highly experienced professional, sensitive, and with a big heart, who has always been friendly towards me.

Contents

The Find

Everyone has a unique history and a special life. Some people—prophets, great philosophers, musicians, artists, kings, heroes, and so on—have left a mark on the history books. Good or evil, those who have stood out are remembered by posterity—people like Julius Caesar, Napoleon Bonaparte, Adolph Hitler, Josef Stalin, and others. At their demise, the lives of ordinary people are like dead leaves swept away by the wind when fall arrives. They sink into oblivion, as history pays them no mind. In addition to the history of individuals, there is that of nations, but no book can include the biographies of all the people who formed the nations of the world.

In truth, if it were possible to write an enormous history book, it should record the life stories of everyone who has populated the earth over the centuries and millennia, for each living being has something different and particular to say, often worthy of being handed down through the generations.

Everyone follows their own special path; it is impossible to find two lives that match perfectly. Even members of the same family have different stories. It is like seeing birds in the sky. They may look identical, but they are all different in both shape and character. There are long and short lives, and the loss of someone young is like a bud cut by the gardener before it blooms fully.

In Greek mythology, the Fates, three ladies dressed in white, symbolized man's fate. The first, Clotho, spun the thread of life on her spindle; the second, Lachesis, measured its length by her rod; the third, Atropos, cut the thread of life at her will. Nobody was able to oppose them. Even almighty

Zeus was powerless against the Fates; he was unable to change a person's fate even if he strongly wished it.

Countless people over the years have wished to know their destiny and future. For that reason, there have been astrologers, magicians, wizards, and oracles to consult. In ancient Greece, the Oracle of Delphi was renowned, as was Cuma in Italy. Inside the temples, usually sacred to the god Apollo, virgin priestesses, called sibyls, told people their future, and it seems that their predictions were always exact.

Not only in mythology, but also in the Bible there are instances of the prediction of the future. In fact, the prophets were inspired people that told of future events. They predicted the destiny of Israel and facts relating to the life of Jesus, as in the case of the Prophet Isaiah who lived around the eighth century BC.

Nowadays, horoscopes and astrological forecasts rage. Even disbelievers read their daily astrological forecast in the newspaper or on the Internet, or they listen to it on the radio or while watching television.

The issue about the existence of destiny more or less remains unsolved. People's lives look like numberless straight lines, each one a different color and nuance, which emanate from a common center. Like the rails of a railway, they never meet, and each of them follows its own predetermined course. According to some theologians, and even in some passages from Martin Luther and Saint Paul, the trajectories of our lives follow a route already set. They believe that God has prearranged everything.

Poets, philosophers, and writers think in the same way. Free will is just illusion; man cannot act apart from the events that drag him here and there like a flag that changes direction according to the wind. It is as if a great architect had already designed a path for every living being to follow, as a director does when giving the actors roles in a play.

When I was a high school student, I asked my philosophy teacher this question: "If God is omnipotent and all-seeing, he knows what is going to happen in the future, since he is beyond space and time. Therefore, where is our free will? If the life to come is already plotted and known, what can people do to change a scene already set up?"

She was a beautiful lady from Catania. All the schoolboys had fallen in love with her. As for me, I was enchanted by her Junoesque bearing and the way she arranged her black hair, which she gathered up and kept fast with a hair slide every day new. She had the habit of sitting at her desk and testing the students who stood by her. We schoolboys couldn't help but take a peek at her legs when she was sitting on the chair and her skirt was pulled up a little bit.

Despite her beauty and gracefulness, she was strict and demanding. She gave me her answer by paraphrasing Saint Augustine: "If I see a man standing on the edge of a ravine, I know he is going to throw himself down. Yet, he is free to give up his resolution to die." She meant that despite the fact that the future is already known, our free will remains.

Her answer didn't convince me then, and I am still not convinced. In my opinion, if God knows our future and the events to come, it means that our lives run along tracks that have already been set.

The length and quality of every person's life is different. Many lives are gloomy from the beginning, others are luckier. Since life on earth is unstable, most lives are made of ups and downs—that is, continuous alternation of joys and sorrows. Some personal stories consist of struggle: to make a living, conquer the heart of a loved one, come to power, attain freedom, and so on. However, each life is like a piece of a huge jigsaw puzzle in the sky. You cannot find two identical pieces.

I am fond of technology, but when I see youngsters looking at their smartphones all day long, a question arises in my mind: "Is this the goal of life?" And whenever I see a self-employed worker or an employee working tirelessly on Sundays and public holidays, I ask myself again, "Is this what our Creator wants from us?"

On that point, I cannot help thinking of a surveyor from my town. He was Mario. I had known him since I was a child. He was a good-looking boy, a few years older than me. Whenever I saw him in the street, he was always surrounded by friends. I don't remember ever seeing him alone. He really enjoyed his life. Being tall, stout, and cheerful, he married a very charming wife and had a daughter. He had a job at a state firm that did road maintenance and was an indefatigable worker. His office was by the side of the Palermo-Catania freeway. Quite often, when I went to Catania by bus on Sunday, looking out the window, I spotted his car in the parking lot near his office.

Life is impermanent and changeable! Mario, the cheerful boy in his youth, turned into a cold office worker. His job was everything he had in his life, but it was also an escape from something he considered unbearable. His family appeared to be close-knit in public, while in the privacy of their home things went differently. His wife, Laura, detested him, while his daughter, Marisa, didn't esteem her father. Work was a diversion for him and an escape from the burden of his family. If you run away from situations that cause you stress, anxiety, or uneasiness, you have the illusion of ridding yourself of unbearable problems, but you cannot overcome your plight by escaping; instead, you should cope with your issues and solve them.

One day, the tireless surveyor, Mario, was found dead in his chair with his head laid on the desk in his office, a revolver still gripped in his hand. That was evidence that his overzealousness was just an escape from his family problems.

I have seen people reading books continuously. At first glance they looked very cultured, but observing them carefully, I noticed that their so-called love for books was just an escape from reality.

Even going to Mass may be an escape. I once noticed a man that attended a 6 p.m. Mass and then headed for a seven o'clock Mass in a different church. He had nothing to do, so he moved from one church to another just to kill time.

A dear friend of mine who was a Protestant pastor once confessed to me that he had had many arguments with members of his congregation and had been on the verge of quitting his office, but he didn't because he didn't know what he would do without his church.

In Enna, there was a shop seller who had a notions store. Even though he became too old to run his business and no customers bought anything from him, he continued to keep open his shop just to have a way to spend his time. Otherwise, he had no idea what he would do.

A trader of building materials struggled daily to run his business. He was always overwhelmed with debts and had a lot of trouble honoring his bills of exchange. Finally, he went bankrupt, and all his worries vanished like snow in the sun.

One day, I stumbled across him. I didn't know he had quit his job. Seeing him, I had the feeling that he was much too flabby; moreover, he was pale.

"How is business?" I asked.

"I don't work anymore!" he answered with a disconsolate air.

"You should be more relaxed now without anything to do. You have no worries!"

"No, it is not quite that easy. When I worked, I had lots of worries about my customers, my suppliers, the bills and taxes to pay, and I had many things to do. I had so many concerns that I couldn't sleep at night, but I felt alive and satisfied. Now, with nothing to do, I am like a dead man."

Some individuals seek shelter inside their family or get married to feel safe and stable. Somebody becomes engaged to a person who is a second-choice lover. They cannot get the one they truly desire and resort to living with someone they don't love just for the sake of safety.

Sometimes, making friends seems to be a daily challenge. People go to dance schools, gyms, bars, and similar places hoping to make friends, but the more friends they get, the more they feel alone, because their search for friendship comes from the void they have inside. Running after friends might be an escape from reality as well. People fear remaining alone and flee from their loneliness to fill their inner void through friends.

All the cases mentioned above are clear examples of escaping from reality, from life. As for me, I have always avoided watching too much television or sitting in front of my computer for too long, for this too can be an escape from reality.

I don't set myself up as an expert. I am just a good observer of people and situations. I have realized that anything we get involved in so much that we become identified with it takes us away from real and authentic life, which requests that we live it fully and in all its facets.

What is the meaning and goal of our lives? Over the years, everyone has tried to answer this dilemma. If our lives are predestined, we don't need a goal, for our aims and targets have already been laid out in heaven long before we were born. So why strive for a target? We could just live as it naturally happens and go with the flow of destiny as migratory birds do when they follow the airstream. We wouldn't need to improve ourselves to overcome our shortcomings that prevent us from reaching our targets.

Not everyone has a goal. Some people spend their lives with no purpose, others have short-term or long-term goals. There are innumerable variations in people's ends, for, as I told above, every life has its own story which is different from another.

Since I am not sure about the existence or nonexistence of destiny or predestination, I want to do my best to learn more about this issue, but also about life, death, and the end of life. To do this, I collect data and information, not only through my travels, but also by reading different kinds of books, even those old and rare.

The public library in my hometown is located within a few rooms of an old palace that long ago belonged to Andrea Chiaramonte, who was one of the eminent noblemen in Sicily at the end of the fourteenth century. He fought against the Spanish but was defeated by them. They arrested him and, after a short trial, sentenced him to death by beheading. He was executed in Palermo in front of the Steri Palace where he had established his court. Meanwhile, his family members forfeited all their assets in Sicily, including the prestigious palace in Enna, which later was split into three parts. One part was given to the Franciscan friars, one was used as a court of law, and the smallest one as a civic library.

The ancient and precious volumes are kept on the highest wooden shelves. To reach them, you need a special ladder provided by the attendant. One day, I was on the ladder looking for a book that told the history of my town, when something that looked like a scroll fell onto the floor after having slipped from a gap between two big volumes on the Spanish Inquisition in Sicily that were placed on the highest shelf. Therefore, the scroll was supposed to be a part of them or connected to them.

I got down from the ladder and bent down to pick up the strange roll, which at first sight contained sheets of paper tied up with a string. Thinking they were precious, rare writings, I headed for the director's office to hand in the yellowish bundle of sheets.

I knocked on the door of the office and a man with a stentorian voice prompted me to enter. As soon as I saw the manager, I recognized him. He was one meter and ninety centimeters tall, which is unusual in Enna, where the average height is a bit more than one meter and sixty-five centimeters. Whenever he walked in the streets with his German shepherd, he stood out, but I didn't know he was the boss of the local library. His nose was quite red, with small hollows similar to those of a raspberry, a clear sign of his tendency to drink too much wine. However, he was well-mannered.

"Please, sit down. How may I help you?"

"I found this bundle of sheets on the highest shelf in the main reading room. I think it belongs to the library."

"When did you find it?"

"Just now, not five minutes ago."

The director untied the roll and unrolled it on his desk. Then, he sneezed several times. "Sorry!" he said. "I am allergic to dust."

"That is no problem!" I replied.

The roll contained handwritten pages. The paper was yellow with age and had a nauseating, moldy smell. The director examined the material carefully. The writing was readable, even though some lines were a bit discolored. From the expression on his face, I had the feeling that he wanted to get rid of those old papers as soon as possible.

"These are not in the list of the things that belong to the library, but I want to ask the attendant. He's worked at the library for almost forty years. He is near his retirement by now and knows everything about the old volumes in the library. Who knows, maybe he can give us some useful information. Abraham!" he called out.

Instantly, an old, short man with greasy, white hair and prominent jawbones came along.

"Have you ever seen this stuff?" asked the boss.

The attendant, who wore thick glasses for shortsightedness, came near the director's desk and bent his head forward to have a better look at the papers. He took off his spectacles to see clearly and eyed the stinky sheets narrowly, leafing through a few pages.

"No, sir," he said. "This is the first time I've come across this kind of stuff in our library."

"Okay, this means that the shelves need better cleaning!" said the irritated director. "Tomorrow morning, you must remind the cleaner to dust and mop all the shelves properly, starting with the upper ones. Now, go toss this filthy stuff that is soiling my desk and my hands."

The attendant showed annoyance and replied, "The cleaner does her job every morning beyond reproach. As soon as she comes, she dusts off the volumes on the upper shelves and then the others. Finally, she sweeps and mops the rooms."

I was so engrossed in the squabble between the two that I didn't pay attention to the attendant, who was already carrying the roll away under his arm, but I soon returned from my reverie and turned towards him when he was about to open the door and leave the room.

"No, please don't throw away those sheets of paper. I can use them," I said to the attendant.

The old man turned back and looked at the director, waiting for orders. "*Res derelictae, res nullius,*" said the director with his thundering voice.

"What does that mean?" asked the old man.

"It means that whoever finds a derelict thing has the right to take possession of it if it is not reclaimed by the rightful owner. This gentleman," continued the director, pointing at me, "has the right to keep what he has found. You can give him the material."

The old man stepped back and handed me the papers. I folded and bound them with the string and left the library, rushing home.

Outwardly, they looked like historical records. I had the impression of having stumbled across a rare precious report about an *auto-da-fé*, which were held in great numbers across Sicily at the time of the Spanish Inquisition. According to some historians, 114 autos-da-fé were celebrated in Sicily from 1501 to 1748.

The word auto-da-fé comes from the Portuguese *auto da fé*, meaning an act of faith. It consisted of a public ceremony where a sentence of the Spanish Inquisition was carried out. Before the enforcement of the judgment, the condemned person was paraded between two lines of people, their hair was shaved, and then they were dressed in a donkey cap and a sack, on which were painted the grounds of the judgment. If it was painted with a full Saint Andrew's cross, it meant that the condemned person had repented in time to avert the execution; a half cross showed that he had been just fined, while the flames meant that he had been sentenced to death at the stake.

A solemn Mass attended by city authorities and a large gathering of the townspeople was celebrated where the auto-da-fé took place. People came together in great numbers, as if there was a festival, and many street vendors flocked from the nearby towns and villages to sell cakes, carobs, licorice, and similar things.

In Enna, death sentences were enforced in the largest square, which is called Municipality Square. Near the scaffold was the small Church the Lady of Sorrows, where the convict received the confession of sins and Holy Communion before filing towards the stake. Recent excavations in the Church of the Lady of Sorrows brought to light a crypt where those condemned to death spent the last hours of their lives.

It was also possible that the roll contained a report of one of the many capital sentences passed in Sicily against sodomites. It has been reported that at the time of the Spanish Inquisition, from 1547 to 1640, about one hundred capital punishments were enforced against homosexuals and people who had had "deviant" sexual intercourse, like oral or anal sex. Copulation with animals was also liable to bring a death sentence. In fact, any sexual activity not directed toward procreation was considered a capital sin. Sometimes, the confession of those sins was wrung out by torture, even though at the time of the Spanish Inquisition it was not necessary to torture the suspect, because the mere sight of the instruments of torture was enough to persuade the alleged culprit to confess all their sins—or whatever else the inquisitor wanted them to confess, for that matter.

While heretics went directly to the stake to be burnt alive, homosexuals and sexually indecent people, as an act of mercy to make their death less agonizing, were usually strangled or hanged before being burned at the stake. In any case, death sentences were enforced publicly to serve as a deterrent to others.

The main difference between the Medieval Inquisition and the Spanish Inquisition was that the former was directed by the pope, while the latter was under the authority of the king of Spain, who enforced the Inquisition's rules not only in Spain but also in the Spanish possessions like Sicily, Sardinia, and Mexico. Spanish kings used the Inquisition not only to judge heretics and witches, but also to get rid of their political opponents, on the pretext they were heretics.

One of the most atrocious instruments of torture was that called "the mouse." The inquisitor inserted a live mouse into the vagina or the anus of the person suspected of heresy or witchcraft. The head of the small rodent was directed towards the inner organs of the prisoner. Sometimes the anus or the vagina was stitched closed. The little rodent, striving to find a way out, penetrated the victim's body, scratching and biting their bowels, and provoking shooting pain.

I was so anxious to arrive home that, lost in my reverie as I was, I didn't even see the people in the street. I thought about how strange it was that one person's trash was another's treasure. I was sure of having found a document worth more than all the volumes in the library of Enna.

Once at home, I dusted off the sheets and laid them onto my desk, eager to decipher them. I wanted to know all the details of the trial against the heretic that had been sentenced to death and the exact protocol the inquisitors applied.

The handwriting was clear and readable. Nevertheless, the more I leafed through the pages, the more I got disenchanted.

Unfortunately, the papers didn't contain either a report of an auto-da-fé, as I had hoped, or a detailed account of a death sentence of the Spanish Inquisition against homosexuals.

The first page held the title "A Hidden Sicilian History," and about three hundred numbered pages followed. The script was anonymous; its author could have been a man or a woman, young or old. There was no evidence to trace the author.

I read it line by line, day after day. To my surprise, the events told in the manuscript didn't belong to the remote past. How was it possible that such recent happenings were written on such old, filthy paper? One of the plausible answers was that the author had stocked a considerable amount of paper at home, which had then turned yellowish due to the dampness of the place where it was stored. That was not unusual in Enna, where the fog wrapped up the city very often and not many houses were fitted with a heating system.

I don't know why, but I doubted the author knew what kind of research I was doing and had purposely put the roll on the top shelf to make me find it.

I also wondered why the author didn't try to publish their work. There were a few probable answers. First of all, it is not easy to be a published author, and if you want to publish a book yourself, you have to spend some money. Perhaps he couldn't afford it. There was another likely explanation: the author was so shy and introverted that they didn't feel comfortable asking anybody for help in getting the manuscript published.

Nevertheless, the writing denoted the presence of a person of action, someone strong and extroverted. The only answer I thought acceptable was that somebody had told the events to the author, who then wrote a tale that didn't come from their own experience or imagination.

As soon as I finished reading the story, I was undecided as to what to do. In fact, in my opinion, the tale was full of tortuous reasoning, and some passages were so absurd that nobody would believe them. It looked like a script for dead people. In fact, some characters seemed to have returned from their graves to tell their lives to a world in which they no longer belonged.

Perhaps the manager of the library, who intended to throw away the useless, yellowed old sheets of paper, was right. But, after much mulling over what to do with the strange finding, I at last realized that it might be worth something. It was absolutely not trash, for it contained some useful information about the life and traditions in Enna, a mountain city in the center of Sicily.

I was hesitant about typing the contents and considered giving the work back to the library, but I was not sure if the manager would accept the gift. After ruminating for a while, I came to the decision to translate the story into English and have it published. I opted for the translation of the manuscript instead of maintaining the original Italian, because by doing so I thought it would fulfill the author's will. Indeed, he or she had intended to hand the tale down to whoever found it, in the same way somebody does when they fit a written message into a glass bottle and entrust it to the ocean. By translating and publishing the story in English, it would be more likely for it to cross the ocean and reach faraway lands, for there are people who can read a book written in English in almost every country.

A Hidden Sicilian History is not a great literary work. Its contents are deep, and it is neither engaging nor gripping. Furthermore, the translation from Italian into English is not perfect. English is my second language indeed! Although I tried to translate the manuscript perfectly, a careful reader may find errors in the English version, above all in the word order, because the two languages have a different syntax. However, *A Hidden Sicilian History* may be useful to those who want to learn something uncommon. As for me, I found the manuscript quite boring at times and full of abrupt digressions, but some details are really unique.

I decided to publish the work because, in my opinion, chance events don't exist. In other words, if I found that script, it was not by chance; a superior will wanted it, and maybe the author chose me as a means to spread their thoughts. Furthermore, apart from its literary style, which is not lofty, the manuscript is worth reading because of the considerable amount of information it contains. It will definitely broaden the reader's mind.

Enna is a small city, but over the years it has fostered the hopes of great spirits and people that have devoted their lives to missions in faraway lands, like Blessed Girolamo De Angelis (1567-1623), a Jesuit friar who left his hometown of Enna to follow his spiritual path. At the beginning of the seventeenth century, he went to Japan to spread the Gospel, but he fell into fierce persecution against Christians and had his life ended by being burnt at the stake. Enna is the birthplace of good writers like Nino Savarese and Napoleone Colajanni—the latter was also an honest politician and sociologist—and musicians like Francesco Paolo Neglia. The spiritual path followed by the main character of this story is worthy of note, though minor in scale.

Not many towns in the world can boast so peculiar a lifestyle. It is possible that if I hadn't published *A Hidden Sicilian History*, some of Enna's oral traditions would have been lost forever.

Events happen because they have to happen, not by accident. On Earth, there is an invisible thread that links those who have the same spiritual feelings, regardless of their race or skin color. They belong to the same spiritual race. The real races are not physical but spiritual, and you can feel it clearly whenever you have the chance to come across someone with similar feelings and spiritual nature. Through that bundle of paper sheets, the author wanted to create an invisible chain of spiritual beings, which he intended to become broader and broader.

What happened to the original lost manuscript? After I translated it into English, I retied the sheets of paper with the same string they had when I found them a year before, and then, unbeknownst to the library staff, I took the scroll back to the library and put it on the top shelf between two volumes on the Spanish Inquisition, and it is still there.

Here is the translation . . .

Chapter One

The Church of Santa Croce

Ladies and gentlemen, let me introduce myself to the reading public. My name is Vincenzino, and I am one of the characters in a drama performed some time ago on the stage of the deconsecrated Church of Santa Croce in Enna.

The small house of worship had a single nave and was located on Via S. Agata. If my memory serves me right, it could have been about fifteen meters long and eight wide. The facade was gray, the gable roof was covered with red clay tiles that had lost color over the years, and a small rose window with stained glass at the top of the central facade gave it a touch of artistic style. A few stone steps led to the green wooden entrance door.

When the church was deconsecrated, the sacred objects were removed from the nave and from the sacristy: vestments, holy pictures, statues, ostensory, chalice, and so on. Some objects were moved to the Church of La Donna Nuova, in the upper part of Enna, others to the nearby Parrish Church of San Cataldo.

The stage, which occupied the entire width of the nave, was erected in the same spot where once was the altar. Of all the statues and holy paintings that once crowded the walls, only one about two meters high portraying the Virgin Mary on the crescent with a crown of twelve stars on her head and a snake under her feet was left on the far right of the stage.

We used the ex-church for religious conferences and for theater and musical comedies. Children also came and played ping-pong or table football, but when there was a performance, the ping-pong table and the bagatelle were put away in the sacristy, and the nave was filled with chairs for the audience.

Our director, Paolo, was a middle-aged stout man with a limping walk due to an untreated fungal infection in his feet. He had been the sacristan of the small church and had developed a deep passion for theater and poetry over the years. He had also written a lot of poems in Sicilian and enjoyed reciting them in front of his friends. He was unmarried and lived with his single sister, Maria, who was also the costume designer for our theatrical group.

The house where Paolo and Maria lived was very old; it had been built at least a hundred and fifty years ago and was connected to the church. I can say that Paolo was a lucky man, because his sister took care of him the way a wife does with her husband—except having sex, of course. Since Paolo was terribly messy, Maria tidied up the house all the time.

Unlike Paolo, who was dark-skinned, Maria was blond with green eyes and always with a smile on her face. I don't remember ever seeing her angry or sad. She was a curvy and attractive woman, three years younger than her brother, and had had a few occasions to get married, but for one reason or another, her engagements failed. I had the feeling that she unconsciously broke them so as not to leave her brother, whom she was very fond of!

As a sacristan, he'd had the task of keeping clean the place and locking the wooden chairs, which were stacked at the entrance. In fact, a long time ago, the churches in Enna were furnished with just two or three rows of pews, usually reserved for those who had acquired the right to use them as a result of the donations they had made to the church. All the others who wanted a seat during Mass or a religious function had to rent a chair from the sacristan, paying a small fee. Nowadays, Mass is held every day in Catholic churches, but before the Second Vatican Ecumenical Council, it was said only on Sundays and holy days. Instead, the Benediction was celebrated in the churches every evening on the weekdays.

After each function, Paolo took care of cleaning the hall; moreover, he restacked the chairs and fastened them with an iron chain that he padlocked.

After the Church of Santa Croce was deconsecrated due to the shortage of priests, Paolo lost his job as a sacristan, but he still had money to live on. While remodeling his house some time ago, he found a clay piggy bank in a walled-up niche full of gold *marengos* (coins minted in the early 1800s to celebrate Napoleon Bonaparte's victory over the Austrians in the village of Marengo, Italy). On the other hand, his sister worked as a nurse at the local hospital and contributed towards the living expenses.

As for our play, Paolo organized the work by making each actor perform his own life story on the stage. According to him, life is just a play, or sometimes a tragedy, but never something real.

He selected seven actors, three women and four men. The choice of seven players was not random. Being the number of creation, seven had a special meaning in Paolo's mind. Actually, the number seven is recurrent in the Bible and also in life: seven are the days of creation, seven the musical notes, seven the colors of the rainbow, and so on.

The three actresses were Cettina, a comedienne as lively as a goldfinch, very short with a melodious voice. The audience couldn't help but laugh just at seeing her gesturing while at the same time saying jokes. Elvira, unlike Cettina, was quite tall with bobbed black hair. Her voice sounded like the chirping of a nightingale. Giulia, was one of the most elegant and polished women in Enna. She was a teacher of Italian language and literature at the high school in Enna. Even though she was almost as short as Cettina and a bit ugly, her refined manners made up for her physical defects and gave her an irresistible charm.

As for the male actors, I was a bit awkward and shy at first, but Paolo pushed and encouraged me so much so that he turned me into a real actor, uninhibited like the others. He said that my tone of voice was deep, manly, booming, and without dialectical inflection; on the other hand, my height was a little above the average, and my emerald green eyes and my auburn hair had a great effect on the audience. The other three male players were Gaetano, Carlo, and Elijah, who were professional actors, accustomed to acting in theaters full of audience. They had performed not only in Enna, but also in other cities in Sicily. They agreed to act on the stage of the small theater of the Church of Santa Croce only for the sake of their friendship with Paolo. The most theatrical of them was Carlo. His voice was a continuous alternation of high and low tones. In my opinion, he was too melodramatic. Gaetano was the most handsome and talkative of us. He would have been an excellent player, but he had the disadvantage of speaking with a heavy Sicilian accent—too heavy indeed. Paolo tried hard to change his inflection, but it was to no avail. Elijah had the same name as Saint Elijah the Younger, a great saint from Enna. Perhaps because of his name, he liked to talk about religions, and he actually had a great culture on the subject, but as far as theater was concerned, he was a mediocre actor, in my opinion.

Paolo's sister, Maria, had designed and sewed seven tunics, each of a different color of the rainbow. My tunic was yellow. In the play, the actors sat on white chairs facing the audience. When the performance began, the house lights were turned off, the curtain opened, and an usher with a dark-blue cloak buckled around his neck with a gold-colored buckle lit a line of candles that formed a horizontal number eight, the symbol of infinite space and time. At the rear of the stage beside the candles, two musicians with a guitar and a violin constantly played their background music. Whenever it was their turn, one of the actors stood up, slowly turning their body towards the audience, and with a lofty tone started telling some episodes in their life.

Paolo said that this kind of play had a cathartic meaning, which was equivalent to inner cleansing, beneficial to the actors and to the audience as well.

At the comment that the play would take a long time to get to the end constructed this way, Paolo replied that time doesn't exist; it is just human work. It is our limited mind that creates the concept of space and time, but in the universe, it is always now, and there are no distances between one side of it and another.

Every day we performed that play, and a few people alternated in the hall of the church, now turned into a theater house. For Paolo, it was important to play with a loud voice without lowering the sound at the end of the words. For him, words had to be uttered in their wholeness.

It didn't matter if we moved along the stage or stood unmoving like statues. We were free to gesticulate as much as we liked. For our director, theater meant freedom of expression. Life is freedom as well.

Someone objected that actors were not normally allowed to freely express themselves, because they had to follow a script, but Paolo said that it was not like that in the beginning. Anyway, his job as a director was to restore the primeval freedom of expression, which was typical of the actors on stage. All the players alternated according to Paolo's direction. He was a kind person as well as a qualified director.

When my turn came, the lights in the church were put out. Everything became pitch black, except my yellow tunic. The background was the starry sky and the candlelit number eight silhouetted against the sidereal space. As soon as the musicians struck up their instruments, I got up from my chair, and a stage floodlight followed my movements. I headed for the center of the stage and started off by telling a few episodes from my childhood and adulthood. I confined myself just to telling what, in my opinion, was most significant, for my aim was to pass something interesting and educational onto the audience, leaving aside whatever might sound trivial.

Chapter Two
The Estate in Pollicarini

Sebastiano was my father's uncle, although he was only five years older than my father. This is because he was my grandmother's younger brother, and the age difference between my grandmother and Sebastiano was eighteen years. He was born at the beginning of 1900 in the old neighborhood of Saint Peter and showed a disposition to acts of bravery from a young age. In 1917, despite being just seventeen, he volunteered for active service during the First World War.

Later, with the rise of Mussolini, he became a member of the Fascist action squads, taking part in the march on Rome. As the Fascist Party became established, he fit in first as one of the Blackshirts and then got a job at the Fascist Federation of Enna. Apparently, he had an important role in the party. Thanks to him, my Uncle Salvatore got a contract as a hauler of military supplies in Ethiopia. Moreover, he was the one who helped my family's emerging business by ensuring the needed political support.

His wife, Annette, was ten years older than him. They were childless, and he considered his nephews and nieces as his own children. Angelina was the oldest, followed by Salvatore, Giuseppe, Francesco (my father), Mariano, and the youngest, Amelia. He loved all of them, but he was particularly fond of Salvatore. They were almost the same age and had an astonishing likeness, so much so that they looked like brothers. He admired Salvatore's heart, because he always put the family's well-being before his own.

My grandmother, Maria, died very young, when Amelia was still a little baby. When my grandmother fell ill with the disease that led her to death, she was so weak that she could not breastfeed Amelia, who was then in danger of dying as well. At that time, powdered milk was not available, and cow or goat milk was not always right to give to newborn babies. Some people used donkey milk, which was believed to be similar to human milk, to feed babies in extreme situations, but this kind of food was not always within reach.

No one in the family seemed to be able to save Amelia's life. My grandfather, Giovanni, was resigned to losing his wife and his daughter, but Salvatore did not lose heart and began frantically searching the streets and alleys, trying to find a wet nurse that could feed Amelia. He got information and knocked on many doors to find a woman with a baby that would take Amelia on her breast as well, but he was met with many refusals, for most of women had milk enough for only one baby. At last, just when his hope was about to die, he found a lady that had recently given birth and who would accept Amelia to her breast as well. He took his dying sister into his arms and rushed to the wet nurse. Thanks to her elder brother, Amelia is still alive. Every time Sebastiano recalled this episode, he got a lump in his throat and his eyes moistened with tears.

After Mussolini's death, the Fascist Party was suppressed and its reconstitution forbidden by the law. Of course, the Fascist Federation of Enna was also banished and Sebastiano lost his job.

What to do without a job? Sebastiano was in his forties, and the economic crisis after the war was biting the small city of Enna. Many people were starving, and if it hadn't been for food aid from the Americans, many townspeople would have died of starvation. As for me, even though my family was not poor, the food was not abundant. When I recall those times, I remember always being hungry.

To clothe us children, my mother reused things. I wore the woolen sweaters and underwear that had belonged to my elder brother, and my younger brother reused my clothes once they became too tight for me as I grew taller.

Fortunately, Uncle Salvatore had bought a plot of land for his family in a district called Virardi during the Second World War. When the war was over, he purchased another estate for himself and for his brothers in an area called Pollicarini, so Sebastiano was employed to take care of his nephews' properties.

When I was eight years old, I got typhus, and the next year I again got typhoid fever because I had eaten too many unwashed loquats. After fifteen days of fever, my body was heavily weakened and my weight went down. When I looked at my legs, they resembled two thin wires. My parents were very worried about my condition, so they decided to send me to the countryside for summer holidays and entrusted me to the care of Sebastiano.

The estate in Pollicarini, with its ancient house, had belonged to a knight named Greca. It was the first property the nobleman sold to finance his political campaigns. Greca was a rare example of a person who ruined himself by engaging in politics. He was born of rich and noble parents and got married to a young noblewoman named Caterina. Their union produced a daughter, but their marriage didn't last long. According to many, one day Caterina lost her balance while shaking a blanket on the balcony of her house and fell headlong onto the street. The truth was that she committed suicide.

Outwardly, his wife's suicide didn't affect Greca's behavior. He continued his political career as if nothing had happened. I still remember him with his big belly, wearing a gray suit and chatting with people in front of the city hall. Inwardly, he was not as unperturbed as he appeared. In fact, his wife's suicide had turned his life into hell.

When a loved one commits suicide, the reactions of their family members are often contrasting.

One day, I had the chance to meet a lady whose son had married a girl from Argentina. At first the husband and wife led a happy life, but as time passed their ties began to deteriorate. The husband's character got more and more gloomy until he put an end to his young life.

His wife returned to her country, but his mother couldn't accept that her son had passed away so suddenly. She was shaken to the extent that she couldn't even get rid of the furniture that had belonged to her beloved child. She wanted to buy an apartment in order to keep all her son's belongings inside. Finally, she bought the apartment and arranged her son's kitchen, bedroom, living room, laundry, and everything that had been in some way connected to him. She recreated the atmosphere of her son's home, thinking him still alive. Every evening she went to that empty apartment, prayed, and imagined talking with him. She also bought a garage to keep her son's car, and she paid for car insurance and taxes every year. For her, it was unthinkable to sell her son's car.

A twenty-year-old university student named Mario was engaged to an eighteen-year-old schoolgirl named Claudia. They dated for three years, but he felt that he was too young to be engaged. Furthermore, he couldn't bear the excessive influence the parents of both families had on their lives. He wanted to extricate himself from the commitment, but he didn't know how to get rid of the tie that he considered too tight for his age.

Nevertheless, Claudia's mother continued to press her daughter, who could do nothing to keep the engagement alive. The exasperating situation finally led Claudia to kill herself. Both families blamed Mario as being guilty of driving Claudia to suicide. The police even investigated him for allegedly inciting the suicide.

From that day on, Mario's life changed radically. Although the prosecutor dropped the charge of incitement to suicide, he continued to feel guilty for the rest of his life and atoned for his bad deed by leading a life marked by his dedication to helping his neighbor as much as possible. Obviously, his willingness to do good deeds was not his natural disposition, but he suppressed his evil instincts to become a good man and make up for his alleged sin.

Greca's reaction to his wife's suicide was the complete opposite. He wanted to forget whatever he could remember of his wife. He joined the political fray and began to sell his properties in Enna, one by one, to buy two hotels in Taormina, where he at last moved to spend the rest of his life. He left the furniture, pieces of cutlery, Chinese vases, and valuables in the house in Pollicarini. He wanted to erase the memory of the tragedy that had marked his life at any cost.

The house had been kept in good condition and had many rooms. Sebastiano took a small room with a bed for himself where he spent the night. When I came to stay with him in the house, he added a bed in his room for me.

The house had two stories, as well as a small room in the loft that we could enter through a winding wooden staircase. I only remember going to that room once or twice with Sebastiano. He kept his chicks there, for he figured that magpies were not able to snatch them while they were in that room.

The person that worked the land lived in two rooms on the first floor. Other rooms were used as a stable and a wine cellar, as well as places for a wood-burning oven and a wine press. The henhouse was detached. There were two she-asses in the stable, co-owned by my family and the agricultural laborer.

A bit over the courtyard near the roost there was a cistern where the rainwater from the roofs was conveyed to be used to drink. Near the cistern there was a stone basin with some water for the bees to drink. The beehive was a bit further out and looked like a little house. Sebastiano had planted a long line of prickly pear cactuses to keep people away from the bees, which were vicious.

The house still kept the shape it had when it was built. Everything had been left intact: the black piano, the sofas, the tables, the chairs in the dining room, and even the stonework kitchen with its fine, decorated tiles, which opened onto a wide terrace encircled by railings on three sides.

Many portraits on the walls revealed the figures of Greca's ancestors. They gave a sinister look to the house, but Sebastiano wanted to keep everything intact to respect the memory of those who had passed. At that time, there was no electricity in the countryside, and we used an old oil lamp that had been left by the previous owner to provide some light.

The closets were still full of clothes. There were evening dresses and suits. I remember seeing a black waistcoat with a vest pocket watch. I tried to imagine the atmosphere in the house, and I could feel it was not happy. Many times, despite appearances, rich people are the most miserable of all.

Anyway, even the rich die, and now they are in another dimension, or maybe they have disappeared into thin air. What happens when we die? What happened to the Greca and his wife? Did they leave some imprints in the house, or at their death did they just slip away and vanish like the flame of a candle when it is blown out?

We started the day with a cup of coffee made by Sebastiano. He didn't want me to call him Uncle Sebastiano, even though he was old enough to be my grandfather, because if I did, he would feel too old. In fact, his spirit was still young, and his body was also young. Despite the fact that he was sixty, his legs still looked like two tree trunks, and his rosy cheeks had no wrinkles. Only his white hair showed that he was no longer young.

Usually, after a cup of coffee and some slices of bread and biscuits we went hunting—or rather, he was the hunter; I just followed him. We set off around five in the morning when it was still dark and the air brisk. As we walked and the darkness of night gave way to the half-light of dawn, the air got a bit warmer.

To hunt, we used our three white long-haired dogs. Although they were mongrels, they had exceptional noses. Obviously, I didn't have a weapon and confined myself to walking behind Sebastiano. He carried a double-barreled rifle, a cartridge belt around his waist, and a bunch of strings where he tied the animals he killed.

He made the cartridges himself, and for that purpose, he used a kit made of a precision balance to weigh both the gunpowder and the pellets, and a tool to push the gunpowder and pellets inside the case. According to him, a good hunter must be able to make his cartridges himself, because a different kind of gunpowder and pellets are needed depending on the game you are going to hunt. The weather was also important in selecting the proper gunpowder. If it was dry, he used the gunpowder of such and such brand; during moist or cold weather, he employed a different brand.

Not many times in my life have I seen scenery comparable to that which I beheld when I went to hunting with Sebastiano. I'll never forget the sun rising from the flanks of the volcano on Mount Etna. The great mountain was still covered with snow, the sun was visible to the naked eye, and the morning star was silhouetted against the sky like a brooch on a blue, reddish mantle.

While we walked, our dogs tried to rouse rabbits, Greek partridges, or hares. Suddenly, in the distance, a rabbit moved quickly towards its burrow, but Sebastiano's unerring eye didn't give it a chance. I rejoiced over that rabbit's death, unaware that with passing time I would change my opinion about hunting, for I would become incapable of even hurting a fly. I would come to love all creatures. But at the time, I was very cruel to animals and insects. In the upper level of the hen house at Pollicarini, Sebastiano had created a shelter where the domestic pigeons could nest and reproduce. When the young pigeons had grown enough to be eaten, we took them from the nest and killed them by drowning. I enjoyed drowning the small creatures, even though I didn't much like their meat.

Another cruelty I used to commit was killing the flies on the windowpanes by burning them little by little. First, I burned their wings with a lighted match, and then when they couldn't fly, I tortured them with the tip of my burning cigarette until they died.

If I happened to catch a mouse, its death would be atrocious. I'd smear it with gasoline and then light a match and set fire to the tip of its tail. The mouse would catch fire and run for a while until it died.

What I was not able to do was another cruelty that some people of my town committed. Whenever two dogs were making love, they remained stuck to each other for a while, because the male's penis could not withdraw from the female's vagina. A stupid, dull boy would fetch a shovel and strike a blow between the two dogs to get them separated. This appalling action usually resulted in the death of the male dog.

Sebastiano said that hunting was a noble sport and a good hunter had to respect a code of honor, which consisted of not killing more animals than he needed for eating, respecting and loving nature, and never lighting a fire to drive out a wild animal. He never used a ferret to get a rabbit out of its burrow, because it could kill many rabbits inside the burrow, giving rise to useless slaughter.

Moreover, he recommended I put prudence before greediness. "Never jeopardize the life of a dog when you shoot game," he said. "When you are shooting, the scope must be clear. Refrain from shooting near farmhouses or in poor visibility."

Sebastiano taught me how wild animals live. The rabbit is an animal of fixed habits. It spends all his life in the same territory, while the hare lives in the flatlands and changes its territory continuously. There are animals that live long, like the crows, while there are insects, like the mayflies, that live just one day; they are born in the morning and die that night.

Sebastiano looked after me like a father, and every time I had a relapse and my fever rose, he made me eat bread and honey. In his opinion, honey is rough and can remove throat inflammation. However, thanks to him, my health improved and my legs became fuller.

We usually hunted until nine in the morning and then stopped because, according to Sebastiano, it was too hot for the dogs to smell the rabbits. Once at home, he gutted the rabbit or the bird we had caught, and after a few hours he cooked it.

Once the sun was high in the sky, it was impossible to hunt or work the land, so Sebastiano, the farm laborer, and I stayed in one of the rooms on the first floor waiting for lunch. It took several hours before we could have lunch, so we sat on the bench and just waited. Nowadays, this kind of thing is inconceivable. People always have something to do—watch TV, listen to the radio, play on the Internet, or talk on the phone—but at that time we didn't have such devices. Television hadn't been invented yet, and we needed electricity to listen to the radio.

While we were waiting, my attention was caught by the singing of the cicadas that filled the silence of the countryside. I asked Sebastiano to show me one of them, but he said it was not possible because they lived on the high branches of the trees and it was not easy to spot them. Anyway, those long waits in the sunny summer mornings gave me the ability to endure waiting. We confined ourselves to waiting until lunchtime.

Sebastiano and I ate our meals on normal plates, but the farmhand ate more than we did and put his meals on his special dish called a *lemma*, which means "big bowl" in Sicilian.

The daily dish was pasta with cabbage and potatoes seasoned with olive oil. Meat was too expensive and not easy to get. Only when Sebastiano killed a rabbit or a bird did we have meat. On special occasions, the farmhand wrung a chicken's neck. In any case, we couldn't preserve meat because we didn't have a fridge. To keep a watermelon or a melon cool, we put it into a basket and then down into the cistern where the water was quite cold. The only thing we preserved for a long time was cheese, which was yellow because of the use of saffron in its preparation and stuffed with black pepper grains. In the evening, our food was lighter and consisted of cheese or poached eggs that Sebastiano, in a kind manner, forced me to eat.

The table was laid by the farmhand, who never shorted us good wine. I was too young to drink alcohol, but Sebastiano poured a little red wine into my glass, diluting it with water. In his opinion, good wine makes good blood.

In the afternoon when the air got cooler, we went around the land to check if everything was okay and the farmhand had done an acceptable job. Sebastiano took particular care in the vineyard, which had to be dug often and sprayed with dry sulfur at the right time. A belated spraying could compromise the harvest.

Whenever he spotted walnuts left on the ground, he picked them up. That seemed quite strange to me.

"What are you going to do with those two walnuts in your pocket?" I once asked.

"I'll take the walnuts home and put them in the pile on the terrace to dry. I want to increase my nephews' finances!"

At night before going to bed, we sat on the terrace gazing at the starlit sky. There was not much illumination in Enna at the time, and in the countryside, there was no power at all. We had an oil-fueled power supplier in the house in Pollicarini, but we used it only on special occasions. So, we put our oil lamp on the marble top of the kitchen table, set two chairs on the terrace near the walnut heap, and sat just watching the sky.

Moths thronging around the glass of the oil lamp cast their shadows on the walls of the kitchen. The moths' shadows projected on the walls looked much bigger than their actual size and made a pyrotechnic display that mesmerized me. From time to time, our dogs barked at other roaming animals or passersby, and the sky seemed an immense blue space where every kind of heavenly body twinkled. There were so many spots of light that even counting to a billion would not be enough. Some sources of light were very bright, while others were barely visible. Sometimes meteors appeared and disappeared, streaking the vault of heaven.

Sebastiano taught me the constellations and the influence of the moon on the earth. "Whenever I sow a field with wheat," he said, "I consider the cycle of the moon. You cannot sow a field at random, but only when the moon is waxing. In that way, the seeds absorb energy from the moon and the seedlings will be strong."

"Today is the fifteen of August," Sebastiano said one night, "and in the neighborhood of Fundrisi, in Enna, they are celebrating the mid-August feast of the Madonna."

"What kind of celebration is it?"

"Tradition says that Mary, Jesus's mother, didn't die, unlike all other human creatures. She fell asleep and the angels took her to heaven."

"What is that long line of clouds in the sky?" I asked.

"Those are not clouds, Vincenzino. It is the Stairway of Saint James, also called the Milky Way. Through it, souls go up and down. They come from faraway stars, stay on the earth for a while, and then migrate towards new lands in the sky, always passing through the Stairway of Saint James."

"Where are the sky boundaries, Sebastiano?"

"There are no boundaries in the sky. It is infinite, with neither beginning nor end."

"That's impossible! I cannot imagine anything without a limit. Everything has a boundary. For instance, our estate borders other neighboring properties."

"If you are convinced that there is a border in the sky, tell me what there is beyond the border, Vincenzino."

"Another universe, of course!"

"And where is the border of the second universe? And that of the third and so forth? As you see, we cannot find the last border, and we cannot understand the universe because our minds are limited. It is like trying to teach our dogs to read. You'll never succeed."

"When was the universe created, Sebastiano?"

"According to some scientists, it seems that the universe is expanding; in fact, both stars and planets run away from a center. In other words, there was a time when all the matter of the universe was concentrated in only one spot—like a storehouse where bricks are packed. Then suddenly the storehouse exploded and the bricks were cast into the space. They started moving in different directions and are still moving."

"Who made the storehouse explode?"

"I don't know, Vincenzino. Christians say that it was God who did it. Atheists, who are people that don't believe in God, think that the explosion happened naturally."

"What was there before the explosion? Has the storehouse always existed or was it made by someone?"

"I am not able to answer your question, Vincenzino, but I am sure that when you become an adult, you'll study this subject and find the answer. Now, it is the time to go to bed."

"Do you know, Sebastiano, where all those souls are going that you say come up and down through the Stairway of Saint James?"

"We'll talk about that tomorrow. It's too late now."

In the small room where we slept, before falling asleep under the light of the moon and stars that filtered through the shutters, Sebastiano told me his war feats.

"You have to know, Vincenzino, that I was on the front line when I served in the army. During the Second World War, I was first sent to Croatia and then to Cyrenaica, and the sound of the bullets whistling close to my ears became familiar. One night in Croatia, our platoon was crawling towards the top of a hill, but the enemy was doing the same on the opposite slope. Suddenly, we heard the rat-tat-tat of enemy gunshots. Can you figure out what happened, Vincenzino?"

"I have no idea, Sebastiano."

"Well, the officer that commanded our platoon panicked, and instead of leading his troops to attack, he began to tremble with fear and was on the brink of having a nervous breakdown."

"What did you do without a commander, Sebastiano? Did you run away?"

"Not at all, Vincenzino! I scolded the commander. 'What kind of man are you? I will lead the troops to attack if you keep shivering in your shoes!' But he said, 'I don't want to die! I am still young!' I said, 'You have to die one day or another, but it is better to die and leave a scent behind you, instead of stinking if you escape as a coward.'

"The young first lieutenant was shaken by my words, and he gathered his strength and led our platoon to victory."

"Sebastiano, how is it possible that you went to war twice, always stayed on the front line, and never got even the tiniest injury?"

"It was not my destiny to die or be wounded in war. Remember, Vincenzino, even though you plan your future very carefully, you cannot succeed without God's will. Some people say that you can win your battles only if they are just and according to your destiny. Once there was a great commander named Napoleon Bonaparte who had planned his last battle at Waterloo very carefully. On paper he could not lose, but many unpredictable hindrances got in his way."

"What were those adverse conditions, Sebastiano?"

"Many! Above all, the torrential rain that lasted two days and turned the battlefield into a quagmire. He was forced to delay the use of his most powerful arm, the artillery, which was not effective on a muddy ground. That day, some of his generals made mistakes as they had never done before."

"Do you mean we have to consult a fortune teller before doing anything, Sebastiano?"

"No, I don't mean that, but I want you to learn this principle: do your best in your life, but keep in mind that the earth is a tiny spot in the infinite universe governed by good energy. All actions must conform to the good, universal energy. In the end, only goodwill prevails. Therefore, keep a pure heart always. In this way, you will win all your battles."

As time passed, I often asked myself if the feats Sebastiano told me were true or the fruit of his imagination. Either way, he left the inclination toward dignity and bravery in me, and above all to be a good and honest person.

The condition of my body improved greatly while I stayed with Sebastiano. The healthy, natural food and the salubrious air of the countryside strengthened me both physically and emotionally. I was not the thin boy of two months earlier; now I was even stouter than many boys my age. My parents could hardly believe I was their son, for even my mood was much more cheerful.

Nevertheless, staying in Enna didn't help me. I suffered from the strange atmosphere of my hometown, which was not very congenial to me.

Chapter Three
Enna Seventy Years Ago

When the Second World War was over, most women in Enna didn't work outside the home. They were housewives, dependent on their fathers, and once they got married, they were submissive to their husbands. You saw ladies dressed in black in the streets, the symbol of sorrow. The close relatives of those who died wore black to show their grief. Every time a person died, the walls on the streets were covered with death notices as if the whole city was mourning.

The duration of mourning varied according to the degree of kinship with the dead person, but the following criteria were usually observed: if an uncle, or a cousin, or someone not a close relative had died, the woman dressed in black for three months. If a child had been lost, the woman dressed in black for five years. If a sibling had passed away, his or her sister dressed in black for three years. If the dead person was the husband, the widow dressed in black the rest of her life. I never saw my grandmother wearing clothes that were not black. She had lost two children and her husband.

As for men, the duration of mourning was much shorter than that of women. They usually wore black suits for a few days, and then confined themselves to wearing a black tie, or a black armband, or a narrow black band around their jacket collar, or a black button on their jacket or on their shirt collar.

In the afternoons, after having done their chores, the housewives sat on their chairs by the window and watched the people walking in the street.

At that time, Via S. Agata was unpaved, and in the early morning you could see goats in the streets and the shepherd milking them and selling their milk to the housewives. It was a very fresh product. The goats were white in color, long-haired, and quite tall with upright coiled horns. Nowadays, there are people in the cities who have never even seen a goat!

One day, I was playing with other boys my age near the Church of San Cataldo, when one of my mother's cousins passed by.

"How dare you play here!" she said with a stern face.

"Is it forbidden to play?" I asked.

"Don't you know that your grandfather died?"

It was the first time I had heard that someone in my family had died. My parents hadn't told me about his death. Hearing those words, I immediately stopped playing. It was also the first time I had experienced the feeling of guilt. I really felt guilty for not observing the mourning of my grandfather's death, and I immediately ran home. My parents were not there, just the maid.

"Is it true that my grandfather died?" I asked.

"Yes, it is."

"I want to go see him."

"Do as you like," said the maid, "but children shouldn't see corpses!"

"I am not a child! I want to go anyway. My grandfather is not a corpse!"

As I insisted, she washed me and dressed me up, and then I rushed to my grandparents' house. I was entering what had been my grandparents' bedroom when my ears were flooded by my Aunt Carolina's cries.

"Little Vincenzino, you haven't been here for a long time!"

She was right. I had not gone to my grandparents' house for two months. I felt even more guilty.

The dead body had been placed in the middle of the room. He wore white gloves and a gray suit. As soon as I arrived, I gave a quick look around the room full of people sitting on chairs that had been arranged along its perimeter. I spotted my mother and headed for her.

"Go kiss your grandfather's hand," she said.

I did as she had told me and then took a seat next to her. A man came in and cried desperately. He was not one of our relatives, but just a worker in the sulfur mine my grandfather owned.

After the dead body had been kept in the room for two days, the moment of separation came. Two gravediggers entered carrying an empty coffin. At that moment, everybody cried and screamed with pain. My grandmother blocked one of the diggers and tried to prevent him from taking away her loved one, but unfortunately it was not possible.

The coffin was carried by my grandfather's friends on their shoulders to the nearby Church of San Cataldo, and after Mass it was set on a hearse dragged by two black horses. There were thousands of people at the funeral, and all of them followed the hearse to the cemetery. At that time, there were not many cars in the streets, so whenever there was a funeral, the streets were closed to traffic. Sometimes the municipal band played a funeral march for very rich or special people.

When the funeral was over, we returned to my grandmother's house. I was horrified to see a squabble between my Aunt Carolina and my mother. Aunt Carolina accused her sister of having been absent during her father's disease. Actually, she was right. My mother said that she didn't know about the seriousness of his disease because my father had hidden it from her. My aunt's daughter cried desperately. As for me, I didn't cry, but that didn't mean that I was not grieving over my grandfather's demise. Often, we don't openly express our sorrow, or we suppress it, while others show openly what they feel.

After the funeral, we had a tasty dinner. For eight days we were served breakfast, lunch, and dinner by our close friends. All the family members gathered around the table. In Enna, you could not make the time of mourning at your will. It had to last eight days. During this time, besides being served delicious food by our relatives and close friends, we received visits from our neighbors and acquaintances.

The food we received was more delicious than anything I had ever eaten before—so much so that a doubt arose in my mind: "Is this a time for mourning or a party?"

After eating, we returned to the double bedroom to receive those who came to visit and offer their condolences to us. I sat next to my mother and observed the scene. The visitors entered the room and gave condolences to the family members, starting with my grandmother, and then they sat on the chairs scattered across the room and remained silent or talked with some of the family members.

My grandmother and her daughters were dressed in black. My father and Aunt Carolina's husband wore black ties. As soon as a new visitor came in, my mother and Aunt Carolina put a sad expression on their faces. Then they started chatting with the newcomers. While they chatted, their faces were quite relaxed, but whenever somebody entered the room, they stopped chatting right away and took on a sorrowful look. In fact, it was mandatory to show a contrite face; otherwise, folks might think they didn't mourn the loss of their father.

Since then, I have learned the difference between "to be" and "to look like." The change in my relatives' faces in showing grief meant that appearances had great importance in people's eyes.

The custom of judging by appearances was widespread in Enna.

Even today, not only in Enna, we tend to judge by appearances and fail to see what is really hidden inside every human being.

Chapter Four
My Two Uncles

After my grandfather's death, his house had a sinister look for me. Almost every evening after dinner, my mother and I went there to visit my grandmother, Angelina, my only grandparent still alive.

There was no TV or Internet at that time, but human warmth made up for lack of electrical devices. Relatives, friends, and neighbors gathered at somebody's home and spent their evenings together talking about this and that.

It was cold during the winter in Enna. To warm up the rooms, people made use of braziers burning charcoal slack. It was customary to cook small pieces of sausage or a few potatoes, wrapped in yellow, thick paper of the kind used to wrap pasta, in the charcoal. We children vied with one another to eat a small piece of that delicacy.

Since the climate was colder than today, the roofs of the houses were white with snow almost all winter. Whenever I came home from school, I had the bad habit of warming up my frozen feet and hands in front of the brazier. The sudden contact of my cold hands and feet with the heat of the brazier caused me chilblains. My fingers and toes had purple hues and itched. To cure them, I wore thick woolen socks and gloves.

My grandmother's house was the meeting place for the families of her daughters, who were Aunt Carolina and my mother Rosa Maria, the family of a neighbor nicknamed "The Fat Woman," and the family of my grandfather's brother, Armando, who had recently returned from Venezuela.

During one of these meetings, Uncle Armando told us that my grandfather's friends tried to discourage him from buying the house, for the place was haunted by ghosts. After that, he was unsure whether to buy or not, but in the end, he decided to make the purchase because he had been told that the story of the ghosts was a trick plotted by the tenants who wore white sheets at night to look like ghosts. They staged the show in an effort not to be evicted.

Was it really a staging of the tenants? That evening, I didn't miss a single word of what Uncle Armando said. At the end of the story, he added a detail that made my blood freeze in my veins. He said that one night while he was looking out on the balcony of his house, he thought he saw two flames chasing each other on the roof of my grandfather's house.

After that, I had doubts about the farce staged by the tenants. I suspected the house was really haunted. One day I asked my mother to tell me the truth.

"Is it true that ghosts haunt your mother's house?" I asked her.

"What are you talking about, Vincenzino?"

"Uncle Armando said that one night he thought he saw two flames running after each other on the roof."

"Don't put all your trust in what Uncle Armando tells. He drinks too much wine. When he is drunk, he mistakes candles for lanterns."

"Do you believe in ghosts, Mom?"

"No, I don't, Vincenzino, but I want you to know that even though I've never seen ghosts in my father's house, I was not happy when I stayed there. My father was too strict with his children, and my mother often beat my brothers until they bled. You have to know that your name is Vincenzino as a sign of respect to my younger brother, Vincenzo. He was a great brother, and I loved him more than my own eyes. Every time my mother hit him, I interposed myself between them and often was beaten instead of him.

"My father had such a stern look that we couldn't meet his eyes. Furthermore, he couldn't stand it when children cried; therefore, we had to stifle our crying even when my mother beat us. Laughing was not allowed in that house, because it was considered imbecility. All we could do was just study or work.

"Only boys continued their studies. After attending primary school, the girls stayed at home helping do chores, or in the best of cases they learned the art of embroidering. I went to the Franciscan convent every day to learn how to embroider. I really enjoyed life in the convent. Surely, I would have become a nun if it had been my choice, but without my father's permission, I couldn't do anything. Therefore, I used the art of embroidering I had learned from the nuns to embroider my trousseau.

"That house was really ill-fated. One of my younger brothers, Biagio, died of malaria at the age of ten; the other, Vincenzo, died when he was nineteen. It was an awful experience for me. I would have given away one of my organs to save Vincenzo's life, but unfortunately nothing could be done for him."

"What disease killed Uncle Vincenzo, Mom? Was it malaria as well?"

My mother let out a deep sigh, and then she looked around, uncertain what to say to me. Finally, she found inspiration and gave me an answer that seemed to be plausible.

"No, it was another kind of disease. One day, he went out with a ballerina and died."

"What is a ballerina, Mom?"

"She is a woman that dances on the stage of a theater."

"How is it possible to die just by walking with a ballerina? Maybe somebody killed him."

My mother tried to change the subject. "Your Uncle Vincenzo was very handsome. His blond hair and green eyes were the envy of his friends. At school he was not—"

"I want to know how he died, Mom!" I insisted.

"You are too curious! You are very young now. Let's go to the bedroom. I want to read you a poem I wrote for Vincenzo last night. For me, this poem is wonderful."

We went downstairs, my mother opened one of the dresser drawers, and picked up an accordion-shaped piece of paper. As soon as she unfolded it, her eyes misted over with tears.

"I loved my brother, Vincenzo, more than anything else, even more than my children. Now," she said in a trembling voice, "I will take this poem to my mother's house, and I'll put it in the drawer where I have placed my other poems, Vincenzo's writings, and his diary."

I didn't quite understand the poem my mother read, because my attention was focused on her tears, but I pretended to listen to her until she finished reading, so as not to displease her.

I found it strange that Vincenzo had died because of walking with a ballerina, so I wanted to find out if it was a real story or just one of my mother's lies. I decided to ask Aunt Carolina, who knew the truth for sure.

Chapter Five
My Grandparents' House

My grandparents' house was an old Sicilian-style, four-story building. It had been made partly from building stones and partly by digging out the rock. The rocky part was the first floor, which was used as a stable, a storeroom where my Aunt Carolina's husband kept his builder's tools, and as a wine cellar. A bit further, a henhouse had been realized by digging out another side of the rock.

In front of the house there was a wide vegetable garden that we could access both from a gate that looked onto the public street and from the front door of the house. To go to the second floor, where my Aunt Carolina lived with her family, it was possible to go through a steep, dark staircase dug into the rock that swarmed with small rodents or pass through another gate in the upper part of the street. I usually opted for the latter.

A courtyard was at the entrance of the upper part of the house. It was a common area for both Aunt Carolina and Grandma, while an external stone staircase linked the courtyard to the third and fourth floors where my grandmother lived alone. It was Aunt Carolina who took care of the henhouse and the vegetable garden.

Every evening, the hens came back from the garden to the poultry pen, and my Aunt Carolina then inserted her forefinger into the hens' vent to check if they were ready to lay their eggs the next day. Not all the hens used their straw nests; some preferred to lay their eggs in a recess in the vegetable garden. So, it was important to know how many eggs were expected, in order to find the ones that were in some corner in the garden.

On the third floor there were the landing, the lounge, and the wide double bedroom with a balcony that looked out onto the garden. After her husband's death, my grandma kept that part of the house dark. The blinds were always down, and it was pitch dark inside. I had the feeling that besides her personal grief, which she manifested by wearing black clothes, the third floor of the house was also in mourning because of the darkness of the rooms. A narrow, dark staircase led to the fourth floor that had a very small bathroom, two small rooms, a kitchen, a large dining room, and another balcony.

My Aunt Carolina was always busy making bread, cooking, or doing other chores. Whenever she saw me, her eyes and lips conveyed her pleasure. That day she was in the courtyard. She had just wrung a chicken's neck and now was plucking it after having dipped it into hot water. Afterwards, she would pass the chicken over the fire for a few seconds to burn out the small feathers left.

Aunt Carolina was forty or so, and her hair was beginning to turn gray, but she was still a very beautiful lady, though a little bit plump. Her main feature was her smile, which she showed copiously, except for the rare circumstances when she was angry with somebody or something bad had happened to her.

These days, a subtle wrinkle crossed her forehead. She was worried because her husband didn't have a job and they might have to emigrate to northern Italy where it would be easier for him to get a position as a builder.

"Hi, Vincenzino. Don't you want to go play with the other kids today?"

"I am not a kid anymore. I am a grownup!"

My aunt burst out laughing. "Okay, Vincenzino, I see you are wearing long trousers. So, you are an adult now, are you?"

Without making any comment, I went straight to the core of my inquiry.

"Did you have two brothers, Aunt Carolina?"

"Yes, I had two brothers, but as you know, both of them died young."

"Could you tell me something about them?"

"Why come to me? You can ask your mother. She knows everything about them."

"Yes, I know, but my mother is not very talkative. She is too serious and always thinks about this and that. Her mind wanders in the clouds. She doesn't seem to care about talking with me much."

"Okay, as you like. I'll tell you something about my youngest brother. His name was Biagio. He looked like my mother. He was a good student, but whenever he had the opportunity to play football or other sports, he did, without caring much about studying. One day, my father presented him with a bicycle, and he was happy. He covered long distances on it, and he even dared to cycle from the town of Villarosa, which is on the plain, to Enna, which is on the top of the mountain.

"He had a strong likeness to my mother, to such an extent that he looked like Grandma with short hair."

Aunt Carolina went into her bedroom and from one of the drawers took an envelope that contained many pictures of her beloved ones, including one of me riding a papier-mâché horse that the photographer kept in his studio to photograph children. At the sight of my Uncle Biagio's photo, I was left speechless. He was standing at attention and wearing a black suit with children's trousers. His resemblance to my grandmother was astonishing.

"Sometimes," said Aunt Carolina, "he came home exhausted, and your mother, who was fond of him, washed him from his feet to his crown. Unfortunately, at the age of ten he got malaria and died."

"I didn't know there was malaria in Enna, Aunt Carolina."

"At that time, malaria was widespread in our area. Later, Mussolini eradicated the disease from our territory through a massive anti-malarial campaign. Nevertheless, not many people died because of it. Biagio was unlucky because he contracted the pernicious malaria that had no cure.

"But let's change the subject!" continued Aunt Carolina. "I don't want to talk about sad topics. I have cried so much in my life that I don't have any more teardrops to shed. I want to show you my wedding photos."

She opened her album, which contained pictures of her daughter receiving her First Communion with her mouth wide open and the priest in the act of putting the Host onto her tongue, her son riding a mule, her husband in a military uniform holding a sword, and herself with her husband on the day of their wedding. But at the sight of another picture portraying baby Biagio in her arms, her eyes got misty, and she closed the album and put it back into the drawer.

My aunt was almost crying at the thought of her brother when I, without giving her enough time to pull herself together, abruptly introduced my second question.

"How did your brother Vincenzo die?"

My question took her completely aback. She stammered for a few moments and then lost her self-control. Her words got stuck in her mouth, her lips dried, and then she exploded.

"You bad little rascal! Every time you come here, I get nervous. You should not come when I have a lot of work to do. Your mother has a maid, but I am alone in my house! I have to cook, bake, wash, hang out, and take in the washing. I have no time to chat with you. Go to your mother and let me work!"

I left her and rushed home. My aunt had behaved very oddly, and the feeling increased in me that something mysterious or unmentionable was linked to my Uncle Vincenzo's death. A few suspicions grew in my mind. One possibility was that my grandmother had beaten him with a stick so harshly that he died. Another possibility was that he had had a relationship with a married ballerina and her husband had killed him out of jealousy. A third possibility was that he had been kidnapped or the Mafia had killed him for revenge against my grandfather.

Many hypotheses were whirling through my head, and I often let my imagination wander about the possible causes of Uncle Vincenzo's death. Maybe Vincenzo, by chance, was the eyewitness of some dirty crime and was killed to hush him, or he killed himself. This last possibility was the most likely. My mother had told me that he died because of a ballerina, a dancer in the theater. They were usually very beautiful. Yes, likely it was a matter of suicide. Uncle Vincenzo fell in love with a ballerina and she did not live up to his expectations, or they were in a relationship for a while and then split up. Perhaps Uncle Vincenzo's pain at the loss of his beloved ballerina was so unbearable that he came to the point of putting an end to his young life.

The silence from my mother and Aunt Carolina would be understandable then. In Enna, suicide was considered an infamous action. Even priests refused to officiate a funeral in the church for a person who had killed themselves, unless the close relatives of the suicide showed the priest a medical certificate attesting that the suicide had been from suffering from a nervous breakdown and they didn't have rational power at the moment of making the decision to put an end to their life.

Those were just conjectures in my mind. To know the truth, I needed to get Vincenzo's diary. I was sure there was something written about the events that led to his death. I knew the diary was kept inside a drawer in my grandmother's house along with my mother's poems. But where? The only way to solve the problem was to sneak into her home, get the diary, and then put it back into the drawer after reading it.

Quite often, my grandmother, who lived on the fourth floor, went downstairs with my Aunt Carolina to bake or wash or cook something together. I just had to find the right moment to enter my grandmother's house undetected. The only problem was that I was terrified at the thought of being alone in a place haunted by ghosts. Furthermore, my grandmother had the bad habit of keeping the shutters closed, which gave a dark, ghostly look to the third floor. But to know the truth, there was no other way. I had to overcome my fears.

One day, Grandma and Aunt Carolina were making bread. Thinking it would take a lot of time to bake it, I asked my grandmother permission to use her bathroom on the fourth floor. As soon as I entered that dark house, panic gripped me, and I was on the verge of giving up my investigation, but curiosity and the love for truth prevailed. Nevertheless, I was seized by such a fear that I felt pain in my stomach, and now I really did need to go to the lavatory. So, I closed the door behind me and went up directly to the small bathroom on the fourth floor, passing through the pitch darkness of the staircase.

While I was sitting on the toilet, I thought I heard the crying of my grandfather's sisters while the coffin was being taken away by the gravediggers. Now I was visualizing the same scene. I could hear those cries as clearly as I had heard them a few years before. Was it a hallucination? Who knows! Maybe ghosts really exist! Perhaps they were still haunting that house. Or maybe I was too shaken or an easily frightened boy who mistook the shouts of the children playing across the street for the shrieks of pain at my grandfather's death. However, I was too shaken to enter the bedroom where Vincenzo's diary was possibly kept. I gave up on my quest that day, intending to continue it another time.

I only slept in that gloomy house a few times with my grandmother. She didn't use the double room after her husband's death. It was the biggest room in the house, and it was there that my grandfather's dead body had been exposed for two days. She had moved to the upper floor into a small room beside the kitchen. When I stayed with her, we slept in the same single bed. It was uncomfortable for me, but that was my grandmother's will.

Before going to bed, my grandma and I checked the house to make sure that nobody was hidden under the beds, inside the closets, or behind the furniture. Once we finished checking every corner of the house, she put a chair close to the main door.

"What is the chair for?" I asked her.

"If a wrongdoer comes, he will hear the sound of the chair and think that somebody is living in the house and will give up trying to come in."

I found my grandmother's behavior odd at the time, but I am sure she was not the only one to have some kind of pet phobia.

She prayed a lot and even before going to bed. Some prayers were the well-known Hail Mary and Our Father, and others were traditional prayers of Enna. Other prayers were taken from the small holy pictures that contained written invocations to God, Mary, or the saints on the back.

My grandma taught me these traditional prayers, which I still say in Sicilian every night before sleeping, even now that I am old. The first prayer is:

I MI CURCU NE STU LETTU

I mi curcu ne stu lettu
C'è a Madonna supra u pettu
I dormu e idda viglia
su c'è cosa m'arriviglia

I SLEEP IN THIS BED

I sleep in this bed
There is Mary over my chest
I sleep and she watches over me
If something bad is going to happen she will wake me.

The second prayer is:

CCU GESU' SUGNU

Ccu Gesù sugnu, ccu Gesù staiu.

Stannu ccu Gesù I paura un'aiu

Sacciu a curcata,

Un sacciu a livata,

L'arma mi sia sempri raccumannata

A Gesù

I AM WITH JESUS

I am with Jesus; I stay with Jesus.

As long as I am with Jesus, I have no fears.

I know I am going to sleep

But I don't know if I will awake.

My soul is always commended

To the protection of Jesus.

Chapter Six
Aunt Filippa

In Enna, housewives believed that whenever a kid was seized with strong fear, he grew parasites in his bowels. It was believed that parasites, if not treated in due time, could pass from the intestine to the stomach and then climb up along the esophagus, finally coming out through the mouth. In more serious cases, they could form a blockage in the throat, causing death by asphyxiation.

There are different kinds of intestinal parasites. The most common worms in children's bowels are pinworms and roundworms, but the latter are very dangerous because they can perforate the intestinal wall, slither into the bloodstream, and find their way into the lungs. They can be 15-20 centimeters long, a few millimeters thick, and have a reddish hue.

One day I found a roundworm in my underpants. Another day, while I was in the toilet, I noticed one that was striving to get out of my anus. Terrified, I cried out for my mother's help.

"Mom, Mom! Come quick, I have a roundworm in my anus! It wants to get out, but I can't grab it!"

My mother rushed up the stairs to the bathroom and pulled out a thick roundworm almost twenty centimeters long from my anus. Obviously, when I was at my grandmother's house trying to get Vincenzo's diary, I built up so much fear that I weakened myself. Due to stress, I lowered my immune system, giving rise to the growth of intestinal parasites.

"What to do?" I asked my mother with a worried face. "I don't want to live with these roundworms in my belly!"

My mother put her finger around her chin and pondered for a few moments. Then she faintly smiled and seemed to have found the solution to the problem.

"We have to go to Aunt Filippa!" she said.

Many years ago, most of the houses in Enna were detached. As time passed, single-family houses were demolished and replaced with big buildings full of apartments. Nowadays, people who live in apartments seldom meet one another, and many don't even know their next-door neighbors.

When I was a child, I used to hang out on Via S. Agata. Aunt Filippa was not really a relative, but everybody called her "Aunt." Therefore, she was the aunt of all children in the neighborhood. She was particularly skillful in ridding children of their intestinal worms. To do that, some kind of small donation was needed, I guess.

My mother had prearranged the meeting with her, and one afternoon we knocked on her door—or, more accurately, on her window. In fact, she used to sit behind the windows of her house to watch the passersby and the children that played in the street.

Her daughter came to welcome us and invited us to take a seat in the living room. While we were waiting, I took a look around the room. There was a glass sideboard that contained small, decorated cups, glasses, and dishes, a round wooden table with a thick embroidered cloth on it, four amaranth-colored upholstered chairs around the table, and a sofa.

My mother seemed to be very friendly with Aunt Filippa's daughter. In fact, they had been schoolmates at elementary school. Aunt Filippa arrived after a few minutes wearing a black dress—she was a widow—and thick glasses on her nose. Grey hair framed her white face. As soon as she saw me, she gently caressed my hair.

"I will help this cute boy with all my strength," she said. "First of all, we have to check if Vincenzino has some sort of evil eye inside him."

I looked up at my mother with an inquiring look, but she seemed indifferent.

"What does evil eye mean, Mom?" I asked.

"Let Aunt Filippa work, and don't ask questions!" answered my mother with a harsh voice. So, I just continued sitting on the chair, resigned to wait for whatever was going to happen.

Aunt Filippa opened the sideboard and took out a soup plate and a small cup. She put the plate on my head and asked my mother to hold it fast. Then, she poured some water into the plate and olive oil into the small cup. Finally, she dipped her finger into the small cup of olive oil and dripped some into the water.

I remained with that plate on my head for a few minutes. Aunt Filippa was not convinced, and from time to time she dripped more olive oil. Finally, she scrutinized the shape of the drops.

The drops could take different forms. They could remain as they were, become wider, or even disappear completely. If the drops maintained the same shape they had when they were dripped, it meant that there was no hex on me. If the drops became wider, there was a real hex. Sometimes the drops disappeared completely, and that meant that there was a lot of hex. In my case, the drops disappeared, and for that reason Aunt Filippa dripped olive oil several times.

"This cute little boy has a lot of hex," she said, "but I'll take it out of him. I swear!"

To do that she made special signs around the plate and said a special prayer, which she had learned from her mother one day on Christmas Eve. It was a secret prayer that had been handed down from generation to generation. Then she asked my mother to look at the plate carefully.

"Look, Rosa Maria! If the drops of oil combine to form one large drop, it means that the evil eye has been removed; otherwise, that is, if the drops remain separated, another treatment is needed, and Vincenzino will have to come back here next week," said Aunt Filippa.

Fortunately, the drops of oil merged together as if attracted by a magnet. Aunt Filippa then concluded, saying that I was now hex free thanks to her prayer.

At the time, I barely understood her method of removing the hex, but with passing time I realized that what Aunt Filippa had done probably had a scientific basis. Words, thoughts, and feelings have vibrations. Everything vibrates in the universe. It means that each kind of vibration affects both organic and inorganic matter, including the shape of the drops that Aunt Filippa used to diagnose the evil eye. In other words, if my body vibrations were good, the drops assumed a certain shape; otherwise, they got broad or sometimes disappeared.

However, the real reason my mother and I had come to her was not to get rid of my evil eye but for the intestinal worms.

I looked up at my mother again and shyly asked her, "What shall we do about my roundworms?" Once again, my mother told me to keep silent and wait.

Aunt Filippa removed the plate from my head and put it, along with the small cup, on the near table. She then asked me to lift my T-shirt and bare my belly. Finally, she made certain arcane signs on my stomach and at the same time said a special secret prayer in a low voice, which she repeated the three times. Since I was a curious boy by nature, with very fine hearing and an excellent memory, I heard and imprinted in my mind the secret prayer to cut roundworms, which I now disclose both in the original Sicilian and in English:

RAZZIONI PPI TAGLIARI I VIRMI

Tagliu li virmi ne stu curpu
Tagliu uttu e tagliu novi.
Tagliu li virmi ne stu cori.
Luni santu, Marti santu, Mircuri santu,
Iuvi santu, Venniri santu, Sabbatu santu,

A duminica di Pasqua.
Mori lu vermi e 'n terra cadi.

PRAYER TO CUT ROUNDWORMS

Cut the roundworms in this body
I cut eight and I cut nine.
I cut the roundworms in this heart.
Holy Monday, Holy Tuesday, Holy Wednesday
Holy Thursday, Good Friday, Holy Saturday,
Easter Sunday.
The roundworm dies and falls onto the floor.

When her prayer was over, she recommended I drink a small glass of olive oil with squeezed lemon and raw mashed garlic the following day in the early morning. I followed her instructions, and I have to say that I actually excreted a lot of roundworms. Some of them were dead and some looked dazed.

Chapter Seven
Pietrino

I was very shaken by the voices I heard at my grandmother's home. I also didn't appreciate my Aunt Carolina's reaction, who offended me by giving me the epithet "bad little rascal" and kicking me out of her home. Therefore, I decided not to go to that haunted house for a while. As for my Uncle Vincenzo's diary, I opted for postponing my investigation indefinitely. Maybe when I was a few years older my boldness would increase and I would be able to enter the bedroom where my grandfather's dead body had been exposed and where Vincenzo's diary was likely kept. Who knows, perhaps Vincenzo had also died in that room!

I spent my teens hanging about on Via S. Agata where my family lived, going to school, studying at home, and whenever it was possible playing with other boys in the neighborhood. Across the street from my house was a carter who worked with his two-wheeled cart pulled by a draft horse. He had a small store where he sold building materials, and he also delivered them to the builders by his cart.

I was enchanted by that huge horse and the fantastic scenes depicted in bright colors on the cart, and whenever I had the chance in the afternoons, I leapt onto the cart and went around Enna with the carter. The horse was harnessed with a tall plume of feathers on its head and harness bells around its neck. The cart had multi-colored figures painted all over its sides that depicted the feats of paladins like Roland and Charles the Great. It was not a big cart, but it could carry a fair amount of goods like gypsum, sand, cement, bricks, and tiles.

The carter was not able to read and write or count numbers beyond ten. He was just a good hard-working person, but his wife was skilled in reading, writing, and doing arithmetic. Thanks to their children's help, today they are one of the richest families in Enna.

My playmates were my cousin Emanuele and my friends Carlo and Pietrino. I was the youngest; the others were two years older than me. We formed a group called "The Gang of the Horn," but we had nothing to do with a gang, despite the name. Our symbol was a white flag on which a horn had been drawn. I don't know who made the flag, but it was probably Pietrino, who was endowed with manual skills like his father.

The city of Enna lies on a flat mountain a thousand meters above sea level. The main characteristic of the mountain is that it has deep cliffs on almost all sides. Enna has been inhabited since ancient times because of this peculiar feature, which made the city inexpugnable. The Arabs besieged Enna for a long time. They conquered a great part of Sicily except my town, which was considered impregnable. They were eventually able to enter the city by using a secret path that a traitor from Enna had taught them.

One day during the Second World War, a garrison of Italian troops came to Enna in the late afternoon. They camped in an area not far from the edge of a ravine. During the night, the Americans launched an airstrike. The soldiers tried to escape the bombs and ran away from their camp, but unfortunately, they didn't know that my town lay on the edge of a cliff, and they all died when they plummeted into the chasm.

Basically, our Gang of the Horn devoted itself to exploring the territory. We used to run along the edges of the cliffs and search caves that were disseminated all around the area. In old times, people lived in those caves, and it is still possible today to see evidence of some of the old dwellings. In a cave, we saw a lot of juts that the owners had dug out to put lamps, food, and tools. Nobody lives in such caves today, but sometimes people use them to keep animals like goats, poultry, mules, horses, or donkeys.

One day we had just explored a cave on the edge of the ravine that had two entrances and four rooms. On our way back, my cousin lost his footing and fell into the ravine. Only a tiny shrub prevented him from plummeting at least two hundred meters down. He hung in midair between life and death, cried out, and tears welled in his frightened eyes. We were all petrified with fear, unable to do anything to save Emanuele's life, but Pietrino summoned up his courage, put his legs astride a log that stuck out from the rock, bent his body, stretched his arms, and finally clutched Emanuele's hair. He lifted my cousin slowly until he could catch hold of the same log Pietrino was sitting on, and they finally both came up safe and sound.

I remember a Christmas when Pietrino's father made a big Nativity scene at his home, which occupied almost half of the wide living room. His father had built cardboard castles, houses, and streets similar to those at the time of Jesus's birth. Christmas trees aren't part of Sicilian culture and tradition. Nowadays, many families dress Christmas trees, but at that time they made the Nativity scene and gathered around it to say their rosary.

Our Gang of the Horn was a united group, and we loved one another. Carlo had been born with a harelip. He had been operated on, but he still had some difficulty speaking, and it was not easy to understand him. Nowadays, people with physical imperfections are tolerated and helped to fit into society. Most countries have special classes for disabilities, but at the time of my childhood it was different. If you had a physical defect, the other boys mocked you, and you felt humiliated.

I had some problems properly pronouncing the letter R, and I also stammered sometimes. In order to overcome this, I trained myself in pronunciation at home, lest my schoolmates mock me. I used to put a few little stones into my mouth and then tried to utter words that contained the letter R. That method worked, at least for my stammer.

You seldom saw people with disabilities in the streets of Enna in the old days. A weak person was an object of derision of boys. The ideal man was strong, cunning, and cheerful. Therefore, many families secluded their members who had some kind of physical or psychical imperfection, lest they become an object of mockery.

Carlo was not able to pronounce words properly, and for that reason the other boys gave him the epithet "gnie-gnie." Actually, it was difficult to understand him, but our group could figure out his speech. Pietrino, who was the leader of the Gang of the Horn, gave orders to defend Carlo whenever other boys mocked him.

At that time in Enna, the quarter wars raged. Gangs of teens had formed dangerous gangs according to the area they belonged to. Their gangs were not peaceful like our Gang of the Horn. In fact, they attacked anyone who didn't belong to the same neighborhood. They used stones, arrows, slings, and even chains. More than one boy had been blinded by pointed arrows made from the iron of umbrellas. Therefore, we couldn't go with our flag to explore quarters different than ours.

The oddity of life is that Pietrino, who had saved Emanuele's life, was not able to save his own. Cruel fate cut the thread of his life off prematurely.

There was a time when the Asian flu spread in Enna. Most of the children that contracted the virus got over it. Unfortunately for my friend Pietrino, the clock of his life was going to inexorably stop. As soon as he had taken ill with a high fever, his parents called their family doctor. He examined Pietrino and diagnosed him as suffering from the Asian flu. He prescribed some medicine to fight the virus.

As the days passed, Pietrino didn't recover. Fever hovered around high levels, and his body was reduced to skin and bone. When his parents realized that their son's health was getting worse and worse, they took him to the hospital. Pietrino had blood tests, and the doctors found out that he was not suffering from the Asian flu but from typhoid fever. They started the proper therapy, but it was too late. A complication arose; a tremendous hemorrhage occurred in his bowels and Pietrino's life was slipping away.

One afternoon, my cousin Emanuele informed me about Pietrino's bad condition and asked me to go to the hospital with him to visit.

"Of course!" I said. "Where is Pietrino? How can we find him in the big hospital?"

"I know where to go and how to find his room," answered Emanuele.

While we were walking to the hospital, my cousin informed me about the glaring mistake the doctor who had diagnosed Pietrino the first time made.

"How is that possible?" I asked.

My cousin and I meandered through the hallways of that big hospital until we finally found Pietrino's room. As soon as he saw us, his face beamed. He tried to get up from his bed to show us that he was still the leader of our Gang of the Horn, but he didn't have enough strength and fell back onto his bed. He didn't have the strength to speak. Seeing his pale face and dimmed eyes sunken into dark eye sockets, I realized that Pietrino was going to die.

A few days later it happened. The dead body, as was customary, was placed for two days in the living room where his father had once made the Nativity scene. Pietrino wore a gray suit with short trousers. When his mother saw me, she cried desperately, tears streaming down her face.

"Vincenzino! Vincenzino! You will not come here anymore. Your playmate has left all of us forever."

I never did go to Pietrino's home again, but every year on the Commemoration of the Dead on November 2, I visit him at the graveyard.

His father built a family chapel. At first, all the family members gathered around the tomb every year. Then, within a few years, all five children died from diverse causes—some because of a car accident, others because of disease. It was a family marked by cruel fate. Eventually, Pietrino's mother also died.

Every year when I went to pray before Pietrino's tomb, I saw his father sitting in front of it. I had never seen such a strong man. His wife and children died before their time, but in spite of everything, he stood up to his adverse fortunes. He looked as strong as the gigantic cypress that stood near his chapel. He seemed to be immortal, but at the age of ninety-eight he also gave up his ghost.

I have looked at doctors with suspicion my entire life, but who knows? Maybe fate exists and it decides regardless of human will.

"Who is the doctor that treated Pietrino the first time?" I asked my cousin Emanuele one day.

He told me his name and, as I didn't know him, he pointed him out to me. He was very tall and enjoyed a good reputation. As for me, as soon as I spotted him, I wanted to spit in his face. I pondered over and over how it was possible to mistake a diagnosis of typhus for the Asian flu. In my opinion, that stupid doctor should be struck off the professional register! Every time I met him in the street, I was tempted to slap him, but unfortunately that was not possible. However, over the years I reexamined the concept of guilt. In fact, in my life I made some mistakes similar to that of the doctor. Everybody can make a mistake. No one is infallible.

When Pietrino died, it was the second time I had been touched by death in my life. With Pietrino's death, our Gang of the Horn came to an end. He was the leader of our group, and no one else was in a position to lead us. Meanwhile, from time to time, Vincenzo's diary crept into my mind. I had given up detecting it because of my cowardice.

I decided to confront situations instead of fleeing every time I was seized with fear. I had to figure out a strategy to enter my grandmother's double room. To overcome my fears, I should not think about ghosts and dead people. My anxiety would not help me. Therefore, once I entered my grandmother's house I should stop thinking and go directly to my goal. So, I did.

One day, my grandma left the front door ajar. She was at Aunt Carolina's to bake bread. I took advantage of the favorable situation and sneaked into the house. Then, instead of thinking about anything, I went straight to the double bedroom. I was determined to overcome my fear and thought, *If I can succeed now, I'll be a winner in life. But if I give up now, I'll be a loser and a quitter all my life.*

I opened the door of the lounge and then the bedroom, but I made the mistake of not completely closing the doors. The bedroom was pitch black because my grandmother kept the shutters completely closed. I groped my way to the shutter in the bedroom and raised it a little bit to see more clearly. Once there was enough light, I headed for the big closet. I opened the door and saw a hunting rifle in the back, similar to Sebastiano's. On the shelf there was a big revolver that I had never seen before. Curious, I took the handgun and unsheathed it.

I was scrutinizing that big revolver when my grandmother's voice resounded in the hollow house. She was sure of having closed the door to the lounge, and the light that filtered through the shutters of the bedroom made her certain that a wrongdoer was inside.

"Who is there?" she spoke out with quivering voice. Obviously, she feared having an unpleasant encounter with a thief.

I was paralyzed by fear and feelings of guilt for entering the bedroom without permission. As my grandma flung open the door of the bedroom, she saw me with the revolver in my hand. She screamed so loudly that even the neighbors could hear her. Aunt Carolina, worried by my grandma's shrieks, stormed into the bedroom, where I was still frozen by my feelings of guilt. She then got close to me and calmly took the revolver from my hand. Then, feeling more relaxed, she started railing at me. "You little monster! How many times have I had to warn you not to come here? You should stay with your mother and let us live in peace. I can't look after you. Next time you come here, I'll beat you!"

I left the house with my tail between my legs. Due to stress, I wet my trousers and underwear. I decided to give up trying to find Vincenzo's diary.

Chapter Eight
My Mother's Poems

I attended middle school in my hometown. My parents were so eager to make me a good student that they also provided me with afterschool teachers. I was at school and afterschool all day long. Studying became an obsession for me. Moreover, the relationship with my new schoolmates was different than in elementary school, where I had felt my friends more spontaneous and naïve.

I remember a dream I often had at that time in my life. I saw the earth like a big rocky ball; then, the end of the world came, and I was crushed by that huge rocky sphere. Obviously, my grandfather's and Pietrino's deaths had made a strong impression on me. Someday, death would knock on my door as well, and I would not be able to send it back as an unwelcome guest.

Later, I no longer had those kinds of nightmares, but death would remain the most important theme in my life. I constantly asked myself, *If God doesn't exist, what is going to happen when we die? Is it possible that we are the ones who create God in order to have the illusion of not disappearing into thin air forever when we die? Maybe God is just a projection of our insecure minds to give us a footing to live without anxiety and worry about the hereafter.*

I kept mulling over death without ever finding a definite answer. With Pietrino's death, I lost the only real friend I had. I didn't consider my schoolmates trustworthy friends. I spent some time with a few of them, but they had little sympathy for my problems. They couldn't understand why I worried about death instead of enjoying life.

The only friend I had left was Sebastiano. He had found a temporary job as a foreman at a building site. It lasted a year, and then he found another job as a mink breeder. On Saturday afternoon, I met him at his workplace. I loved watching him prepare mince for the minks. While he worked, he never stopped talking politics, which was his great passion. His hair was completely white, but he was still a strong man. He kept his hair short and crewcut, according to military style. His beard was shaved as deeply as if he was going to undergo a review by his commander.

"Vincenzino, you have to know that the actual Italian ruling class is made of the same type of people that were in the ranks of the Fascist Party."

Then he showed me a newspaper whose ideas were similar to his.

"In this newspaper, there is evidence that the Fascist Party leaders have turned themselves into champions of democracy.

"There was more democracy under Mussolini than there is today!" he continued, getting worked up. "Nowadays, to get a job—any kind of job—you need your political connections. The different parties pretend to fight against one another, but that is just a farce. In fact, both the ruling and the opposition party have power. Do you believe that it was Mussolini who led Italy to the Second World War? Not at all! Vincenzino, you have to know that behind the shoulders of every politician there are hidden powers who actually decide the destinies of nations."

"Who are these hidden powers, Sebastiano?"

"The lobbies! There are many lobbies in Italy, as there are in all the nations of the world. One of the most dangerous lobbies is made of the magnates of industry. They sell most of their outputs to the States, and whenever there is a war, they take the opportunity to sell more goods. The weapon industry is based on war. The more wars there are, the more weapons that are made. Mussolini paid with his life for his faults, but no one who belonged to the hidden powers paid anything. They are still rich, produce and sell weapons, and increase their earnings more and more."

Then he took a picture from his shoulder bag and showed it to me.

"Do you recognize this man?"

"It looks like the mayor of Enna," I answered.

"You are right. That is our mayor, but this picture was taken in Mussolini's time when he wore the Fascist uniform, which included the black shirt. Now he's turned himself into an antifascist, but the truth is that he seized the opportunity offered by the new pseudo-democratic regime to continue his political business in the same way he did under Mussolini.

"When Mussolini was alive, there was no Mafia. He stamped out it almost completely. Almost all mafiosi were arrested or sent to prison. I say 'almost' because he arrested only the so-called small fry. He couldn't catch the big shots because they belonged to the economic and political power. Both the political and economic class formed lobbies, otherwise called Mafia organizations, to control the economy of the country. In other words, the big Mafia was within the Fascist Party, and for that reason he couldn't eradicate it completely."

"May I ask you for advice, Sebastiano?"

"Yes, of course. You can ask me whatever you want, and I'll be happy to help you."

"I want you to help me get my Uncle Vincenzo's diary."

"What do you need that diary for?"

"I want to know how Uncle Vincenzo died. Both my mother and Aunt Carolina have been reticent to talk about his death. I am sure that in his diary I can find a few clues to trace the cause."

"Do you know where it is kept?"

"Yes, of course. The diary is in my grandmother's house in one of the drawers of the closet in the bedroom, along with my mother's poems."

"Well, that means that it is very easy to get the diary. All you have to do is ask your grandmother for permission to see your mother's poems. Once you have spotted them, you can pick up the diary."

It was the most natural and straightforward way to get Vincenzo's diary. Why didn't I think about that before? Why did I run all those subterfuges to get into the bedroom surreptitiously? Indeed, I had the habit of walking along blind alleys without seeing that there was an avenue in front of me with all the doors flung open. Now Sebastiano was opening my mind, teaching me not to complicate my life with useless reasoning. I had to act in a more straightforward and simple way to hit my targets.

"Thank you, Sebastiano! I'll do as you have suggested, and this time everything will be alright."

One day I went to my grandmother's house and nonchalantly asked her, "Can I see my mother's poems?"

"Yes, of course, Vincenzino. They are in the lower drawer of the bedroom closet. You can go there to see the poems, but don't touch the guns!"

Sebastiano was right! He had paved my way to get Uncle Vincenzo's diary. I headed for the bedroom and opened the windows one by one. The light entered the room and the ghostly presences seemed to fade away.

I opened the lower drawer, which was filled to the brink with slips of neatly folded paper. I dipped my hands in to find a notebook or something similar and fathomed with my fingers here and there until at last I felt something that seemed to be a notebook. I took it out very carefully and found that it was a rather thick, black notebook. It was exactly in the middle of the drawer, as if my mother's poems were the bed and the blanket for it. I leafed through the pages and felt sure that it was Vincenzo's diary. My heart was pounding as never before, but I kept calm and gently put the diary inside my T-shirt to take it home.

Meanwhile, I wanted to have a look at some of my mother's poems. A quick look showed that they had been composed with her brother in mind. According to my mother, Vincenzo was not dead, for he continued to live in another dimension. I picked one of the folded pieces of paper, and inside it was written this poem:

FLOWERS

My beloved brother,
When you cross the river of eternal life,
May the angels strew your way with flowers.
Your heart is pure and stainless
And your soul will never die.
You are now in a faraway land
Where the moon always shines
And the sun never sets.
Before long we will hold hands again,
To walk together until the end of space and time!

I didn't know my mother had such an unschooled talent! I unfolded two more small sheets to read two more poems:

THE MOON

O moon! Over the eras,
You have been giving inspiration
To poets, artists, and philosophers.
I know the reason. It is because
The souls of our loved ones live on your surface.
We cannot see them, but they are
Still alive and watch over us and teach us

And love us.
Someday, o moon, I will abide on your bright face too,
With my brother Vincenzo and the angels,
And we will protect and guide to the straight path
Our beloved offspring.

RIVER

I see a river with emerald-green water.
It flows calm and marks the border between life and death.
If I could, I would build a bridge to unite the two worlds.
But I cannot. I am too frail, too powerless. I am just a human being.
Only God can build such a bridge.
For now we are separated, my beloved brother,
And Charon will keep ferrying souls across the river.
But one day, a new light will guide me to you,
And we will stay together in our star, which is the same
As that from where we came.

I kept reading the poems, but almost all of them had the same nostalgic tone for her beloved brother, Vincenzo. I refolded the sheets precisely and tidily, so as not to arouse suspicion about Vincenzo's missing diary. I closed the windows one by one, lowered the blinds, and the darkness again took over that part of the house.

With the diary well hidden between my belt and T-shirt, I sneaked out, homeward bound. I closed my grandmother's main door behind me and was coming down the stone staircase when my Aunt Carolina came out from her house and beckoned me to join her.

A complication! If she sees the diary, I am ruined! I thought. *What to do? I have to make up an excuse!*

"I cannot come to you, Aunt Carolina, because my mother is waiting for me."

"Please come over here, Vincenzino, just a few minutes. I have something special for you."

I had been raised to obey my elder relatives, so I couldn't refuse my aunt's invitation.

"I have just made some bread. I'll take it out of the wood-burning oven in a few minutes, and there is a special surprise. I have prepared some buns just for you."

We went downstairs where my aunt baked her bread, and she took out a few buns from the oven. They smelled of fresh Sicilian flour, and their color was between white and yellow. My aunt sliced one of the buns with her long knife and seasoned it with olive oil, ground garlic, salt, and black pepper. Then she offered it to me.

While I was eating with gusto, she noticed something sticking out from my chest. "What is that? What did you do at Grandma's?" she asked.

This time I didn't want to raise any suspicion about something I had stolen, so I answered without thinking much. "This is my armor, Aunt Carolina!"

"Armor? What is it for? Are you leaving for the war?"

"No, the problem is that some friends of mine mock me and try to attack me, so I have to protect myself."

"I knew you were a bit strange, but not to such an extent."

I swallowed the bun in two or three mouthfuls and then rushed home.

Chapter Nine
Vincenzo's Diary, Part One

Now I had to find a safe place to hide the diary and read it peacefully. I thought about putting it into my school bag so that nobody could find it. This way, the diary was always with me and I could read it whenever I wished. It was not a long journal. Vincenzo started writing it at the suggestion of his Italian language teacher in 1933 when he was twelve, about six years before he died. It was the time when Vincenzo began to be attracted to the opposite sex.

At the Church of Santa Croce, I showed our director, Paolo, Vincenzo's journal. He selected the most significant pages and slightly rearranged the style and the times when the events took place, so as to make an orderly and flowing account.

October 1, 1933

My name is Vincenzo Chiaramonte. I was born in Enna on April 4, 1921. I have two elder sisters, Carolina e Rosa Maria. My younger brother, Biagio, died of malaria last year. I still wear a black band on the collar of my jacket as a sign of mourning for the death of my brother.

I am blond with green eyes. Obviously, I must be descended from some Nordic people who conquered Sicily long ago. We live in a large house with a vegetable garden. My father works in his sulfur mine near Villarosa and usually comes home with his mare only once a week, on Saturday afternoon. My sister Rosa Maria is learning embroidery from the nuns and goes to the Franciscan convent every day, while my sister Carolina is a housewife.

Our Italian teacher suggested we write a diary to improve our current Italian, which is full of Sicilian terms and idioms. I didn't even know the term "diary." The teacher said that by keeping a diary we can know ourselves better and can also learn to write in Italian fluently.

I like my Italian teacher. She is close to retirement by now. Her nose is aquiline, and her face is framed by gray hair. She looks strict, but she has a good heart. Last year, I didn't get good marks in Italian, so I want to follow her advice and write my diary with the help of my Italian language dictionary.

October 2, 1933

Today was my second day of school. I attend the second grade of middle school. My class is composed of boys only. There are no mixed classes in Enna. Maybe it is possible to have mixed classes in more open-minded countries like those in Scandinavia, but in Enna, a city steeped in prejudices about sex, this is unthinkable.

The girls have their class close to ours, but we have recess in the same schoolyard. I noticed that all the girls have flat breasts, except one who is grown and has two round, attractive breasts. Her name is Maria. Today at recess she was talking with a friend of mine about her oral test in Latin. Once again, I looked at her breasts and fell in love with her. I then realized that love and physical attraction coincide. Love is like an animal instinct.

However, I am too young for her. She prefers boys older than her, and that makes me terribly jealous. I have no hope to conquer her heart.

October 10, 1933

My progress at school is not good, because I think of Maria all the time instead of studying. I cannot help but talk about her with my sisters and friends. My sister Rosa Maria says I should forget her and only think about studying, but I am not able to suppress my emotions. I have a fire inside me that burns and clouds my mind. I cannot live without her!

October 12, 1933

I don't know how, but my mother found out about my crush on Maria. I suspect that Rosa Maria informed her for my own good, because she wants me to study without distractions. Today Mother scolded me harshly and forbade me to think of Maria, otherwise she would beat me hard.

October 22, 1933

Maria has disappeared from my dreams, not because of my mother's reprimand, but because she has fallen in love with another boy. This morning I saw them in the grove near the cemetery. They were walking hand in hand, when all of a sudden, he kissed and hugged her. Maria flushed and shivered, but she let him kiss her. Maybe it was her first kiss.

October 23, 1933

My mother was at my school this afternoon to ask the teachers about my progress.

"Your son doesn't study enough. He always has his head in the clouds. If he continues to go wrong, we will fail him for sure." That was the teachers' unanimous verdict.

When my mother came home, she cried out, "Vincenzo!" Hearing her voice, my blood ran cold. I knew she had been at school, so I figured that my teachers had not talked well about me, and now my mother was ready to beat me harshly.

She reached me while I was reading a book at the table in the dining room. As soon as I saw her, I stood up while she tried to get hold of me. We both ran around the table, I fleeing and my mother pursuing me. At last, she gave up.

"I'll tell your father that you're not making any progress at school, and this will be worse than my beating."

Actually, I fear my father more than my mother. He is very strict, but I hope she has just threatened to tell him I am not a good student. She probably will not tell him anything.

October 25, 1933

Two days have elapsed, and my father has not been at home. He works at his sulfur mine all week, but today is Sunday and he enjoys staying at home. He came home yesterday afternoon and will leave tomorrow in the early morning. He brought a hare, which he killed with his shotgun on the way home. My sister Carolina, who is an excellent cook, will cook it in tomato sauce, but I will not enjoy this delicacy, because my legs shake at the thought that my father knows what my teachers said.

At lunch we sat around the table. My sister Carolina put in the middle of the table a bowl of pasta topped with hare sauce, fried eggplants, and grated sheep cheese. My mother sat next to my father, who was the head of the table. Rosa Maria and I sat facing each other, while Carolina, after serving the pasta, took a seat opposite my mother.

My father said nothing to me. We all enjoyed the food, and I had the feeling that the worst had passed. But unfortunately, it was not like that. After eating, my father looked me in the eye, and then he looked me up and down. Obviously, my mother had told him something about me. He then abruptly spoke.

"Tomorrow, you must get up at four o'clock in the morning. You must help me saddle the mare, and then we will go together to a certain place."

I didn't ask him where we would go the following day. I just confined myself to nod. I was too afraid of my father and literally petrified with fear.

October 26, 1933

It was 3:30 in the morning when my mother woke me up.

"Get dressed within ten minutes, because your father is waiting for you!"

I looked at my mother with my eyes wide open and obeyed her without saying any word. I got dressed and went down to my parents' bedroom where my father was waiting for me. As soon as I entered the room, he took his revolver from the closet and loaded it with six bullets. He then fastened his cartridge belt around his waist, put on his blue hooded cloak, and buckled it near his neck. Eventually, he took his double-barreled gun from the closet and slung it over his shoulder.

"Now we are ready to go," he said with a stern face.

I was breathless. I couldn't imagine what was going to happen. I had a bad feeling, but I didn't have the courage to ask him what he was going to do with those arms. I followed him down the stairs that led to the stable. The light of the lamp was feeble, but here and there I saw some mice running through the straw. My father took the packsaddle from a hook in the wall and put it on the mare, which was startled. Finally, he pulled the girth tightly.

"Take the reins and the saddlebags!"

I did as he wanted, and then he asked me to get a small barrel of wine, a bottle of water, and an acetylene lantern. We would use the lamp on the road.

He lifted me with his strong arms and put me on the front of the packsaddle, and then he walked the mare up to the exit of the vegetable garden. He closed the gate and leapt back into the saddle.

Our mare walked briskly through the empty streets of Enna. They were illuminated until we reached the Janniscuru Gate, but little by little as we advanced along the country road, it became darker and darker.

My father took the acetylene lamp and lit it. "Hold it!" he said.

I grabbed the lantern from the hook, and I have to say that it actually lit the road in front of us. It wasn't heavy, but the smell it gave off was disgusting!

I had heard from my mother that there were bandits along the roads who mugged passersby, but I blindly trusted my father. He was strong, and nobody dared confront him. My only worry was what my father would do to me. I was sure my mother had told him I was a bad student, so I expected punishment, but I couldn't figure out what kind. At last, I summoned up my courage to ask him.

"Where are we going, Father?"

"Shut up!" he said with a voice so firm that it made me shiver with fear. We kept going through the pitch-black night while I held the lantern in my hand.

After about half an hour of riding, I saw a long line of men, young men, boys, and ragged children walking slowly on the road with the acetylene lanterns in their hands. They looked as if they were souls heading for the Valley of Jehoshaphat near Jerusalem on the day of the Last Judgment.

"Where are all those people going at night?" I thought. I could never have imagined so eerie a scenario. It was as if I was dreaming, but the lantern in my hand, which was now getting heavy, dispelled all my doubts. I was awake, as were all those people walking along the edge of the road in the middle of the night.

It was almost dawn when we arrived at a place with many cylinder-shaped stone mounds that gave off smoke on the top, while below a yellow liquid leaked through a crack in the stones. Of course, we were already in the area of my father's sulfur mine.

As soon as they saw him, three mine laborers headed for us. They all bowed to my father and kissed his hand. One of them took the reins of the mare, while another laborer took my father's cloak. A third workman was waiting for my father's orders.

"This is my son, Vincenzo. I want you to show him the mine, both inside and out," my father said to him with a commanding tone.

The laborer nodded.

"It will be done, your lordship!"

He helped me dismount and then, holding my hand, led me to the smoking stones I had seen before.

"These are furnaces," he said. "We put the sulfur ore inside and smelt it. At least two-thirds of the molten sulfur is lost in the air as sulfur dioxide. The remaining third flows into wooden casts. We wait until the sulfur is cold, and then we take it out of the wooden casts and load it into trucks. We export sulfur all over the world. It is used in agriculture as a fertilizer, to make gunpowder, as an insecticide, a fungicide, and so on. Nevertheless, I have to say that all the people who work here breathe toxic fumes due to high levels of sulfur dioxide in the air. Sooner or later we all get sick. We are doomed to die young. Therefore, I advise you to stay as far away from this sulfur mine as you can."

We kept walking around the area until we finally came to an entrance to the mine that had been dug into the ground. The upper part of the tunnel and the walls were propped up by wooden piles and beams. A narrow staircase led underground.

"Is it not dangerous to go underground? I don't think these wooden posts are stable enough," I said.

"Actually, accidents happen every now and then, but we must go down. Otherwise, your father will reprimand me. Anyway, don't be anxious. You are safe with me," he said, holding my hand tightly.

We went underground for about a hundred meters. The stairs became steeper and slippery, and the air got hotter. We continued down the staircase until we arrived at a wide area from where a few tunnels branched off. They were propped up precariously.

Along the stairs and the galleries, I saw an uninterrupted line of children who were carrying that nauseating acetylene lamp in one hand and a heavy weight on their shoulder. The ore was stuffed into canvas bags or baskets. The children wore small bags stuffed with rags on their shoulders and heads to soften the harshness of the ore. Stooping under the weight and with labored breathing, they went upstairs slowly, giving out a painful moan with every step. I had the impression of seeing human-shaped moles which didn't like to come out in the daylight.

"What is the average age of those children?" I asked.

"Their age ranges from seven to eighteen years. They cannot grow well because the air here is too rarefied and humid. Moreover, they carry weights that are too much for their young age. They cannot stop on the stairs to take a rest, or the entire long train of carriers would stop. Their bodies are misshapen, and they will never grow taller."

We kept going down and finally arrived at the end of one of the galleries. The air there was hot and unbearable. I saw a few men completely naked because of the stifling heat. With picks in their hands, they dug out the ore. Near them, children filled baskets and canvas bags with the ore, while other little laborers helped other children put the loads on their shoulders.

"Every pick man has at least thirty children at his disposal. He cannot do his work without children that carry out the material he digs out. For this reason, he makes an agreement with children's parents. The pick man gives the parents money in exchange for their children's work."

I was itching to leave that goddamn underground place. I wanted to breathe freely in the daylight, but the laborer, who had to follow my father's orders, took me all around the mine to see more naked laborers and misshapen children.

"One last thing," the laborer said. "You have to know that accidents are not infrequent in this mine. Some are caused by the accidental collapse of the props, but the most serious tragedies happen when the laborers come across firedamp, which explodes when it comes in contact with the flame from the lanterns. A considerable number of both pick men and children, sometimes dozens, are left trapped in the bowels of the mine. Their deaths are appalling. The oxygen runs out little by

little, and they die of suffocation. It is like when mice are walled up in their hole. Can you imagine their deaths?"

When I got out of that infernal mine, my legs were quaking. My mouth was dry and my face pale. The hand gave me some water, and we both sat down on a bench near my father's office. From there, I could see those who set fire to big logs below the furnaces, while other laborers loaded the blocks of melted sulfur into wheelbarrows and then carried them to the trucks.

My father didn't allow me to enter his office, so I had to wait outside. Two hours later, a hand came with our mare. It was the sign that we could go home.

On the way back home, my father broke his silence.

"Did you visit the mine?"

"Yes, I did."

"Did you see all those children working hard?"

"Yes, I did."

"Well, now I'll give you an option—you either make progress in your studies, or you will come and work inside the mine like those children you have just seen. You can be sure that if you fail as a student, I will take you to work in the mine!

"You can consider yourself a privileged boy, because you are given an option, while those unlucky children have no choice. They belong to large families with six, seven, sometimes twelve children. Their parents cannot afford to support them, so they entrust them to the pick men for a handful of money."

"Okay, Father, I promise. From now on I'll be a good schoolboy!"

October 27, 1933

I went to school with my tail between my legs, firmly resolved to study hard and not fail. Otherwise, the mine's doors would be wide open to me.

During recess I saw Maria. My heart had a start, in spite of the fact that she was now in a relationship with another boy. In *order not to think of her, I envisioned working along with those misshapen children in the bowels of the sulfur mine. I turned my back on her and headed for a group of schoolmates that were chatting cheerfully.*

November 6, 1933

I have struck up a friendship with the son of the Enna police chief. His name is Roberto, and he is a few years older than me. The police station is near my home, and the officers' quarters are next to the station. We wrestle quite often. He should be law-abiding, seeing that he is the son of a policeman, but he spurs me to perform illegal acts.

November 10, 1933

Roberto told me I had to steal an apple from a market stall. "It is very easy! Don't be shy! You just have to go near the stall, and when the greengrocer is inattentive, grasp an apple and run away at lightning speed."

I don't know why, but I have the tendency to blindly do what my friends tell me. If a friend of mine tells me, "Look! There is a donkey flying," I believe him. I am one of the most gullible boys in the world.

In the late afternoon while my friend was waiting for me at Garibaldi Square, I headed for the fruit stall. My heart was pounding like a drum, but I finally grabbed an apple and ran away as fast as I could. Once I joined my playmate, I gave him the apple because I don't like their taste much. He ate the apple with gusto and then congratulated me.

"Now you are a real strong boy," he said.

November 18, 1933

Roberto incited me to commit another act of bravado. "If you want to be a real man, you have to go to Saint Francis Square, and whenever you see a kid playing or walking there, you have to slap him and then run away."

I did what he told me. In the evening, at the time when the square swarmed with kids, I got near a little kid, gave him a slap in the face, and then ran away.

My bullying lasted only a few days, because this evening after I had slapped a little boy, his father ran after me and caught me. When I was in his hands, he spanked me harshly. His face expressed rage and his words were fiery.

"I'll teach you how to behave in society. Next time I catch you slapping a kid, I'll send you directly to jail!" His words terrified me, and he didn't want to release me. I was so frightened that I wet my underwear and my trousers.

Obviously, from now on I will take care not to slap children anymore.

November 21, 1933

After that regrettable episode, my playmate disappeared mysteriously. I couldn't see him in the streets anymore. Maybe his father was transferred to another city.

I looked for him at the Belvedere and Piazza Mazzini where he used to hang about, but there was no trace of him. Even though his company is not good for me, he is still my friend. I finally decided to go to the police station and ask for him.

At the entrance, a policeman stopped me.

"Where are you going?"

"I am looking for Roberto, the police chief's son. He is my friend."

"Roberto is not here anymore," the policeman said.

"Where is he?"

"He is in Bronte now. It is a town at the foot of Mount Etna. There is a big seminary there. His father has enrolled him in that school so that he becomes a priest."

A priest? I can't imagine Roberto as a priest. He likes to live as a gangster. Who knows, maybe he can better himself and become a good man by studying and living in the seminary.

Many people change their inclination in the course of their lives. I hope Roberto is one of them.

November 25, 1933

After Roberto disappeared from my life, I made friends with a boy three years older than me. His name is Giovanni. He is very tall for his age, and when we stroll together, he looks like my father—or at least like my uncle. We like to walk in the high street and along the Belvedere.

This evening he got an idea.

"What about having a bet?" he asked.

"What kind of bet?" I replied.

"In Enna, to start a relationship between a boy and a girl, we stop a girl who is walking in the street and make a declaration of love."

"What does a declaration of love mean?" I asked.

"It means that you have to propose to her."

"I have never done that! I don't know how to talk with a girl about love."

"Don't worry!" Giovanni said. "Our bet is not about which of us is able to conquer the heart of a girl. Our bet is about how many refusals each of us collects. The one that scores fifty refusals will win a free beer at the tavern."

"Okay, I agree. Let's start tomorrow," I said.

November 26, 1933

This evening I stopped three girls. The first walked with me for a few minutes. I proposed to her, but I was too crude and was met with a kind refusal. The other two girls didn't want to walk with me and almost ran away.

November 27, 1933

I kept courting girls, but no one wanted to start a relationship with me. On the other hand, I noticed that Giovanni didn't stop any girl. He just wanted to make fun of me!

November 28, 1933

I decided to put an end to this harmful companionship. In fact, by constantly being mocked by Giovanni and being met with all those refusals from the girls, I was losing my self-esteem and becoming the laughingstock of the entire city.

December 20, 1933

Last night I slept in the bedroom with my parents. They slept in their big bed and I in the smaller one. Suddenly, I heard my father's voice say, "Is Vincenzo sleeping?" My mother didn't answer, but I answered yes. My parents didn't notice that it was me who had answered. Obviously, they were too excited.

After a few seconds, I heard my mother gasping. I was worried about her. I thought she couldn't breathe. I was about to get up from my bed to run to help her, but I didn't because I had the feeling that my parents were doing something dirty. I couldn't sleep all night, and when I woke up, I felt a sense of disgust at their bad behavior.

January 10, 1934

Last night I didn't sleep in my bed, but in the double bed with my parents. I didn't sleep in the middle between them. I set myself at my mother's side. I was sleeping well when I was awakened by my mother's body, which swung towards me. She kept swinging sideways for some time, and I couldn't sleep. I got the same sensation of nausea and disgust about my parents, who were having sex in the same bed where I was sleeping.

March 6, 1934

A friend of mine told me about his sexual activity. He said that he used to masturbate several times a day. He explained to me how to do that.

"It is very easy!" he said. "Just hold your penis with your hand and then shake it up and down. After a while you will have a sensation of pleasure, and some white fluid will well from the mouth of your penis."

I went to the bathroom and did as my friend had taught me.

May 10, 1934

I went to the bathroom too often and aroused my father's suspicion. Today he looked through the keyhole and saw me while I was masturbating.

"Who taught you to do that?" he asked with his terrifying voice. I didn't have the strength to answer him, but the blood ran cold in my veins.

When I got out of the bathroom, my father grabbed me by my arm. "Give me your hand! Give me your hand!"

He struck me on my hand so many times that it became red. "Don't do that dirty thing anymore! Otherwise, I will chop off your hand!" he shouted.

From now on, I will not hide in the bathroom to masturbate. I will do it when I am in my bed. Even though I will wet my underpants, they will dry soon and my mother will wash them.

June 2, 1934

Today, my mother asked me, "I have seen a few unsightly yellow stains on your underpants. Are you sick?"

I was terribly embarrassed and couldn't answer.

"Answer me!" continued my mother. "If you have any disease, we will call the doctor or take you to the hospital."

"No, there is no problem, Mom. The fact is that yesterday I ate too much yellow cheese," I lied. "That is why my urine is

yellowish, but now I will eat more vegetables and it will become normal again."

My mother swallowed my lie and didn't seem to suspect anything. As for me, I swear that I will not masturbate again, even though I predict that I will break my oath frequently.

December 8, 1934

Today is the Feast of the Immaculate Conception, which marks the beginning of the Christmas holidays. Every year on this day, the feast is celebrated in the Church of Saint Francis, also called the Church of the Immaculate Conception.

In the morning, my mother, my sisters, and I went to church for Mass; the bishop of Piazza Armerina officiated. It was a great event, because the bishop seldom comes to Enna, except to confirm the boys and girls who have already received their First Communion.

My mother, who is an earnest Catholic, wanted all of us to be blessed by the bishop.

"When you come close to the bishop," she told us, "remember to kneel and kiss the ring he wears on his finger."

There was a long line to see the bishop. When I arrived by him, I was seized by awe and my legs were shaking, but I finally kissed his ring, and he repaid me with a smile and a loving caress.

My father was not with us because he was working at his sulfur mine. He has many workers under him and cannot leave the mine unattended.

In front of the church there was a long line of market stalls. They sold lupines, bilberries, and another tasty fruit called holy oil. In the square, which we citizens of Enna call Saint Francis Square, even though its real name is Piazza Vittorio Emanuele II, the city band played their wind instruments, drums, and cymbals nonstop. Then a litter with the statue of the Virgin Mary on it came out of the church. At least fifty brethren dressed in white robes and blue mantillas bore the heavy litter on their *shoulders. The city band followed the litter, and we got into the procession behind the band.*

The number of processions during the year in Enna is considerable. Every quarter has its own patron saint, who is taken in procession along the streets on the day of his or her feast.

When the procession was over, my mother bought four small paper bags of lupines, one for each of us.

December 13, 1934

Today is the feast of Santa Lucia, a saint from Syracuse who was martyred under the emperor Diocletian. She is the patron saint of the blind and people with limited eyesight.

As usual, there are processions on her day, and the statue of the saint is carried on a litter along the streets of Enna. On this day, many families in Enna make a special meal called cuccìa. *It is a ritual meal that was made in ancient Greece on the day of the commemoration of the dead. Nowadays in Sicily, the cuccìa is cooked on the day of the Feast of Santa Lucia. It is made from boiled wheat seasoned with chocolate or sweet ricotta, honey, and pieces of candied fruit. On this day, my sister Carolina cooks cuccìa in a big cauldron and then invites all our neighbors to taste it. Even though I don't like cuccìa, I really enjoy the coming and going of our neighbors who crowd my home all day long.*

December 21, 1934

There was a joyful atmosphere at home today. My aunts joined my mother to prepare buccellati. *They are typical Christmas sweets made from pastry filled with mashed almonds or dried figs. I was really happy to see my relatives gathering at my home and my mother chatting with them while they were making the buccellati.*

February 8, 1935

I wanted to become a Catholic priest and devote my life to God and Jesus, but after pondering my decision for a while I opted not to go to seminary. What prevents me from dedicating my life to Jesus is the fact that I don't feel I am able to suppress my sexual activity and my feelings for people of the opposite sex.

Being a Catholic priest means accepting a life of depriving oneself of sexual impulses. How can priests do that? In my opinion, many of them are homosexual. You can recognize a gay priest by the way he talks and acts. The inflection of his voice and his gestures clearly denote that he is a gay. Other priests are not gay but have some kind of secret relationship with women. Sometimes when their illicit love is unveiled, it is cause for scandal and they have to leave their ordained life to marry their lover. That happened a few times in Enna.

As for me, I am not able to take the vow of celibacy and suppress my sexual instincts, and above all, I don't want to give up my ordinary worldly life. Therefore, I have decided to follow Jesus in my daily life by doing my best to be a good person that abides by the precepts contained in the Gospels. It is not necessary to become a priest to be a good Christian!

The Catholic religion considers masturbation a deadly sin. Therefore, every time I masturbate, I rush to the priest to confess my sin. He doesn't tell me the reason why masturbation is a sin but confines himself to giving me absolution. I have decided to stop confessing, because I find it absurd to confess a sin and promise not to sin anymore when I know in advance that I will masturbate over and over again.

June 20, 1935

My afterschool teacher is quite strange. On the one hand she beats me, but on the other she has the habit of lifting up her skirt and pulling her nylon stockings up. When she does, she shows her thighs almost up to her groin. I am very embarrassed, and I try not to look at her. Her thighs are nice, but my awe of her is too great to think of her when I masturbate.

November 1, 1935

I am a high school student now. I got good grades in the entrance examinations. I am happy about getting rid of my afterschool teacher who used to beat me and show me her naked thighs, but now I am out of the frying pan and into the fire.

My new afterschool teacher is a man. He has the habit of beating me too. When he gives his lessons at his home, he wears a bathrobe and slippers. His bare feet stink so much so that sometimes I get a headache.

December 10, 1935

Today I was with another student, a girl, at the afterschool teacher's house. He was not in the room where he teaches us, but his sister was sitting in front of us. I started to play with the other student and touched her breast. The sister informed the teacher, who came in the study room and asked me to follow him to another room. Once there, without saying a word, he beat me more harshly than ever before. He punched me in the face and other parts of my body. Then he hit me with a hail of blows.

I will never forgive that teacher for that. He should have explained to me in words that my behavior was wrong, but he didn't. He just used his brutal power against a defenseless student. I cannot inform my parents because they trust the teacher more than me. They would say I am wrong.

March 7, 1936

I have two close friends at the high school. One, Renato, has the reputation of being a very good student. He is short, square-built, with a dark complexion. His hair and eyes are as black as a block of coal. The other, Fabrizio, is just a friend of his and doesn't belong to our school. He is always stuck to Renato, and as a consequence he is also my friend. He studies at the technical high school. He is a boy of medium build. In spite of his shoulders stooping a little, he is strong, and his brown, deep eyes show aggressiveness and defiance.

March 8, 1936

Today Fabrizio asked me, "Why don't you sit next to Renato in the class so you can copy his work and be a successful student?"

I answered, "I don't need to crib off him, because I am able to do my work by myself."

When I arrived home, I told my mother about the episode. I was proud of having turned down the proposal of copying Renato's work, but instead of praising me because I wanted to be independent and diligent at school, my mother rebuked me.

"You are stupid and silly," she spoke out. "Renato is a good student and can help you be successful. You should accept his proposal. Sit close to him at school and copy his work!"

I was astounded. I could never have imagined my mother acting that way. Obviously, what mattered to her was that I pass the final exam; it didn't matter how. It was important to her that at the end of my school career I got my certificate of degree, even if I didn't deserve it.

That way of thinking is widespread in Enna. A certificate of degree is considered more important than actual good grounding. In fact, by having a doctor's degree, you can get a job in the civil service through good political connections.

Nowadays, the competitive state examinations in Italy are all fixed. Membership in the Fascist Party or the closeness to this or that Fascist Party leader is a prerequisite to getting a good job or making progress in your career.

March 9, 1936

I followed my mother's orders and sat at the same desk with Renato. The consequences were disastrous. I stopped thinking with my mind and slavishly followed what he suggested to me. In the afternoons, when I didn't go to my afterschool teacher, I studied with him. Our way of studying was that he read the schoolbooks and then repeated to me what he had read, and I in turn repeated to him what he had said to me. In other words, I didn't read books anymore but confined myself to memorizing what he explained to me.

October 23, 1936

Fabrizio bullies me. He is very arrogant and mocks me continuously. Today, I tried to fight back, but he punched me. He is stronger than me and more aggressive. What to do? He is Renato's friend, and it's important I follow my mother's orders: "Follow Renato all the way, because he is a good student!"

I cannot breakup the friendship between Fabrizio and Renato, and now it is too late for me to be an independent student. In fact, I depend on Renato for my school progress. I am used to copying his work, and now I am unable to do my work by myself. Renato has become indispensable, and cribbing off him is a habit or, worse, an addiction for me.

By enduring Fabrizio's bullying, little by little I have quenched my natural sense of boldness. I get desperate whenever he mocks me. This morning he called me "queer." I felt humiliated, and my pride was wounded. This time I attacked him, but he soon reversed our positions and hit me very hard.

I cannot help recognizing his superiority. In fact, he is stout, stronger, and above all more aggressive than me. Every time he calls me "queer," I pretend not to hear him, but inside I am devastated. By acting this way, I have learned to be a victim of somebody else's power, and I will surely be a loser in life.

November 4, 1936

Fabrizio and Renato are proud of getting money from pederasts. They even boasted that a rich pederast used to give them two lire if they allowed him to masturbate them.

"Where did you meet that pederast? I want to get money from him as well!" I asked.

"Usually," they answered, "we meet him at the cinema. If you go to the cinema in the early afternoon, you can meet pederasts as well. As a rule, they hang about on the Belvedere in the evening or they go to the cinema in the early afternoon."

November 5, 1936

Today I went to the cinema at four in the afternoon and took a seat in the middle of the balcony, waiting for a pederast to come.

At a distance, in the same row, a distinguished gentleman was sitting pretending to watch the movie, but he had different ideas in his mind. He wore a blue jacket and a red tie. He had the air of belonging to a high class. He moved from the end of the row towards me and sat down two or three seats away. I watched him out of the corner of my eye. I thought he might be a pederast and give me some money.

All of a sudden, he moved close to me. It was evident that he intended to do something with me. In fact, the balcony was almost empty and there were a lot of seats available. Nevertheless, he was apparently not interested in me and kept watching the movie. He was sweating profusely and looked uneasy and tense. It seemed that a tremendous struggle was happening inside him. He unbuttoned his shirt and loosened his tie. It was too hot for him, so he took off his jacket and put it on his legs.

Little by little, he moved the jacket towards me and slipped his hand onto my genital area. He lowered my zipper, put his hand into my underpants, and took out my penis. I was not interested in his masturbation, but I didn't want to disappoint him, so he kept touching my penis. After about ten minutes, he left. Apparently, he had already satisfied his perverted sexual need.

I didn't get money from him. Maybe I should have asked him for money when he got close to me before allowing him to masturbate me. If I had had Renato's or Fabrizio's boldness, I would have acted differently, but I was too sheepish to have the strength to cope with that pederast.

I don't know if I will tell Fabrizio and Renato tomorrow about my meeting with the pederast. I will probably say nothing, because they will think I am a really stupid boy and will mock me for not being able to get money from the pederast.

January 8, 1937

Renato and Fabrizio convinced me to play hooky. Renato claimed that he was able to perfectly forge the headmaster's signature. He showed me the faked signature, which did actually look identical to the headmaster's.

In my school, every time you miss a class, a note written by one of your parents needs to be shown to the headmaster, who generally accepts the excuse and admits the student to class. Then the student has to show the note signed by the headmaster to the teacher in the classroom.

"It is very easy!" resounded Fabrizio. "The teacher in the classroom only checks the headmaster's signature, not your parents' note. Therefore, you can write the excuse note by yourself and Renato will forge the headmaster's signature."

"That is absurd!" I replied. "The teachers know my handwriting, and they will smell the trick."

"That's no problem!" said Renato. "Fabrizio doesn't belong to our school, and no teacher knows his handwriting. So, he can write the excuse note and the teacher in the class will not suspect the swindle. I can then forge the headmaster's signature. It's so easy and simple!"

I was so gullible that they convinced me to skip school. I had never done a fraud in my life. My parents are very strict, and if I don't tell them the truth, they beat me harshly. Above all, my mother doesn't endure me lying to her. Whenever she discovers I have told her a lie, she hits me wildly, sometimes even on my head.

We spent our hooky time at Lombardia Castle. It is a stronghold whose origins are lost in the dim and distant past. It stands on the highest place in Enna and dominates the valley, which in the springtime has a green color, while in the summertime it takes on a yellow hue due to the withering of the herbs from the scorching sun and the lack of rain. The castle is very old and stands on a rocky spur. You could say that the rock itself is a natural stronghold. In some stretches, the nearly sheer rock face is about twenty meters high.

Of the six towers left, the one in better condition is the Pisana tower, which, according to some historians, takes its name from the Roman consul Lucio Pisone, who took the stronghold by storm at the time of the slave revolt. Tourists from all over the world come to the top of the tower to see the scenery that encompasses a great part of Sicily.

Fabrizio wanted to show Renato and me how fearless he was. "Are you able to climb the rock face?"

"That is impossible!" we both answered. "It is sheer!"

"I'll do it!" he said, looking firm while his voice betrayed a hint of worry.

Renato and I tried to dissuade him from his mad idea, but he was stubborn. He took off his shoes in order to adhere better to the rock, and then started his crazy climbing. I was sure he would fall headlong, but to my surprise, little by little, he climbed the rock face and then climbed down from another side where the cliff was less steep.

We spent the morning around the castle area. From time to time, Renato approached some tourists to practice his English. At the time, we studied French as a foreign language at school, but Renato had taught himself English.

Finally, Fabrizio wrote the excuse notes for Renato and me, while Renato wrote a note for Fabrizio and forged the headmasters' signatures. Around the time our parents expected us to come home from school, we parted.

Oddly, today my father came home unexpectedly from the sulfur mine and questioned me about what I had done at school.

"Did the teacher test you today?" he asked.

At his question I blushed throughout my face.

"Why are you blushing? What happened to you?" continued my father.

I didn't know how to justify my blush, so I gave him the first answer I thought of. "Yes, today I was tested in Latin."

"How did you do? Was your teacher satisfied?"

"The test went so-so," I answered.

"Tell me what your teacher asked you and what your answers were."

What stressed me most was the fact that my father, who had studied only in elementary school, wanted me to tell him Latin. Anyway, after my continuous refusal to talk Latin, he finally gave up.

January 9, 1937

Today I had to enter class with a forged excuse note. My legs were quaking from the time I left home, my heart was in my mouth, and a wave of blush pervaded my whole face. What would I do if the teacher suspected the scam?

In the past, students had been suspended from school throughout Italy for disciplinary offenses. That happened in Enna in the classical high school. One day, a student unsatisfied with his final grades tore all the notices off of the school board where the names and marks of the successful and failed students were posted.

That was a serious offense, while my transgression was, in some way, forgivable. But who knows! Sometimes criteria to assess students' behaviors vary according to the person who is doing the judging. A venial fault may be considered a capital sin by a person that observes the rules strictly. As for me, the worst would happen if the headmaster informed my family of my hooky.

I met Renato at the school entrance. He looked quite calm and was going to show the teacher his fake excuse note with nonchalance. But I was not calm at all, and my legs shook as if I had a vibrator under my feet. It was impossible to show the teacher that excuse note, because I was sure that my hands would also be trembling when I handed the note to the teacher. It is absolutely impossible for me to lie.

What to do? I decided not to go to school and play hooky for the second time. This time I didn't go to the castle as I had done with Renato and Fabrizio, because somebody seeing me alone in that place at school time could inform my parents. Therefore, I went to the billiard room. I am not a good billiards player. Furthermore, I was not in the right mood to play. I confined myself to watching the others shoot pool, but the thick cloud of cigarette smoke that permeated the room made my eyes water.

After noon, I headed for my home.

January 10, 1937

I couldn't sleep well last night. The headmaster appeared to me in a dream and pointed the way out of the school to me. At the thought that I should tell my parents the truth, I woke up panting, my body damp with sweat.

I had to confront my ordeal, but I didn't have the boldness to show the teacher that goddamn forged excuse note. Furthermore, it referred to only one day of absence from school, but now I had been out for two.

I spent my third day away from school at the billiard room.

I went home at the usual time. As soon as I crossed the threshold, I saw my mother, who oddly was standing in the landing. She came close to me and then landed a punch on my eye, using all her might. If she had had the strength of a man, she would have sent me to the hospital. However, her fury was so high that she continued to beat me so badly that I reeled under her blows.

Then she started shouting. "I met Renato's mother by chance this morning! She told me you didn't go to school for three consecutive days!"

My mother screamed as if she were possessed, and meantime she kept dealing blows and kicking me. I couldn't react. I had been brought up as an obedient child. Furthermore, my mother had inculcated in me a sense of passive obedience to her by linking religious punishments to my acts of disobedience.

One day I was about to fight back against her, but her words made my blood run cold. "If you beat your mom, you will be excommunicated!" she said.

"What does that mean?" I asked.

"It means not to be recognized by God."

Fortunately, while she was screaming and beating me, my sisters ran down the stairs and rushed into the vestibule to make a wall between my mother and me. They took me under their protection until my mother's fury cooled down.

January 11, 1937

My mother wrote an excuse for me. To justify my absence, she wrote that I had been unwell. Now I could enter school without a problem. It was the first and last time I played hooky.

January 15, 1937

I saw three girls at the bus stop today. Two of them were the same height, but the third was quite tall. Of the shorter ones, the one with blue eyes and brown hair attracted me. The other two had both brown eyes and hair.

I noticed that every day they waited for the bus at the same stop after leaving school.

January 16, 1937

I pretended I was nonchalantly walking today when I passed the three at the bus stop and had a quick look at them. Abruptly, I changed my mind. Seeing her polished features, I fell in love with the one who is not very tall and has brown eyes. I want her to become my girlfriend, but I don't know how to approach her.

January 17, 1937

After long thinking, I finally approached the girl I liked and asked her to become my girlfriend. She refused, and I felt her refusal like a wound in my stomach.

April 4, 1937

While I was walking to the Belvedere, I fixed my eyes on a green-eyed girl. I liked her and decided to woo her. I approached and asked her to become my girlfriend. She said she would think about it.

April 9, 1937

I met the green-eyed girl again this evening. This time, she accepted my proposal to become my girlfriend. Once at home, I was happy because it was the first time I had managed to get a girlfriend, but I also asked myself if this relationship was not a makeshift solution. In fact, if the previous girl had not refused me, I wouldn't have approached the green-eyed girl. The body and polished manners of the previous girl had attracted me, but what to do! I cannot stay away from girls, so I accepted this stopgap.

October 8, 1937

The relationship with my girlfriend lasted a few months, but today I told her I didn't feel like continuing, so we split up.

February 10, 1938

I met a friend of mine outside of school. He is Nino, and he is four years older than me. He is passionately fond of hunting and owns a sporting gun and two greyhounds from Etna.

"Why don't you come with me this afternoon? I'll show you how to hunt," he said. I told him I had to go to my private teacher for afterschool activities that afternoon and couldn't.

"He is just a private teacher! Nothing happens if you skip one lesson!"

My friend insisted so much that he at last convinced me to go. After all, my afterschool teacher didn't require written excuse notes whenever I missed a lesson.

It was not a great day for my friend, and he didn't catch any prey. At sunset, we went to our homes with empty hands.

As soon as I entered the vestibule of my house, I met my parents' angry stares. They looked like two guards standing there to carry out an arrest warrant. Obviously, the teacher had informed them of my absence. Now they were ready to punish me harshly.

I had a feeling that something terrible was going to happen, so I ran headlong to my room while my parents ran after me. I entered my room just in time to lock the door, leaving my parents outside. I felt safe while I was locked in the room and just hoped my parents' fury would cool down within a few hours.

Unfortunately, events took a different direction I never expected.

My father kept pushing on the door, but the lock held. Despite his efforts, he was not able to force it. Abruptly, he started planting kicks to the door. His rage grew more and more while he continued shouting, "Open the door! Open the door!" But I took good care not to open it.

Suddenly, a blow more violent than the previous ones made a breach in the door, but the lock held. My father kept kicking the door until the breach became wide enough to let a person get through. When the entire door had almost collapsed, my parents stormed into the room like soldiers who had conquered an enemy's position. They rushed at me. I lay on my bed unmoving, resigned to my fate like prey under the predator's claws, unable to wriggle free from it and just waiting to be devoured.

My parents' violence was unprecedented. They both punched and beat me as if they were beating a drum. I was silent and passively bore their ferocity.

My sisters couldn't do anything to rescue me. They feared my father too much, but finally their love for me prevailed. They left and asked one of our neighbors to come because I was in danger.

At the sight of my sisters, who were visibly upset, our neighbor rushed to my aid and grabbed my father by the arm. "Stop beating your son or you'll kill him!" he yelled.

At his words, my father came to his senses and his ferocity diminished. His choleric dark eyes took on a light hue. Calm seemed to return to my grim house after the raging storm. My parents finally released their grip.

I overcame the terrible predicament thanks to my beloved sisters. I am sure that if I commit a serious fault one more time, my father will shoot me with his revolver.

I must be obedient in all ways. Now I want to immerse myself in studying. I am itching to finish my last year at the classical high school of Enna. Then I will move to the University of Catania, free from my parents' haunting presence.

February 11, 1938

The carpenter came to take out the broken door. He couldn't fix it because the frame couldn't be repaired. A new door was needed. While he was measuring the door opening, I sat on the bed pretending to read a book. Now and then he gave me a pitiful look. I was sure he knew, or at least he could figure out, what had happened to me yesterday.

I will stay at home for three days. I cannot show myself to my teachers and schoolmates in such bad condition. My body is covered with bruises.

July 2, 1938

Today was the first day of final school examinations all over Italy, which started with the written Italian test.

Even though this is the day of the most important feast in Enna, since it is a local feast, schools, public offices, and banks were open. At dawn, the city was woken by a hundred-and-one gun salute, and the city band went through the streets. Everybody got dressed up, and the farmers left the countryside and came to Enna. They are not well-off people and only own one formal dress, which they keep in the closet all year and wear on July 2 for the celebrations in honor of Our Lady of Visitation.

The subject of the Italian essay was "Describe nature as it is seen by Foscolo, Manzoni, and Leopardi" (three important Italian writers and poets). While I was absorbed in writing the essay, I heard the sound of the city band passing through the streets and hoped that today would be my feast day of liberation from Enna and from my oppressive parents. It took six hours to write the essay, but in the end, I felt sure I had done good work.

In the evening, I went out to see the procession. Barefooted brethren bore three litters in the procession with the statues of Our Lady, Saint Joseph, and the archangel Saint Michael along the street from the cathedral to the Franciscan monastery of Montesalvo.

July 20, 1938

I passed my final examinations and can now enter the University of Catania. I got through thanks to Renato, who helped me in the written work, and thanks to my father, who fixed my oral examination with the examining board.

Chapter Ten
The Public Whorehouse in Enna

There was a public whorehouse in Enna until 1958. Afterwards, all brothels were suppressed throughout Italy by an act of the national parliament. Enna's public whorehouse was located in the upper town, which looks onto the nearby town of Calascibetta, but it was not far from downtown. Of course, Enna is a small city lying on a plateau, and the distances between one side and another are not long.

To go to the public brothel from Saint Francis Square, which is the heart of the city, you had to go down the main street called Via Roma. When Mussolini came to power, he decreed that the main street in every Italian city, town, and village should be named Roma, which he considered not only the capital of Italy, but also the symbol of the Italian power, history, and traditions.

Walking a short distance down Via Roma, there is another small square called Piazza Balata, named by the Arabs who had conquered Sicily around the tenth century AD, and who remained here for two centuries until they were defeated by the Normans.

Four streets branch off from Piazza Balata. One of them that goes uphill is called Via S. Agata. The main business centers of Enna are on this street. The small Church of Santa Croce was located on Via S. Agata as well. The street that branches off downhill is called Via Pergusa. It leads towards mythological Lake Pergusa. Of the other two streets, one is the continuation of Via Roma, while the other leads to the area where the public whorehouse once was. That street is called Via Vittorio Emanuele II, who was the king when the unification of Italy took place.

Walking uphill on Via Vittorio Emanuele II, on the right there is a little square about one meter higher than the street, which at harvest time once swarmed with folk from all over Sicily. Those people were farm workers who hoped to get hired to reap the wheat which was abundant in the fields around Enna.

Further on is the impressive Church of San Cataldo with its wooden-trussed roof. According to a friend of mine who is an archaeologist, this church overlapped the old Temple of Persephone, named for Demeter's daughter. He could be right, because through a glass floor inside the church it is possible to see old remains that likely denote a preexisting place of worship.

Walking along the external wall of the church, the street gets narrower for a few meters and then leads to the area called *Popolo* (the common people). In this area, the street takes the form of a backbone from where, like ribs, a series of alleyways branch off. As we keep walking, we find the Church of Santa Maria del Popolo (Saint Mary of the People) on the left, the origin of which was the chapel of a convent of cloistered nuns.

Long ago, a great part of the city of Enna consisted of churches, convents, and monasteries. After the unification of Italy, the convent attached to the Church of Santa Maria del Popolo shared the lot of much of the ecclesiastic real estate. It was expropriated by the Italian liberal government. The nuns were asked to leave, and the Italian army turned the convent into a military garrison.

The ex-convent, the square in front of it, and the bordering houses took the appellation of *Colombaia* (dovecote), due to the fact that, before the telegraph was invented, the military detachment used to communicate with other outposts by carrier pigeons that were kept in the state-owned dovecote. The carrier pigeons had the task of delivering messages from one place to another, and it seems that they never got lost. In fact, they were able to cover a distance of a thousand kilometers at the speed of 100 kilometers per hour, bearing the message to be delivered stuck on their claw.

If you keep walking uphill on Via Vittorio Emanuele II, it leads to another street called Via San Francesco d'Assisi. Almost at the end of Via Vittorio Emanuele II, on the right, there is Via Aspromonte, a narrow alley that just leads to the building that was once the public whorehouse.

The brothel was run by a brothel keeper, but the building belonged to a wealthy Enna family and had been leased to an ex-prostitute who had made enough money from her "work." Brothel keepers were often called "queens" and were usually unmarried. If it happened that one of them was married, her husband was called the "king."

One room of the whorehouse was left for a police officer, who had the task of keeping order and checking the personal documents, above all the ones regarding the customer's age. In fact, entrance was forbidden to young men under eighteen years of age. Nevertheless, the brothel keeper controlled everything in advance and kept order. She was always present at the entrance and was very strict with both the prostitutes and the customers.

The brothel's main door was kept ajar till late into the night. A wide red curtain separated the entrance from the rest of the house. Over the curtain there was a hall. The queen's room was on the right, and on the left two steps led to a corridor. At the bottom was the room for the policeman; on the left there were two wide bedrooms, and on the right two waiting rooms.

The bedrooms were equipped with a washbasin, a bidet, an irrigator, and a small closet where tubes containing calomel ointment, thymol, and silver mercury for the treatment that had to be done after every intercourse were kept, and of course there was a bed. It was a big double bed covered with a bedspread and a simple white cotton sheet.

The whorehouse was not furnished with a heating system, so every room had a wood stove with a saucepan full of water on it, which served the purpose of keeping moisture in the air. The hot water was also used to fill hot-water bottles that warmed up the girls and also the chilly customers, who put them on their genitals. Some girls obliged their customers by taking a hip bath, using the bidet, before having sex.

In the waiting rooms, where the customers sat on wooden sofas, there were placards that listed the dangers of sexually transmitted diseases, the preventive treatments to apply, the location of the prevention and treatment dispensaries, and where to go for clinical tests.

In one of the lounges that the girls used to talk with the customers there was a desk where the queen kept the accounts. One drawer held the tokens and in the other she stashed the money. After the customer had paid the fee, the girl got a token, which was the equivalent of a simple sexual intercourse, and at the end of the day the tokens that each girl collected were counted and exchanged into ready money by the brothel keeper.

Behind the desk, stuck on the wall, there was the price list pinned on a wooden board:

- Simple service £ 1
- Double £ 1.8
- Fifteen minutes £ 2.20
- Half an hour £ 3.50
- One hour £ 5
- Towel and soap £ 0.50

From the hall, a staircase led upstairs where there were three more rooms for the girls, the medical room, and another waiting room reserved only for high-class people or someone that wanted to hide his identity, like a priest, a monk, or a married person. The entrance to this waiting room was regulated by the queen, who ordered the doors to all rooms shut, except the one reserved for the police, in order to let in the person that had asked to remain anonymous.

Another staircase led to the basement, which was comprised of the kitchen, the laundry, and the dining room.

The meeting between the girls and their customers took place in the waiting rooms. It was not as easy as you might imagine to find a mutual attraction, because everyone has different tastes. Some people liked a thin girl, and others a plump one, or one with a great pair of tits. Some preferred blondes and others the dark-haired ones. Once the choice had been made, the couple headed for the bedroom, and within about ten minutes the meeting was over. It was possible to stay in the bedroom for a longer time, but in that case the customer obviously had to pay more.

Before having intercourse, the girls examined their customers very carefully, and sometimes they were able to diagnose some of the sexually transmitted diseases.

Some customers took two girls, and sometimes a couple of men went into the bedroom with only one girl. Sexual activities varied widely. Some men liked to have anal intercourse with the girl, some enjoyed the girl sucking or moving her tongue around his penis, while others preferred to move their tongue across the female sexual organs.

A friend of mine, who had been a great haunter of the brothel, told me that before having sex he licked the whore all over her body, from the tip of her toes to her crown. He told me that the time he spent there was the most beautiful in his life. The charming atmosphere of the girls sitting in the lounge was unforgettable. He enjoyed talking and joking with them for a while before going to the room to have sex.

In 1958, when public whorehouses were suppressed by law, he stuck a death notice on the walls of the buildings in Enna: "The public whorehouse of Enna is dead and an era is over. All the men who used to go to that house mourn the loss of their beloved meeting place."

The prostitutes in the whorehouse shifted every fifteen days. The fortnight shift happened by bilateral agreement between the brothel keeper and the prostitutes. The girls were brought there by a recruiter. Once in the brothel, they had to give half of their earnings to the queen. They also had to pay their board and lodging.

In the brothel, the girls took nicknames, which usually reflected the place of their origin or the peculiar "skills" they had. For instance, if one was good at giving a man oral pleasure, she was called the blow jobber.

The girls slept or rested in the mornings; only one of them was on duty and available in case a customer had the pressing need to have sex. In the evenings, all the girls sat scantily dressed in the lounge where the meetings with their customers took place. Some men quite often went to the whorehouse just to chat with the girls. They didn't want to have sex, but just to loaf about. In this case, the queen intervened and asked the person to leave. However, as Enna is a small city where almost everyone knows one another, the queen was able to spot the dawdlers in advance and didn't allow them to enter.

The chat with the girls went on for a while in the lounge. Some people liked to grope the girls before making their choice. Once the customer had opted for one of the girls, she couldn't refuse, even if he was ugly, dirty, or had a penis out of proportion. She had to follow him to the room and satisfy him according to his will.

A friend of mine, who had lived in Enna during the Second World War, told me that when the American troops conquered the city, most of the soldiers were looking for brothels or prostitutes that ran their business at home.

One of the freelance whores lived in Colombaia Quarter not far from my friend's home. He told me that whenever he passed by her house, he heard her crying out with pain. Obviously, there were some problems with the penis size of those soldiers, or the way they wanted to have sex.

Whorehouses in Italy had different standards. There was a classification similar to that of hotels, ranging from five-star to one-star. The whorehouse in Enna was listed at three-star. The difference of the standards of brothels was given not only by the more luxurious environment, but above all by the quality of the female "material." Girls in a four- or five-star brothel had to meet certain criteria: beauty, age, and above all buxomness.

All girls in any brothel had to have their health certificate to work. Apparently, the society of that time was openly male chauvinist, because health certificates were required only for girls, not for men that entered the whorehouse. The fact is that after one year of work almost all prostitutes fell ill with a venereal disease, especially syphilis. When the queen had the tiniest suspicion that a girl had contracted a venereal disease, she asked her to leave the house right away.

In Enna's whorehouse, the new girls all had to undergo health examinations. The outpatient clinic was on the other side of the city, so the new prostitutes were paraded by the queen through Via Vittorio Emanuele II, Saint Francis Square, and Via Roma to go to the doctor. It was a good opportunity for them to be seen by the townspeople and to publicize themselves.

The medical examination consisted of an overall body check-up, but above all, the genitals and mucosae needed to be examined. Then the doctor had to check if gonococcus, the etiological agent of gonorrhea, was present.

Even though the examination was very thorough, it didn't guarantee with absolute certainty that the prostitute didn't have a contagious venereal disease. In fact, all infectious diseases have an incubation period of a few days. During that time, it was impossible to make an accurate diagnosis, and a sick prostitute could still infect her customers.

My friend who lived during the brothel era told me that an outstanding professional man who was married to a noblewoman once contracted syphilis when he had sex with a prostitute in a five-star brothel in Catania. He then infected his wife, who was pregnant. The twins she gave birth were both born syphilitic. It was a real tragedy at that time. Syphilis could not be cured completely, and it affected many organs like the liver, the kidneys, and the central nervous system.

Besides the activity that was run in public whorehouses, there was a kind of underground prostitution. Those prostitutes took a seat in front of their homes—usually located on the ground floor and looking onto the street—and lured passersby. Sometimes the oldest prostitutes took in a young girl.

Those whores were not as beautiful as the ones in public brothels. They were often getting on in years. Their average age was around forty or fifty, but they were the only way for teenagers to have sex. At that time, morals were very strict, and it was even considered improper for unmarried couples to merely stroll on the street. Whenever two engaged people wanted to go together to some place, to the cinema for instance, or just wanted to take a walk, they needed to be escorted by another woman of the family, who remained stuck to them all the way.

For teenagers, there was no other opportunity to have sex except with a whore. Most of the teenagers in Enna had their entry into the sex world through prostitutes that ran their business at home. While whores in brothels didn't need a pimp, for street prostitutes, a kind of protection was necessary. Usually, the pimp was her lover who had started her off on the career as a prostitute.

The greatest danger whenever a boy had sex with a whore was contracting a contagious disease. Some sexually transmitted diseases were not very serious, like pediculosis and candidiasis, while others like syphilis were very dangerous. Gonorrhea was considered much less serious than syphilis, and if no complications arose, it was cured without any lasting effects.

Chapter Eleven
Vincenzo's Diary, Part Two

November 3, 1938

I decided to enter the University of Catania. I had been quite hesitant about which school to choose. I would have liked to be a diplomat, but I thought I would not pass the competitive state examination to be a diplomat without good political connections. I was about to enroll in law school, but after long rumination I gave up, because in my opinion it was not right for me. In fact, to be a lawyer or a judge you must be endowed with a strong personality. I was hesitant and too anxious whenever I had a close confrontation with my opponents. I would have liked to study the classic languages and literature, but I had become accustomed to copying the schoolwork on translations from Latin and ancient Greek into Italian from Renato, and now I didn't have enough confidence in myself to continue classical studies. Finally, I opted to enter the school of medicine, which would allow me to help others and relieve people's sufferings.

Catania is quite far from Enna, so I must live there if I want to attend lectures and seminars.

November 5, 1938

My father has found accommodations for me at the boys' boarding school that is run by Catholic priests. The room is wide and full of light, but the bathroom is shared with the other students. It was my father who chose the room. I would have preferred another room that overlooked the playground, but my father said no because he thought it would take my mind off my studying.

My parents entrusted me to the warden and presented him with one cheese typical of Enna called Piacentino. *My father wanted to know how much freedom I would have. The warden told him that students are free from seven in the morning until ten in the evening. If a student gets home late, he is automatically expelled from the boarding school.*

My father and mother finally left for Enna, and at long last I was alone in Catania. For the first time in my life, I savor the taste of freedom. In fact, I will be far away from my overbearing parents!

November 6, 1938

The beginning of my university experience is a time for taking stock of my life. I want to radically change my way of living. What I wouldn't do if it was possible to go back in time! First of all, I wouldn't copy Renato's work at school. That was one of the biggest mistakes of my life. By cribbing off Renato, I lost my self-esteem, which is one of the most important features of a human. Without it, a human being is like a ship adrift at the mercy of the waves.

Another mistake I wouldn't repeat would be accepting Fabrizio's bullying. Everything is linked in human behavior. If I had not copied Renato's work, I wouldn't have lost my self-esteem, and therefore I would have been stronger and more sure of myself, able to cope with Fabrizio. Surely, I would have found a way to oppose his bullying.

A third thing I wouldn't repeat is the mistake of judging by appearances. So far, I've only approached girls on the basis of the features of their face and the voluptuousness of their body. From now on, I will value the inward side of women much more.

November 10, 1938

I have been approached by other students who are very pleased to have me as a friend. I want to change the way I behave with my companions. I was bullied by Fabrizio in Enna;

here I want to look like I am a strong guy, endowed with courage, dignity, and strength. Unfortunately, that is not my real character, and sooner or later my weakness will come to the surface.

November 18, 1938

A friend of mine advised me to buy a toy pistol. "With such a weapon," he said, "you can appear stronger than you are. All the students will fear you and your personality will be strengthened."

I did as my friend advised. I bought the toy pistol and plan to show it to my new friends.

November 19, 1938

I showed my toy pistol to the other students, but apparently nobody cares about my gun. Even though I have a revolver, I don't look like an aggressive or dangerous boy. After showing it a few more times, I finally opted to throw it away. I still cannot rid myself of the bad habit of doing whatever my friends suggest.

November 22, 1938

Today was my first day of school. In the morning, the lecturer held a lesson about human anatomy. I am enthusiastic about my career and feel I can become a good doctor.

In the afternoon, I read my textbooks eagerly and was sure I would pass my exams without help from anybody. I feel strong, sure of myself, and don't need my father to fix my exams for me to pass them, as it happened in the past.

December 15, 1938

I have a good relationship with the other students in the boarding school. I don't accept it when other students try to bully me. I look quite strong and nobody dares to defy me.

December 16, 1938

My tendency to follow others blindly is not always negative. Staying in Catania at the boarding school, I have struck up a friendship with two very good friends. One of them, Ugo, is from a village at the foot of the Madonie Mountains. He is so shy that he doesn't allow anybody to enter his room. He looks a little bit strange, but he has a good classical education. He reads all kinds of books, because for him culture is all-embracing.

Seeing him so inclined, I started reading books too. So far, I have only read books needed to make headway at school. Now, I want to broaden my cultural scope.

I have to thank Ugo because he put me on the amazing path of books. I will owe it all to him if my cultural horizons broaden.

December 17, 1938

My other good friend at the university is Mario. He is from a town near Syracuse called Noto. He studies at the School of Mathematics. He is a close friend of the warden of the boarding school. He has got the keys to the warden's room, and from time to time invites me to go there. We sit in the armchairs and listen to classical music.

He also teaches me the history of music. "This overture is by Rossini!" Mario explained. "He is famous for his crescendos. This is the 'Moonlight Sonata' by Beethoven. He is a great composer. Did you know that he couldn't listen to his masterpiece, 'The Ninth Symphony,' because he was deaf?"

Mario helped me enter a new world unknown to me. We didn't listen to music at home in Enna. We had a radio with a gramophone, but we confined ourselves to listening to the news bulletin. The only kind of music I had heard before was the Italian national anthem and Fascist songs like "Giovinezza."

February 5, 1939

The celebrations in honor of Saint Agata, the patron saint of Catania, reached their peak. Townspeople wore white habits and ashen-black headdresses. For ten days, twelve gigantic candles on baroque-style litters were borne on the shoulders of guild members as they went along the streets. Today, the litters went ahead of the statue of Saint Agata to light up the street. The patron saint stood on a wagon dragged by hundreds of devotees.

People crowded round the statue and lit big wax candles, which they then handed a man on the wagon. There were so many candles that the wagon couldn't hold them all. Every now and then, it was emptied of all the candles and they were tossed into a truck.

The wagon was dragged along the places where Saint Agata suffered martyrdom. According to history, the saint belonged to a noble family and wished to be a Christian, but the Roman governor wanted to possess her. She refused, and for that she was imprisoned and later executed.

I saw the procession from the sidewalk of Via Etnea. The streets were so crowded that it was impossible for me to get near the wagon, so I watched the bust of Saint Agata from a distance.

There were also many street vendors. I saw an unusual, beautiful red apple in one of the stalls. I asked the vendor what it was, and he told me it was an apple mixed with sugar, the traditional fruit of the Feast of Saint Agata. I couldn't help purchasing and eating that apple before I headed for my lodging house.

I would like to write down more things about Saint Agata and the celebrations in her honor, but I have to stop and study hard. I really want to pass the exams on my own, unlike in the past. I want to show that I don't need Renato's support.

June 22, 1939

I got up this morning telling myself, "I must pass my first exam!" I knew that if I passed my test in anatomy, all the doors of my career would be flung open. As soon as I got out of bed, my heart beat fast. I was aware that I had to strive to keep my nerves and emotions calm or all my studying would be useless. I asked Saint Agata to help me. Above all, I was eager to pass my examination to make my father happy and so he would be proud of me.

There were three professors sitting behind the desk inside the exam room. On the opposite side were some students sitting and watching the interrogations. As soon as I sat down, I gave the professor in the middle, who was obviously the chairman of the examination board, my undergraduate record book. He asked me to sign both that and another register. To my surprise, I noticed that my anxiety had disappeared and I was ready to face my ordeal.

The three professors tested me orally for an hour. With my nervousness gone, I felt able to continue the test indefinitely. Finally, the chairman gave me back my record book, and all three professors shook my hand.

I felt like I'd passed the exam. Mario and Ugo, who had come to encourage me, felt that the test had gone not badly. We left the room, and I opened my record book to see the mark I'd been given. To my surprise, and to the great delight of Mario and Ugo, I had passed the exam with full marks!

I called my parents to give them the good news. They were as happy as me.

June 28, 1938

My mother called me on the phone this afternoon. She was worried about me and told me to eat good food and go to a restaurant from time to time. She asked me if I had seen Renato and Fabrizio, who studied in Catania as well. She overheard that their marks were not as good as mine, and they had even failed a test.

June 29, 1939

It was a very hot day in Catania. Ugo, Mario, and I decided to go to the beach. I had never seen the sea until I came to study in Catania. The color of the sea was fantastic. It looked like an infinite space and took on the same hues as the sky. The water was deep, and many people enjoyed swimming. Mario and Ugo didn't know how to swim and remained under the beach umbrella, while I had no problems floating in the deep water because I had learned to swim at Lake Pergusa near Enna.

July 1, 1939

I go back to Enna once a month to see my family, but tomorrow is a special day for my hometown. We celebrate the feast in honor of Our Lady of Visitation, the patron saint of Enna. Last year I could not enjoy the festival because I was worried about my final examinations in school, but now I am free from school commitments. Moreover, I consider myself a winner because I passed my anatomy exam.

I headed for Theater Square in Catania early in the morning to take the bus back to Enna. This time I wanted to stay home for a week and spend my time cheerfully, even though there are not many things to do in Enna. I usually confine myself to strolling along Via Roma.

July 2, 1939

I was awakened at seven o'clock by the sound of the one-hundred-one gun salute that announced the feast. I got dressed and, at nine o'clock, my mother, sisters, and I went to Mass celebrated at the cathedral. When the Mass was over, my mother and sisters went home to prepare lunch, while I remained in the street to have a look at the stalls on Via Roma and the Belvedere.

While I was strolling, I stumbled across Renato and Fabrizio. They were still inseparable friends. I pretended not to have seen them, but Fabrizio called me in a loud voice, so I couldn't escape them.

"Hi, Vincenzo!" Renato said, smiling from ear to ear.

"Hi, Renato and Fabrizio," I said in return.

"I heard you got good marks on your exams. Is it true?"

"Yes, it is true. I don't need your help anymore. I can manage my studying by myself," I answered with a sneering smile.

Renato tried to show happiness for my success, but a wince on his face showed that he was green with envy.

"Fabrizio and I intend to go to the brothel. Would you like to join us?"

"Are you crazy? If my father found out that I had sex with a whore, he'd immediately shoot me with his revolver. He's a hothead! Do you want me to die?"

"Don't be a stupid, silly boy!" he replied. "How would your father know? We go to the brothel, have our intercourse with a beautiful girl, and then everything is over. Nobody, except Fabrizio and me, will know that you had sex with a prostitute."

"Somebody might see me while I am entering the whorehouse. Enna is full of nosey people who enjoy reporting what they've seen. One of them could tell my father that I knocked on the brothel's door."

"That's impossible!" said Fabrizio. "The front door of the whorehouse is kept ajar all the time. So we're not noticed, we will pretend to stroll in the street, and then we will suddenly turn left and step into the brothel."

"I have to think about that," I answered. "Are you going there now?"

"Not right away," Renato said, "because in the morning, the doors of the brothel are kept shut. This evening, after seven o'clock, is a good time to go."

"Tomorrow there is the fortnight shift!" Fabrizio said. "New whores will arrive in Enna from northern Italy. I overheard that one of them is very beautiful and also works with her mouth."

"Thank you very much, but I cannot come with you. It's very dangerous. We could get a disease. And if that happened, what would I do to cure myself? I cannot tell my father that I got a sexually transmitted disease at the brothel!"

"That is impossible!" replied Renato.

"Why is it impossible?"

"Because the whorehouse is a public establishment run by a brothel keeper who has a license from the government. The prostitutes are checked and tested nonstop by a doctor who is a specialist in venereal diseases, so it's impossible to get one!"

"Let's meet tomorrow at Saint Francis Square at seven o'clock, and then we'll go together. You will have an unforgettable experience," Fabrizio and Renato said with one voice.

"I am not sure whether or not I can come," I answered.

When I arrived home, my entire family was enjoying the merry atmosphere of the feast. My father had shot several wild rabbits and one hare. My mother had cooked exquisite food. On the table were plates full to the rim with steaming spaghetti seasoned with hare gravy. Moreover, there were a lot of side dishes. As for my sisters, they had baked a big fruit cake, set the table, and filled the glasses with red wine.

Very few times had I enjoyed the peace and the gaiety that pervaded my family today. We all sat around the table, and before eating, my father proposed a toast to me. He was proud and happy to have a son who passed his anatomy exam with full marks.

In the evening, we all went to see the procession. My mother and my sisters followed it in bare feet. They had promised Our Lady that they would do so if she granted them the gift of me passing my exam.

July 3, 1939

At seven o'clock in the evening, I was in my room holding one of the books Ugo had advised me to read. It was The Late

Mattia Pascal by Luigi Pirandello. I was reading to myself when my mother entered my room.

"Renato and Fabrizio are waiting for you in the landing. They asked me to call you. If you don't want to see them, I can come up with an excuse. What do you want me to do?"

At my mother's words, I snorted, closed the book, and got out of bed. I was quite hesitant about what to do. I was not enthusiastic about them being in my house, but I was too well-mannered to send them away. So, I got dressed and met them in the landing.

As soon as I saw them, I stopped short.

"I have no intention of going to the brothel. If that's why you've come, you are free to go while I remain at home reading my book," I said in a harsh tone.

"Vincenzo! Don't forget we're your best friends. We just want to go for a walk together like the old days."

Seeing their insistence, I gave in.

We were strolling along Via Roma and the Belvedere when Fabrizio abruptly burst out, "If you don't come to the brothel, it means that you are a gay."

"I am not a gay! I told you why I cannot go. If my father finds out I went to the brothel, he'll shoot me for sure."

They then slipped their hands under my arms and pushed me forward. "Come on, Vincenzo! We are your best friends. Trust us! You will enjoy it. You will have the most exciting experience of your life. It will be like being in paradise!"

I had promised myself that I would only consider girls based on their spiritual qualities. Having sex without love was, for me, like drinking a bottle of cheap wine. However, I had put up with Fabrizio's bullying and Renato's boldness for too long time, and I was still too weak to oppose them.

We kept walking along the Belvedere for a while, but little by little Fabrizio and Renato walked me towards Piazza Balata and then to Via Vittorio Emanuele II. I followed them passively because I was still dominated by their baleful influence over me.

We walked across Popolo Quarter until we arrived at Via Aspromonte, which led directly to the brothel.

The facade looked grim. All the shutters were closed to prevent anyone from the outside seeing in. Between the whorehouse and the edge of the cliff there was a pathway that overlooked the valley and the town of Calascibetta.

Before crossing the threshold, I had a moment's indecision. I walked to the edge of the cliff and had a look at the valley, which was embroidered with the feeble lights of the scattered farmhouses. Calascibetta looked like a Nativity scene, while in the distance Mount Etna was erupting. It was a silent night, and I could even hear the sound of the cowbells coming from the countryside. The landscape reminded me about the simplicity and spontaneity of nature. Making love with a prostitute sounded artificial and unnatural, the exact opposite of the wonderful scenery that spread out before my eyes.

I had a bad feeling about the whole thing. My legs were shaking and my hands were sweating. I thought of my father who, with his revolver in his hand, was ready to shoot at me. I was on the brink of giving up the idea of entering the brothel, but my natural curiosity and tendency to try new experiences prevailed.

Fabrizio passed the red curtain, and a lady dressed in a short silk skirt and a stole made of ostrich feathers welcomed us. She took us to a big lounge where six or seven whores were lazing and chatting while waiting for their customers. As soon as we entered the hall, the girls smiled at us, for they were vying for the customers' attention. Obviously, the more sexual encounters they had, the more they made.

The queen was sitting behind the desk. She asked me to show her my identity card to make sure I was over eighteen. She already knew Renato and Fabrizio, who went directly to the sofa and sat close to the girls. They chatted and laughed with the girls as if they'd known one another for a long time. Two girls leapt on Renato's and Fabrizio's legs, who for their part groped their thighs, breasts, and buttocks.

"Where is that girl from northern Italy who is attractive and works with her mouth?" I whispered in Renato's ear.

"Ask the queen!" Renato answered with a vulgar laugh.

"The girl is not in the lounge," the queen answered. "She is entertaining another person, but she will be here in a little while. Her customer has paid for a simple service, so it will not take much time."

I turned to the staircase and saw a tall, slender, peroxide-blonde girl coming down. She looked beautiful at a distance, but as she came near the queen's desk, I spotted many imperfections that ruined her pale face.

The queen beckoned the girl to join me. What I especially disliked in a lady was a lack of refinement. A gracefulness of bearing and a delicacy of features were essential to me when I approached a girl. I couldn't have sex with a girl whose features and manners were coarse.

I was on the verge of upsetting everything—the brothel, my two friends, the queen, the whore—and running away home, but I was much too polite to let the girl down, who in any case was just doing her job.

"Did you ask for me?" she said, holding my hand.

"Yes, I did."

"Let's go up to my room!"

I had a look around and didn't see Renato and Fabrizio. Apparently, they had gone to the rooms with the girls they had chosen. In the lounge, the other girls, the queen, and two customers looked at me, curious about my hesitation.

I saw that the customers chatted with the girls for a while before heading to a room, but I had nothing to say to the whore that was waiting for me. I was in the place just to have sex. Besides, I was not a good talker, and I sometimes had the sensation that my heart was as cold and hard as a piece of metal. I preferred not to talk when I had nothing to say, because everything I said was as if it came from a robot and not from a human being. I kept watching the girls and their customers, and

I asked myself what they were talking about. And why didn't I have anything to say? My mouth seemed sealed. I had the sensation that my inner soul was already dead and unable to express itself.

After a while of looking at each other without saying a word, the whore I had chosen broke the silence and said, "Let's go!"

"Yes, we can go."

I followed her up the stairs and then into her room. The environment smelled like loose face powder. The furnishings were a console table with an upright mirror, a small closet, a sink, and a double bed. In one of the corners of the room was a wood stove with a pot full of hot water on it. She obviously used the water to wash her vagina after each encounter.

She stripped bare and lay down on the bed. Seeing that I was standing motionless by the bed, she got up and slowly undressed me. She finally took off my underpants and started working on my penis with her mouth. Not one word was exchanged between us. I was about to leave the room and pay my fee in vain, but when she sucked my penis, I couldn't resist and soon became very excited.

Then she lay down on her bed again. "Come to me; don't be shy. Is this the first time you've made love with a girl?"

"Yes, it is," I answered with a trembling voice. She had taken off all my clothes except my socks, so I took them off as well.

"What are you doing?" she said, laughing loudly. "Do you think you are going to bed to sleep?"

I climbed on top of her, but I couldn't find the entrance to her vagina, so she grabbed my penis and inserted it into her. The intercourse lasted a few minutes. When it was over, I felt disgusted. That loveless intercourse left an acrid taste in my mouth, as if I had drunk bitter medicine.

After we finished, she washed my genitals and her vagina. We got dressed and went downstairs. Once in the lounge, she got a token from the queen, who was sitting at her desk. I took a seat on an armchair and waited for Renato and Fabrizio.

They came fifteen minutes later, beaming with joy.

"I climaxed twice!" Renato said.

"Me too!" Fabrizio replied.

We paid our fees and left the brothel. They both kept boasting of their sexual potency.

"Why don't we go to the tavern and drink some wine?" asked Fabrizio.

The subtle thread that had kept my friendship with them alive was broken. I felt a heavy burden walking with them and passively following their whims.

"No thank you," I replied. "I'm going to walk along the Belvedere for a little while and then go home."

When I returned home, my parents were talking about me. I felt guilty of a great sin, and I think my eyes revealed that I was trying to hide something.

"Are you okay?" my mother asked. "Your face is pale!"

"No, I am okay. I just took a walk with Renato and Fabrizio."

"You need to forget them! You are a good university student now and need new and different friends. Those two are not right for you!"

I couldn't understand my mother. Years ago, she spurred me to strike up a friendship with Renato and copy his work. Now she was suggesting I do the opposite: "You must strike up a friendship with new students at the university, Vincenzo!"

While my mother was giving me her advice, I wondered why I had to look for new friends. Friendship just happens. Bonds of friendship are not something to look for. In fact, friendship is a feeling, and you cannot look for something immaterial like feelings or emotions in the same way you look for an item to buy. Friendship and love are feelings that grow inside you when the conditions are the right. I have to confine myself to just living my life and new friends will naturally arrive. No need to look for them.

July 12, 1939

I'm back in Catania at my boarding school. I have to study hard, because I have to pass another exam at the end of this month.

Last night, something unusual happened to me. I couldn't urinate easily. In fact, I got up and went to the bathroom three or four times trying to go. I did it with difficulty, but I couldn't empty my bladder.

July 13, 1939

This morning I woke up with a sore throat. Now, besides my trouble urinating, I have to cope with my throat. What is happening to my body? Maybe I've caught flu and am experiencing its symptoms. I'm sure I'll get over it in a few days!

July 14, 1939

The difficulty urinating and my sore throat persist. I have also noticed that my underpants are soiled with a yellowish, greenish, evil-smelling liquid. My testicles are a little bit swollen, and my eyes have taken on a reddish color.

July 15, 1939

I woke up with a pain in my testicles, my eyes were watering, and the light of the day irritated them. I am worried about my condition. I need to do something. There is a medical student at the school who is about to graduate. I'll ask him for advice.

July 16, 1939

This morning I approached Vittorio, the sixth-year medical student. He told me I looked a little bit strange in the face when he saw me. He said I was pale and my eyes seemed to be suffering from conjunctivitis.

"You are right, Vittorio," I said. "I am not well. Could you examine me, please?"

He brought me to his room, and I lay down on his bed. He examined my throat and eyes, and then I took down my trousers and underpants. As soon as he smelled the stench and saw the yellowish hue of the blotches on my underpants, any doubt vanished from his mind.

"Did you have sex with a whore?" he asked.

"Yes, in the whorehouse in Enna two weeks ago."

"I hope it isn't too late!" he said with a worried expression. "We have to talk with a friend of mine who is graduated and works at the venereal disease unit in the hospital."

July 17, 1939

Vittorio took me to an appointment with his friend at the hospital. He was very friendly and looked like a competent doctor. He examined me meticulously and then expressed his diagnosis.

"You are suffering from a sexually transmitted disease called gonorrhea. This disease is caused by a bacterium called Neisseria gonorrhoeae. To treat it, we use a bactericide called silver nitrate. It has bactericide and disinfectant properties. It is injected through the orifice in the glans.

"There is a very powerful antibiotic called penicillin, but it is under testing and not available yet. Maybe it will be on the market next year. When you go to Enna, go to the hospital right away to have your disease treated. Don't lose time! Treat your disease as soon as possible, before it is too late."

I left the hospital confused. I didn't know what to do. I should go to the hospital in Enna, but it would mean that I have to tell my parents the truth. When my father finds out that I contracted the illness in the whorehouse, he will kill me. Knowing him, I have no doubt about that.

I cannot go to Enna and tell my father that I need to go to the hospital. I fear him too much. What to do?

July 20, 1939

I heard that lemon has disinfectant properties. So, I thought that if I injected a few drops of lemon into the orifice in my penis, the citric acid would kill the bacteria and I'd get over my gonorrhea, and maybe I wouldn't need to go to the hospital.

I cut a lemon in half and squeezed it into the mouth of my penis. When the drops got into my orifice, the pain was the worst I had ever felt. I couldn't endure such terrible pain, and I rolled all over the ground. I thought about banging my head against the wall.

July 30, 1939

My condition is getting worse. The lemon didn't work. I am very weak and feel the urgent need to talk with my parents and go to the hospital in Enna as soon as possible. It is the end of the month and time I normally go home to see my parents.

July 31, 1939

I took the bus at Theater Square, and three hours later I arrived in Enna. I got off, took my baggage from the roof, and headed for my house.

As soon as my mother saw me when I walked in, she put her hands on her head. She didn't have the strength to speak. "What happened to you, my son!" she said in a whisper.

"Nothing bad, Mom, but I feel very weak. Maybe I need to go to the hospital."

"Your dad will be home this evening. We'll talk with him and decide together what to do."

I couldn't stand the light. My eyes were too sensitive. I went to lie down and asked my mom to wake me when my father got home. I was terribly embarrassed thinking about my father knowing the truth about my disease. What would he do? Would he shoot me with his revolver? Or would he punish me in a different way?

In the evening, my father came home and, seeing my bloodshot eyes, he had no doubt. "Vincenzo, don't worry. You will recover your health, but we have to go to the hospital immediately."

August 1, 1939

I went to the hospital and was put in a single room. After visiting me, the general practitioner called for a consultation with the specialist in sexually transmitted diseases. I was terrified that my father would know the truth now.

When the specialist came, he examined me thoroughly and then went out of the room with my father. Obviously, he was informing him about the kind of disease I was suffering from. My father is a very strict and harsh person, but he is endowed with a heart as great as the entire universe. I knew he would try everything possible to save my life.

When he came back into my room, he kissed me on the forehead and then whispered in my ear, "Vincenzo, we must go to Catania. The hospitals there are more advanced. We'll leave tomorrow in the early morning."

Apparently, the doctors in Enna had given up hope of saving my life.

August 2, 1939

My parents and I took a bus to Catania. We went to the venereal disease unit in the general hospital. The doctors there agreed with their colleagues in Enna. It was not possible to treat me because the bacterial infection was widespread now, and there was no broad-spectrum antibacterial medicine available. Penicillin was under testing.

August 3, 1939

The report that I was doomed to die was a great blow to my father. He wanted to try more, so he decided to call a professor from Paris who was a specialist in treating bacterial infections.

August 7, 1939

Today, I received a visit from the luminary at the University of Paris. He entered my room followed by a train of other doctors. He didn't speak Italian.

He carefully examined my tests, talked with the other physicians, and then began a close examination of my whole body. At last, he whispered in French, "C'est la fin!" It's the end!

I studied French at school, so I could understand that the end of my life was drawing near. All my hopes to survive were dashed.

Suddenly, cold sweat ran down my forehead, and I felt as if I was having heart failure. All my dreams were fading away. It was as if all the sandcastles I had been building were being razed by a huge wave.

When I enrolled in the University of Catania, I dreamed about becoming a great physician, a scientist, and an outstanding person in society. I often dreamed of finding my soulmate, who in my imagination was chestnut-haired, curly-headed, and with a never-ending smile on her lips. Now, the fictitious figure of a woman was vanishing in my mind along with all those sandcastles.

August 8, 1939

Renato and Fabrizio came to the hospital to see me. Entering the room, they glanced at my parents and sisters, and then came close to my bed. Hot tears welled in their eyes. After all, they are not bad friends. They love me in their way.

Fabrizio took hold of my hands, but he couldn't control his emotions, and his tears dripped copiously onto my arm. My sisters stood motionless, watching them.

Whose fault is the tragedy that has befallen me? The main culprits are not Renato and Fabrizio. The only person accountable for what happened is me. I was not able to say no to them, and now it is too late and useless to regret what happened.

August 9, 1939

I don't have the strength to get out of bed. I lie in my bed daydreaming and staring at the ceiling. It is said that the person who is about to die has the tendency to look at the ceiling continuously. Maybe it is true, for now I feel an urge to direct my eyes upwards.

I wanted to travel around the world, meet new people, come across new religions, and experience different ways of intending and living life. Now everything has collapsed!

While my body deteriorates hour by hour, I realize that when I planned my life, I didn't consider the imponderable force that no human being is able to control. This force may be named destiny, circumstances of life, fate, or God who undoubtedly knows when our earthy marathon reaches the finish line.

What of all my dreams? In the past, I had fantasized so much so that sometimes I even asked myself whether mine was a real life in a state of wakefulness or I was living in the dream world. My head has always been in the clouds. I used to spend great parts of the day thinking about my future and the achievements to come, but human dreams, plans, and the great things we have in mind are doomed to fail against a power bigger than us, like large waves that impact the cliff but are unable to crest over it.

Even though we carefully organize our lives and futures, there is no guarantee of success, because God has the last word.

August 10, 1939

Now that my fate is sealed, I recall a parable from the Gospel of Luke, which I heard during Sunday Mass.

Once upon a time, there was a rich farmer who had a very good crop one year. The wheat harvest was so abundant that his many barns couldn't contain it. "What to do with all this wheat?" he thought. Then he found the answer to his dilemma.

"I will demolish all my barns, and instead build a very big barn that will hold the entire crop. In this way I'll be safe and peaceful for the rest of my life and won't need to worry about my old age." This was the farmer's reasoning, but his plan failed against a force bigger than him. In spite of all his plans and riches, he died that same day.

Now that I am going to die, I can see the futility of my daily struggles to build a better future.

August 10, 1939

I remember when a friend of mine, who is a painter and a sculptor, invited me to visit his workshop one day. At the entrance I saw a wall covered with his paintings. He was not a representational painter, but a surrealist. I couldn't understand his pictures, which for me had no meaning. His sculptures showed the same incomprehensive style.

I saw a sculpture with a huge figure hovering over a globe that seemed to be the earth.

"The title of this sculpture is 'The Dominion,'" he said. "The ball represents the earth, and on its surface are many small figures who symbolize human beings.

"I have sculpted a bigger man suspended over the ball, holding a scepter in his hand that I have given the form of a war club. This man was able to subdue all other men on earth, but as you see, there's another, bigger figure that holds a bigger mace and hovers over everybody and everything. The man that has succeeded in subduing all, cannot do anything against that figure who is more powerful than him."

"What does this human figure devoid of face who dominates all others represent?" I asked.

"You can call it God if you like. As for me, I prefer naming it fate, which is the only force that dominates human beings."

August 11, 1939

It's four o'clock in the afternoon. My body is weaker and weaker, and now my feet feel cold, as if they were frozen.

While I am dying, I have only one regret: not to have lived my life in my way. The main mistake I made was following advice and recommendations given by others, and that blunder led me to the end of my life. If I hadn't listened to Renato and Fabrizio, who spurred me to go to the whorehouse that day, I wouldn't have contracted the horrible venereal disease and I would now be full of life instead of having one foot in the grave.

If there were another life after death, I would act a different way. I would use my brain not another's. But who knows, maybe there is no life after death, and my existence will end here in this goddamn hospital. In this difficult instance, only faith can sustain me—my faith in Jesus, who was the one who beat death. Thinking about my grave, I am seized by claustrophobia. I am not quite sure whether all vital functions cease to work at the same time when the heart stops beating. I am seized by terror at the thought that I might be still aware at the moment my coffin is let down into the womb of the cold earth and the gravediggers shovel ground to cover my grave.

I was tempted to ask my father to cremate me, but I quickly gave up that idea, because cremation isn't part of our culture and he wouldn't understand me.

My parents and sisters were in the room. I wanted to ask them to take me home, but I didn't have the strength.

I dozed for a few minutes, and in that time, I got the impression of seeing a clear light in front of me and some figures moving here and there. I could see a golden river and a man with a hat standing on a boat who took souls across the river. I rubbed my eyes to see better and was about to ask the boatman to take me to the other side, when the light, the figures, and the boat disappeared, and then I was back in my hospital room.

I can still spot the silhouettes of my family members, but they look blurred. My legs are getting frozen. It seems that a vital force is deserting me. I don't have the strength to write anymore. I'm going to hand my diary to my sister Rosa Maria, because this time is really the end of my life.

Vincenzo's heart stopped beating at midnight the following day among the piercing shrieks of his mother and sisters. His father, even though was racked with grief, stayed outwardly composed.

Only now do I understand why my mother and Aunt Carolina kept the real cause of Vincenzo's death hidden. For them, a disease caused by sex brought dishonor to the family. At that time, sex was a religious and social taboo. That was why my aunt and mother couldn't talk with me, still a little boy, of brothels, sex, and the sexually transmitted disease that led to the death of their brother Vincenzo.

The dead body was taken to Enna and buried in the family vault. My grandfather enlarged a picture that portrayed Vincenzo. It is one meter and twenty centimeters high and sixty centimeters in width. It is framed with fine wood and stands in front of the family mortuary chapel. This was the last gift for his beloved son Vincenzo.

When I finished reading the diary, a teardrop ran down my cheek and fell on the diary, leaving a stain on the words "end of my life."

I kept the diary with me for five or six years. I didn't want to part with it, but I finally thought I had better put it back in the drawer of the closet, along with my mother's poems, at Vincenzo's home.

In the meantime, the situation in my grandparents' house had changed. My grandmother had died of a heart attack, and my Aunt Carolina and her family had migrated to Milan, a city in northern Italy, to find a job for herself and her husband. That haunted house remained empty. The blinds were all shut, and gloom hovered over the rooms. The keys had been handed down to my mother by my aunt and were kept along with all the other keys in a drawer in the dining room.

One day, I took the keys and went to the house to leave Vincenzo's diary in the place where it should stay. I opened first the entrance gate, then climbed the stone stairs in the courtyard and went upstairs. The wooden front door had swollen due to the humid climate and disuse. I had to push it hard to enter the landing.

Once inside, I felt a musty smell. That house smelled of death. I had a feeling of having presences at my side. I couldn't wait to leave. I headed for the double bedroom, lifted the blind, opened the drawer, and set the diary in the midst of my mother's poems.

Suddenly, I heard footfalls coming from the upper floor. Maybe it was another hallucination, as had happened to me when I was just a boy. However, I thought well to leave the house right away. I shut the blinds and ran away, slamming the main door with all my strength to shut it.

It was the fifth time I had come into contact with death. My grandfather, Biagio, Pietrino, Vincenzo, and my grandmother had all passed away. What had happened to them? Had they disappeared into thin air forever, or were they still alive in another dimension? What will become of me once I am dead?

The terror of my annihilation grips me day and night. What if there is no life after death? What to do? At the mere thought that I will simply be sleeping forever, I fall into desperation. Is it just delusion to believe in life after death? Does the immaterial world exist? I mused upon my fear of death, and finally decided that I had to do something to better understand the topic. In my opinion, human beings put aside the issue of death and life after death, even though it may be the most important subject to learn more about.

Time flies very fast, and sooner or later we will die. We have to leave our possessions to our heirs. We have to part from those we love, and we have to quit our identity, our name, and our role in society.

I had no other means to do this kind of research except by using my mind and reasoning and collecting information from learned people and books. I wanted to learn whether or not there is some kind of immaterial entity or energy inside our body. Where does the inner energy go when it leaves the body?

Chapter Twelve
Saint Francis of Assisi

The official biography of Saint Francis was written by Saint Bonaventura, who was appointed this task by the Franciscan general chapter in 1260, thirty-four years after Saint Francis's death.

Saint Francis was born in the city of Assisi on September 26, 1182 and died on October 3, 1226. His father was a prosperous merchant and his mother a noblewoman. He was given the name John by his mother, but when his father returned from France, he changed the name to Francis, in honor of France, the country where he had made his wealth. Coming from a well-to-do family, Francis had the opportunity to study Latin, poetry, music, Italian, French, the Provencal dialect, and literature. It seemed that Francis was destined to follow in his father's footsteps.

According to a few authors, Francis came into contact with the troubadours and the Sufis during his travels to France and Spain. It seems that the Franciscan habit was very similar to that of the Sufis. On the other hand, the parable Francis told to Pope Innocent III to get the Franciscan rule approved was of Saracen origin. These authors maintain that the meeting between the sultan of Egypt, Malic al-Kamil, and Francis during the fifth crusade was possible because they both knew the esoteric language of the Sufis.

Around the age of twenty, Francis joined up with the Assisi army and fought against the city of Perugia, but he was taken prisoner and remained in prison for one year. The time he spent in jail was very hard, so much so that he contracted a serious illness when he returned home. His sickness was the turning point in his life, for he decided to radically change his lifestyle. To that point he had lived a worldly life, but now he chose to dedicate himself to following Jesus's model. He began to give money to help lepers, the poor, and the needy.

Francis's new life and prodigality were not appreciated by his father, who eventually disinherited him. From then on, Francis lived a life of poverty and absolute simplicity. Soon, other young people joined him, giving rise to the monastic Franciscan order. His soul was so pure that he talked with birds, and one day he even tamed a wolf. An example of the pureness of his heart can be found in the *Canticle of the Creatures*, which he composed in 1225.

Saint Francis's life was short; in fact, he lived only forty-four years. After his death, many authors started writing his biography. Some biographies had a hagiographic aim, while others were straightforward accounts, but some data is common to all of them.

Saint Francis was a great traveler. Around the age of thirty, he left his hometown to go to Syria. Unfortunately, his journey was interrupted in Dalmatia for an unknown reason, but probably because he couldn't find a ship to Syria. Therefore, he was forced to return to Italy.

In spite of the failure of his first attempted trip to a Muslim country, he set off on another journey to Islamic lands, this time Morocco. To go to Morocco, he crossed France and Spain. Again, he failed to succeed in his plan because he contracted a serious disease in Spain and once more had to return to Assisi.

His third endeavor to get to an Arab country finally succeeded. He boarded a ship at Ancona in the year 1219, seven years before his death, at the same time the fifth crusade was under way. Once in Egypt, Saint Francis wanted to meet Sultan Malic al-Kamil. Their meeting really happened, and as far as we know, Francis was treated by the sultan as a guest, not as an enemy in time of wars. He received safe conduct and was invited to return to visit Egypt anytime.

From Egypt he traveled to the Holy Land. About two years before his death, he received the stigmata on Mount Verna.

Later, his health worsened, and he died in a small church near Assisi called Porziuncola. At his death, his body was taken to Assisi, and a basilica was later built in the place where he had been buried.

I had the chance to go to Assisi three times in my life. The first time was with my parents on a travel to north Italy. It happened many years ago. Even though I was very young and not in a condition to appreciate Saint Francis's message to humanity, a few things remained etched in my mind. One was the sight of the cilice which Saint Francis wore to mortify his body.

The cilice was a special garment made of goat hair that caused considerable suffering to the person who wore it. The flesh was considered a kind of contamination of the soul; therefore, through the mortification of the body, the soul would be purified.

Hearing the story of Saint Francis from my parents, I was struck by the strength of character of this great man who rebelled against his father in order to follow the aspirations of his heart.

The second time I visited Assisi was while I was traveling on a trip organized by the parish priest of the Church of San Cataldo. We entered the basilica, which was divided into three parts: the upstairs basilica, the walls of which were covered with gorgeous frescoes by Giotto; the downstairs basilica, which contained other works of art; and finally, the crypt where Saint Francis's mortal remains were kept.

The tomb was placed above the altar and was made of gray square and rectangular stones. It was very simple. As soon as I knelt to say some prayers and make a wish, I had the feeling that a kind of energy was radiating from his tomb, and then I asked Saint Francis to hear my prayer.

"Please, Saint Francis, grant me a gift! You are a very powerful saint and can easily make my wish come true. I love

Elisabetta more than life, and I want her to become my wife. There are many hindrances that prevent us from getting married. Please, Saint Francis, remove all the hindrances and help us get married as soon as possible."

At that time, I had fallen in love with a young lady named Elisabetta. She was from Enna as well and taught Latin and Greek at the high school. I courted her for two years and wanted to get engaged to her. We used to stroll along Via Roma and the Belvedere and talk religion. In fact, she was an earnest Catholic, to such an extent that she was once on the verge of quitting her job to become a Carmelite cloistered nun.

While we were walking around the Lombardia Castle, she told me of her pilgrimage to Assisi. "I have been struck by Saint Francis's burial place. I felt a special energy coming from his tomb," she said.

I don't know whether or not it was due to autosuggestion because Elisabetta had told me her feelings, but the same strange sensation was now happening to me. While I repeatedly asked San Francis to grant my wish, I felt as if powerful energy was radiating from his tomb and talking to me.

"I have spent my whole life looking for God," Saint Francis's energy seemed to say, "and now you arrive at my tomb and ask me to grant you a trivial wish, Vincenzino!"

I wondered why Saint Francis considered my desire to marry my loved one to be trivial. As time passed, I realized that I had actually requested something really trivial. In fact, human affairs like love, business, careers, and so on are trifles in comparison to the search and love for God, who is the giver of life.

Meanwhile, Elisabetta got married to another man, and I understood that what I had considered a great love was nothing more than an infatuation doomed to dissolve like the fog dispersed by the wind.

True love is not related to a woman or a person. Love is something you must have inside you. Love comes from your heart and mind, and it stands apart from the appearance and character of the people you come across and the happenings of life.

Later, I married a lady from Greece, and we now live together in Enna. In the evenings after dinner, my wife and I usually stroll along Via Roma and Saint Francis Square, which is surrounded by old palaces on three sides and by the stately Church of Saint Francis on the fourth.

A small green area had recently been attached to the church, with an olive tree and a statue of Saint Francis surrounded by white doves. While my wife and I were going back home and passing by that green, we noticed a fragrance emanating from the area. We turned in all directions but couldn't spot a flower or a tree from where that subtle scent might be emanating. The following days we passed by the same place again, but we couldn't smell anything.

A subtle thread was leading me to Assisi for the third time. My wife and I decided to take a car trip across northern and central Italy. We embarked on a ferry in Palermo and landed in Genoa. From there, we traveled to Pisa, Florence, and San Gimignano.

While we were admiring the numerous towers of the last town, my wife suddenly cried out, "What about going to Assisi? Is it far from here? Do you remember the fragrance we smelt in Enna near the Church of Saint Francis?"

"No, it is not far away. We can go to Perugia first, and Assisi is a stone's throw from there," I replied.

We arrived at Saint Francis's hometown around midday and found lodging in a monastery run by Filipino nuns. We strolled for a while around the medieval city and then arrived at the basilica. My wife was surprised at the sight of the frescoes both upstairs and downstairs.

"Even though I am not a Christian," she said, "and don't follow any religion, I cannot help being astonished by the religious ardor that was behind these great masterpieces."

We went to the crypt and sat on a pew facing Saint Francis's tomb. As soon as I sat down, I had the sensation that the same energy that had talked to me many years ago was now speaking again, suggesting the path I should follow to find out who I really was.

"Purify your heart, mind, body, and actions, and then you'll see God inside you!" Saint Francis said.

What was Saint Francis telling me this time? He meant that the real kingdom of God is inside every living being, but we cannot find it if our mind is contaminated by too many materialistic desires or our actions are not directed towards the well-being of our fellow creatures. I also inferred that prayer and meditation are a good way to purify my mind and get close to God, as long as my actions aim not towards an egoistic goal but to the love of all creatures.

While I was meditating on what Saint Francis was suggesting to me at that moment, my wife suddenly turned to me.

"I have a pain in my heart, and my heart is pounding! I shed tears and I don't know why. I don't feel sad, and I don't know why I am crying!" she said.

My wife is not Catholic and actually doesn't practice any religion, so we couldn't understand why such a phenomenon befell her. Maybe the same energy that had talked to me was revealing itself to her in some way.

I left Assisi with a strong devotion to Saint Francis. Every time I had trouble in my life after that, I thought of him and reminded myself that my worldly misfortunes are a mere trifle. What really matters in life is the search and love for God and all his creatures.

Reviewing my encounter with Saint Francis, I reconsidered what my law teacher had taught me a long time ago. She had stressed the importance of the difference between a piece of evidence and a clue. A piece of evidence is a fact that you have seen or heard, or a way that an event can be proved with absolute certainty—evidence that can direct the judge to return his verdict. A clue doesn't have the strength of evidence, and a mere clue is usually not enough to bring in a judge's verdict, but if the clues are numerous, unambiguous, precise, and concordant with one another, they can be taken into consideration by the judge in order to pass judgment.

In the case of my encounter with Saint Francis, there are five clues that can be admitted as evidence of the existence of another spiritual level that is beyond our ordinary worldly life:

1. *The energy Elisabetta felt while she was praying before the tomb of Saint Francis;*

2. *The fragrance my wife and I smelt near his statue while we were strolling in Enna;*

3. *The energy coming from his tomb that talked to me about the true goals of my life, which were not a mere love of a woman, money, or some other worldly pleasure. Searching for God was the real goal;*

4. *The energy I felt when I went to Assisi for the third time. I realized that the kingdom of God was really inside me. I just needed to purify my mind, my heart, my body, and my actions, and then I would walk on the path that led to the spiritual world;*

5. *The unusual sensation of pain in my wife's chest and the tears in her eyes while she was sitting with me in front of Saint Francis's tomb.*

These days, Saint Francis is the master in my daily life. Whenever I am too worried because my business didn't go well, I remind myself of the teachings he gave me in the crypt in Assisi. The ups and downs of life are mere trifles when compared to meeting God, who stays in the heart of every human.

By minding Saint Francis's teachings, I live my life in a more relaxed way. I am less anxious. I just juggle the events of life as soccer players do when playing a friendly match.

Chapter Thirteen
The Path of Sufferers

By researching Saint Francis's life, I learned that one of the first things he did when he left his family home to start a new life was to help lepers, the poor, and the needy. Musing about that, I found that the way to God for most saints was marked by the help they gave to marginalized people.

A friend of mine, who is an atheist writer, once wrote a pamphlet in which he came to the conclusion that if poverty was eradicated from the earth, the Catholic Church would have nothing to do, because all its teachings are focused on alleviating others' suffering. According to my friend, if there was no suffering in the world, the Catholic Church—and all religions, for that matter—wouldn't have meaning. He stressed that the Catholic Church needs the poor, or the priests and monks would be out of work.

In that pamphlet, he maintained that the creation of a new religion-free humanism, where people with no social class could live in togetherness, was still possible. He often emphasized the old saying, "Religion is the opium of the people." He said that even the Vedas, which are the sacred books of an ancient religion, were written by people under the effect of drugs.

One day I said to him, putting my arm on his shoulder, "My dear friend, what you talk about is impossible. You cannot realize paradise on earth by eradicating suffering. Every person who has depicted an ideal society, like Plato, Saint Augustine, Tommaso Campanella, and many other philosophers, has just made a utopian work. Karl Marx, Lenin, and Stalin, whom you quote continuously, couldn't realize their utopian ideal society ruled only by the working class."

He and I are no longer friends. There was too much difference and misunderstanding between us.

As for me, even though I am not an atheist, I want to use my brain as much as possible rather than believing blindly in religions. Therefore, like my friend, I doubted that the saints who had given up their worldly lives to help the marginalized classes were themselves marginalized, maladjusted people who were unable to fit into their social classes. They escaped from normal lives to find shelter in environments more congenial to them.

Anyway, I had chosen Saint Francis of Assisi as my spiritual guide by now. Based on the extraordinary, miraculous events that happened to me when I was on my knees in front of his tomb in Assisi, or when I passed by his statue in Enna, I considered him a great master. By following his teachings, I wanted the experience of helping the sick as he had done, to see what would happen to me on my way to God.

I gathered some information and then decided to go to Scotland to a center where people with major physical health problems were assisted by specialized staff and volunteers. It was Christmas time, and my wife and I decided to spend our winter holidays individually for the first time after many years of being together. She flew to Athens to stay with her old mother for two weeks, while I went to Scotland to spend my winter holidays at a center for disabled people.

The manager gave me instructions about the use of wheelchairs, both manual and electric, and the functioning of the hoist. Ninety percent of the disabled living there were completely paralyzed and needed to be lifted by a hoist to be put to bed from the wheelchair and vice versa. To have their shower, they had to be hoisted and moved to the bathroom through a linking track in the ceiling.

At lunch, I was asked to feed a young man named Chris. He was completely paralyzed and not even able to stay upright in his wheelchair. From time to time, I pushed him and inserted a cushion between his trunk and the side rail of his wheelchair so that he could assume an almost upright position, but his muscular strength was completely lacking, and his neck was unable to carry the weight of his head, which was constantly bent over his chest.

Despite his efforts, he couldn't keep his trunk and head upright. It didn't appear he was able to raise his head, but whenever a nice girl passed by, he summoned all the strength he had in the innermost recesses of his paralyzed body and raised his head a little bit to look at her furtively. That figure of the opposite sex had the power to light up his face and give vital strength to a body that otherwise didn't have the power to react to external stimuli.

It was impossible for him to have sex because his body was a mass of flesh without any muscular strength, but his sexual urge had not faded. Nevertheless, he was deluding himself at the thought that the girl would return his love.

From then on, I stopped feeding Chris and asked a volunteer girl to do that in my place. I was aware that, for at least a few moments of his troubled life, Chris would be happy. By observing Chris several times, I came to the conclusion that sex is the most powerful ruler of living creatures. It seems that even geldings give a start when a mare in heat comes close.

If my utopian ex-friend had been with me in Scotland at the center for the disabled, I would have said to him, "Your theory about the possibility of creating a heavenly, religion-free world is unattainable!"

"Why?" he would have asked with a commanding tone.

"Because as long as sex appeal rules living beings' behavior, there will be suffering on Earth."

He would have rebutted, "Sex is a positive emotion. The fact that sex is considered a sin is an invention of the Catholic priests, all of whom I would send to the stake."

"Be careful before sending Catholic priests to the scaffold," I would have answered. "All religions have some kind of reservation about sex. In fact, many require purification before the person who has copulated enters holy places.

"Sex always triggers suffering in human creatures. Look at animals! They fight fiercely against one another in order to copulate. There will be a loser that will suffer and a winner that will enjoy its victory. But its triumph will not last long, because sooner or later it will be defeated by a stronger animal, and its life will turn into suffering.

"Look at how lions kill one another to prevail over their opponents. Look at a pack of dogs or wolves and see how they fight and are heavy injured and sometimes die for the sake of mating. I can quote thousands of cases where sex gives rise to suffering. Freud is probably right when he says that most of human behavior is conditioned by sexual energy."

I figured that if my Uncle Vincenzo had not had sex at that goddamn whorehouse, he would still be alive.

"What you are saying is valid for the animal kingdom," my friend would have refuted, "but human beings are different, because for them sex is sublimated by love."

I would have answered him, "Love has nothing to do with sex. True love is totally independent from sex. Human love is tainted by sex drive. Therefore, it is not true love. Family is not a natural institution but a by-product of sex. For that reason, most families turn into prisons after a while, and what was supposed to be a great real love between the husband and wife sooner or later changes into hate. In paradise, supposing it exists, there are neither families nor couples, and nobody gets married. Jesus himself teaches us this concept."

Related to suffering is the concept of power. Everyone wants to be more powerful and rich. This is part of human nature, and no religion or worldly institution can suffocate the want of the individual to excel over his station. This creates suffering, because for every winner there will be a loser who will suffer.

The conclusion is that suffering belongs to human nature, and even though one day physical suffering, diseases, and death will be eliminated, the suffering of the soul will never end. There are no remedies to cure the soul, and the so-called psychotropic drugs only help the symptoms of the disease. They cannot cure the malaise of the soul.

Anyway, the first lesson I learned while I was working with those severely ill people was that instinct is born with living beings and no force can suppress it. Instinct can be kept under control, not suppressed.

Now I want to break a lance in defense of love.

There was a man at the center about seventy-five years old. He asked me to push his wheelchair to the supermarket, for he wanted to buy some oranges and tissues. It was a pleasure for me to do that. His name was James, and he was a man of robust build. His hair was crew cut and showed no signs of grayness, despite his old age. He still had the look of the worker, and for sure, he had been a strenuous, strong worker in his younger years.

When we arrived at the supermarket, he asked me to pick up a ten pack of tissues and a basket of oranges. At the counter, he gave me his wallet to pay for his items. I paid for him and put the wallet back into his pocket.

After we got back to the center, we sat down in the lounge area for a while. I saw him trying hard to take his wallet out of the pocket of his trousers.

"What are you doing, James?" I asked.

"I want to show you my wife's picture, but I cannot take out my wallet. It is stuck to my trousers."

"Don't worry, James. You can show me your wife's picture another time."

James had only one leg; the other had been amputated due to complications deriving from his diabetes. His diabetes was so acute that he had to get insulin many times during the day.

He told me that when he was in good health, he worked in shipbuilding. Two years ago, his wife had passed away from cancer. Thinking of his wife, James's eyes stared into the void, and then he strove again to get her picture.

"Don't worry about the picture," I said again. "Instead, tell me how long you have been married."

"Fifty years!" he answered with a lump in his throat.

"Did you love her?"

"Of course I loved my wife. More than life."

"Now who looks after you?"

"My daughter. We are a very close family."

My conversation with James made me think twice about the non-existence of love on Earth.

Another day, I was asked by the manager of the center to take a disabled person to the shopping center.

"What is your name?" he asked.

"My name is Vincenzino. And what about yours?"

"My name is Gabriele. It is an Italian name because my mother was Italian and my father was English. I can speak both English and Italian. My parents met during the Second World War. My father served in the British Army in a region called Calabria, in the south of Italy. During the breaks between heavy fighting, he met my mother. Their love rose like the sun in the haze of the battles. When the war was over, my father returned to his country, but he couldn't stand being apart from his loved one for long. So, he went to Italy often to see her. Finally, after a year or so, they got married."

"Was it a loving marriage?" I asked.

"Yes, my parents loved each other for more than fifty years. I remember every year when we went to Italy to spend our holidays with my grandparents, my father wanted to give some money to my relatives. They would have been offended if my father had done so. Therefore, we always arrived in Italy with a mountain of presents for them. I always had a good time there, surrounded by the warmth of my grandparents, my cousins, and my uncles. I still have an uncle in Calabria.

"When I was born, the delivery was very difficult and my mother almost died. She had lost too much blood. The doctors fought strenuously to save my mother, and my life faded into the background. As the year passed, my parents noticed that I couldn't stand up. In fact, my brain was not able to give the muscles of my arms and legs the proper commands. I could neither walk nor use my arms. Neither my parents nor the doctors in Glasgow could understand which disease I was suffering from. They thought it might be a psychological issue.

"At the age of two, my parents took me to a specialist in London, who analyzed the situation and made the diagnosis of brain damage caused by the difficult labor. The specialist prescribed therapy and told my parents to purchase a pair of crutches for me. Thanks to the therapy, I made progress, and for a while I was able to walk on crutches. However, I was very shaky on my legs and fell down continuously. It was a battle lost from the beginning.

"Sometimes a mother's love is more effective than medicine though. She encouraged me and spurred me to keep going. Day by day, with constant training, I was able to hold my crutches firmly, and by pivoting on them, I was able to stand up and finally walk. So, I attained my independence."

"Did you go to school, Gabriele?"

"Yes, I went to a special school where every student had a different kind of handicap. Some were blind, some deaf, some morons. Can you imagine what happened there? Nobody could be taught well. I was not able to read, even after five years of attending that school. My mother was very worried. She was convinced that I would never learn to read.

"After a few years, my parents enrolled me in a boarding school. I stayed there for five years and finally learned to read. As for writing, at first it was more difficult than reading, because my brain couldn't properly control the movements of my hand, but I finally succeeded.

"Now my parents are both dead. I have one brother. When I am home, I have a caretaker who looks after me."

"Have you ever driven a car, Gabriele?"

"Yes, but my life can be compared to the ascent of a high mountain and the following descent. I had good mobility for about forty years, but then it started diminishing little by little, and now I am completely paralyzed and in need of a person that can feed me."

"Have you ever worked, Gabriele? What I mean to say is, have you ever had a job?"

"Yes, I am still working! I have worked at a special factory my whole life, where disabled people like me are taken on."

"What kind of work do they do?"

"In our factory, we mostly print, but there are also people who make things by assembling pieces."

"What is your job there?"

"I am a switchboard operator. As you see, my English is very clear. I am also quite talkative. The telephone in the factory rings continuously, and I answer the phone and give the information the customers or suppliers need, or I just put them through to the manager."

The stories told by James and Gabriele about the love that reigned in their families proved to me that love is the driving force of life on Earth. Nevertheless, we humans have a duty to see beyond appearances. By digging deeply into human feelings, we'll discover that what we call love is indeed an instinct that is present in the entire animal kingdom.

When I lived with Sebastiano on the estate in Pollicarini, the farmhand took care of the she-asses he co-owned with my family. We didn't have to worry about the condition of the animals, and the farmer looked after them as if they were his family members. He curried them often. You could see their good health from the brilliance of their coats. Whenever he took one of the she-asses out of the stable, they both brayed, pawed the ground, and got restless. They couldn't endure being parted. Later on, after they were reunited, they showed their happiness by smelling each other.

Was that love? Why shouldn't it be considered love? Love for friends or partners belongs to the nature of all creatures. It can be considered a gift of nature. There is no difference between animals and human beings when it comes to love.

In some species, love is stronger than humans. There are some animals that are monogamous. The pre-eminent monogamous species is the emperor penguin, but there are other birds and a few mammals with strong dispositions to love. The mandarin ducks, also called loving birds, have only one union in their life. When one of the mates dies, the other won't accept another partner and remains alone for the rest of its life.

The logical corollary of what I expounded on above is that the love we have for our children, our friends, and our relatives doesn't add any merit to our being, because the feelings we express don't depend upon our free will and heart. We just instinctively express a kind of love that is not dissimilar to that of animals.

Real love is different—it is unconditional and universal. It goes beyond a couple's love. It has nothing to do with the group, family, or clan one belongs to. Human love is usually on mutual terms: "I'll love you if you love me." Even parental love, which is the strongest, is subject to reciprocity. If a child is disrespectful or aggressive against their parents, they stop loving their child to the point that they can throw them out of their home. The same happens in the animal kingdom, where the mother loves her cubs until they start competing with her. In that case, separation is inevitable.

What I learned in the center for disabled people is that for love to be authentic it must be unconditional. When you love, you have to give without expecting anything in return. Only a limited number of people have shown themselves to be examples of real unconditional and universal love over the centuries. One of those few noble figures is Saint Francis of Assisi.

Only now can I understand the three cornerstones of the Franciscan rule, which are poverty, chastity, and obedience. In fact, to fully love your neighbor, you must get rid of your sexual urges, covetousness, and desire to take the lead. Only when you free yourself from these three hindrances can you start loving. The Franciscan habit has not changed today, and it differs from that of other monastic orders. As it was at the time of Saint Francis, the frock is girdled with a cord with three knots to symbolize the three main vows of a Franciscan friar.

My ex-friend would object, "Don't censure sex, because life is born by sex. If everybody followed your recommendation to practice abstinence, humanity would become extinct. Saint Francis's rule is just as absurd and utopian as the new humanism I dream of. In fact, not only is chastity nonsense, but obedience is also impossible. Think for a minute about what it would be like if everybody practiced obedience. There would be no leaders to obey!"

"The giver of life is God and not sex!" I would answer. "Life was born before sex. God's love and the vibrations of his voice created the universe, human beings included. As for obedience, I say to you that leaders also obey, just not their subordinates. It all depends on what your idea of leadership is. Kings and subjects are not different in the way they obey. If you consider leadership not as an arbitrary act but a service to others, you will see that leaders also cannot shirk their duty of obedience."

One evening I was sitting in the lounge along with the disabled people to watch a singer who was putting on a show. I suddenly had the feeling that that singer didn't recognize me as a normal person. Since I was mixed in with all the ill people, she thought I was one of them. I was about to get up and walk to show her that I was normal, but then I realized that I was really stupid to think that way.

I am not different from the disabled. If I observe them closely, I realize that they have a soul not different from mine, and they are even more sensitive and more clever than me. Thinking like that, I learned my second lesson at this center: souls are all same, and in paradise there will be no difference as to physical form or cerebral abilities.

I have to say that sometimes I had a feeling of repulsion when I saw the condition of some of the guests. Most of them had a hosepipe inserted in their stomach, and their urine flowed away into a bag that we quite often had to empty. Some guests had a hole in their stomach and their excrement passed through the hole and flowed into a plastic bag. Every morning, with the help of a staff member who removed the bag full of excrement, I had to clean the area around the hole to eliminate any traces of feces.

One day I had to look after a young man who was spastic. Sitting in his wheelchair, he was able to move all around the center by pushing the ground with the tip of the only foot he was able to use.

In the evenings, we all gathered in the lounge where a musician or a singer came to cheer up the night. I noticed that all the guests had some kind of reaction to the music. The vibrations contained in human voice and instruments didn't leave them indifferent, even though their bodies seemed insensitive to external stimuli.

The lessons I learned from the disabled I attended to for two weeks were extraordinary. They were weak but showed attachment to life. They didn't wish to die, nor did they give in to despair. They seemed to live normal lives and showed smiling faces, while some volunteers, including me, sometimes were in the grip of anxiety.

They taught me the meaning of unconditional, universal love.

Chapter Fourteen
My Meditation

Saint Francis's words resounded in my mind quite often: "Purify your heart, mind, body, and actions, and then you'll see God inside you!"

I thought meditation would be a good way to purify my heart, mind, and body. I began to research the topic to uncover the path. Most people today focus their attention outward instead of inward. Their main interests are to become rich, famous, have a beautiful partner, and so on. I'm not saying that all these desires are sins. It is normal and plays a prominent role in human society, but if you don't want to act like a machine and want to strive to become a spiritual being, it is necessary to focus your attention inward as well.

Meditation means to look inside yourself and see who really you are. Many meditators say that when you find your real nature, all your worries and longings disappear like clouds blown away by the wind. Your mind becomes empty and you are an organic whole with the universe. Contrary to what some people think, meditation is not escaping from the world. On the contrary, by meditating we can live a better ordinary life and succeed socially.

Meditation, alertness, and consciousness are nearly synonymous. True meditative people meditate not only within the walls of their home, but also while they are working, playing, eating, dancing, or doing just anything. In this case, meditation consists of watching oneself performing any action. By watching ourselves while we are living our lives, our actions cease to be automatic or unconscious. We behave as fully conscious people, always aware of what we are doing.

We humans tend to live according to the patterns and paradigms we learned in childhood. Our family and society funnel us towards fixed tracks, which we then follow automatically without ever asking ourselves whether those tracks lead us in the right direction. If we want to know more about ourselves, we need to drop conditioning given to us as children. When we meditate, we set spirituality before worldly ambitions. In doing so, we go beyond the behavioral models we were schooled in. We follow a new, authentic way—the way to God.

In India and other parts of the world, meditation is a good way to find "enlightenment." Once a person is enlightened, they see things as they really are and not as they appear to our deluded minds.

I read many books about meditation and visited a few places and monasteries where I could study meditation techniques, but now I needed to practice it by myself instead of studying it theoretically. *Vipassana* was one of the techniques I learned. It is one of the most ancient methods of meditation and consists of watching your breathing and watching yourself.

At first, I was doubtful about it. How is it possible that just watching one's breathing can get a person to enlightenment? By deepening my studies, I learned that our minds are like monkeys, always jumping from one thought to another. By meditating, we get free from a host of useless thoughts and focus our attention on the search of our real nature.

Ramana Maharshi, one of the greatest Indian masters, says that when you meditate you have to focus your attention on the question "Who am I?" He claims that if you meditate on that single thought, all other thoughts will be chased away from your mind and in the end it will be empty.

One day I sat on a chair, closed my eyes, and focused my attention on breathing in and out. I was only able to do it for a few minutes because I couldn't prevent thoughts from entering my mind. I then tried to meditate, asking myself, "Who am I?", but by doing so, I mixed breathing meditation with Ramana Maharshi's method and worsened the situation because I jumped from one technique to the other.

A doubt entered my mind. Maybe I feared to meditate and look inside myself. Every time I was about to get my mind free from thoughts, I saw my identity disappear and realized that I was nothing but energy. I've got a name, a family, friends, and good social standing. What would have happened to me if I had discovered that my name, wealth, and prestige were just veils that masked my real being?

There was another hindrance to my meditation. I was concerned about discovering who I really was. Maybe I was not the good and considerate person I appeared to be. Perhaps, I was basically a dirty soul that had been modeled into a good man by my family and society.

Despite that, I decided to continue my attempts to meditate well. Whenever a thought arose, instead of blaming myself for not being able to avoid thinking, I just observed my thoughts as an external watcher. Then, after the disturbing thought disappeared, I went back to watching my breathing. Little by little, I was more able to watch myself and my breathing without being distracted by thoughts, and my mind became quieter. It was a good start, but so far I had discovered nothing about the hereafter, which was the main subject of my quest.

While I was meditating, I looked inside myself to try to see who I really was. I actually didn't think that my body moved and acted automatically. There had to be an energy independent from the body. The problem was to understand whether that energy dies with the death of the body or it survives.

To deepen my study, I decided to go to India to a renowned city called Rishikesh, said to be the best place in the world for meditation. I asked my wife to join me in my spiritual quest. She accepted, and we decided to go to India after the winter holidays.

Chapter Fifteen

Goa

Rishikesh is located in northern India, five hundred meters above sea level. It is not far from the Himalayas, and it is quite cold in the winter. My wife hates the cold and had no intention of going to that cold city in the winter months. She insisted that we find other warmer places where I could satisfy my desire to meditate.

"You can even meditate in our room or in the street," she said. "You don't need to go to a special place to have good meditation."

One of the reasons why I preferred to be alone when I travelled to deepen my spiritual search was that tastes and dispositions vary from person to person, and that difference wound up limiting my freedom of movement. When I was younger and happened to travel with a friend of mine, his views quite often clashed with mine. I liked to visit certain kinds of places, while my friend had different tastes. What to do? You can choose to be alone in your life and have complete freedom of choice, or you can interact with others and have your freedom limited. As for me, I prefer interacting with others even if it means losing part of my freedom.

I reached a compromise with my wife. We would spend the month of January in Goa, a state by the Indian Ocean where the weather is mild and it's possible to swim in the ocean, and then we would move to Rishikesh in February when the weather was supposed to be a little warmer.

We decided to meet in Mumbai after our winter holidays spent respectively in Scotland and in Athens. The plan was that I would arrive at the airport first and then wait about three hours for her. Unfortunately, her flight was delayed, and the route was also changed, so I didn't know which Mumbai airport she would land at. On the other hand, I couldn't collect my baggage because my airline had mislaid it.

I had a few instants of worry, but then I recalled an old saying from Enna: *Ppi tuttu c'è rimediu, tranni ppa morti* (there is a solution for everything but death). Furthermore, Saint Francis had taught me that life's worries are a trifle in comparison with the search for God. Losing my baggage and the twelve-hour delay of my wife's flight to Mumbai were nothing by comparison.

While I was waiting for my wife, I decided to find accommodations in a hotel near the airport. I strolled along the Mumbai streets near my hotel and saw people whose condition was much worse than mine. I was anxious because I couldn't find my wife and my baggage, while homeless people in this metropolis had the sidewalk as their home. I happened to see a young child covered with a thin blanket; only its feet were visible. It wasn't possible to tell if that child was dead or sleeping. A few starving dogs lay down on the same sidewalk. Some dogs were markedly scabby. Apparently, there was not much difference between the dogs and the homeless people who shared the same place. Both of them begged for food to stay alive.

In the streets there was bustle of cars, rickshaws, buses, and motorbikes that polluted the air. I had no doubt that the those who lived alongside the road would not live long. Besides their lack of hygiene and proper feeding, they had to breathe air poisoned by the exhaust fumes.

The owner of the hotel suggested I go to the domestic airport to meet my wife, because the airline she was traveling on used to land there. I did so, and after a few hours of waiting, I finally spotted my wife at a distance, and we both ran to hug each other with joy. As for my luggage, it still wasn't there the following day, so I took advantage of the opportunity to renew my suitcase and wardrobe.

Finally, everything came out right; my mishaps were solved and we could plan our journey to Goa. What couldn't be solved was the problem of the many homeless people sleeping on the sidewalks and begging for a piece of bread. According to the Hindu, the miserable condition of the outcasts is the consequence of the many sins they have committed in their previous lives. There is no hope for them to improve the quality of their living in this life. In fact, they have to make amends for their negative karma until the end of their lives.

We decided to take a night bus from Mumbai to Goa. The coach was drafty, and some of the passengers got a cold. Moreover, there was the big problem of going to the toilet. The bus didn't stop often, and when it did, we passengers, both men and women, had to relieve ourselves on the side of the road, for the coach stopped only for a few minutes.

We arrived in the city of Mapusa around nine in the morning, and from there we took another overcrowded bus to Arambol, one of Goa's beaches.

A picture on the upper part of the bus's windshield showed Jesus, Mary, and another figure who seemed to be Mary holding the baby Jesus on her arm. As soon as we set off, the driver lit a stick of incense and put a garland of flowers around the icon. Apparently, he was Catholic.

Goa had been a Portuguese colony, and as happens to every territory conquered by invaders, the new masters brought not only their armies with them to subjugate the new country, but also their culture and religious traditions. Catholic churches were widespread in Goa. I spotted two churches built in a fashion similar to those I had seen in Mexico.

On the other hand, the same happened in Sicily at the time of the Arab conquest. The Arabs remained in Sicily for two centuries and brought with them good culture in the fields of art and literature. They also improved the agricultural irrigation systems. Likewise, they also brought the new Islamic religion so that Sicily swarmed with mosques. According to some authors, at the time of the Arab occupation there were more mosques in Palermo than in Istanbul. There were also many mosques in Enna, but they were all converted into Catholic churches after the Normans took the Arabs' place in Sicily. One of these converted churches in Enna is that of Saint Michael, whose Moresque features are still visible.

The sandy beach is the highlight of Arambol. It is quite broad and surrounded by coconut palms and other tropical trees. A few fishing boats are alongside the seashore. Judging from the tiny fish the fishermen extricated from their nets, I inferred that that sea was not teeming with many fish.

All along the beach people walked, ran, played ball, did yoga, and played badminton. I even noticed a man playing his saxophone facing the sea in the early morning. It was not possible to hear the sound of that instrument because of the noise of the breakers. I couldn't make out what meaning there could be to playing the saxophone at the water's edge. There was probably no meaning, just someone who enjoyed playing his instrument.

Maybe meditation and prayer are different according to the place where they happen. So, praying by Saint Francis's tomb, for instance, is not the same as praying within an ordinary church. Therefore, I wanted to try a kind of meditation a Sufi from England had recommended to do. *Facing the Indian Ocean with the sound of the waves breaking on the waterline, my meditation would be different,* I thought.

The Sufi had advised me to sit cross-legged with my spine straight and inhale deeply through my nose and exhale through my mouth. He said, "When you inhale, expand your stomach. Confine yourself to watching your breathing. If a thought comes to your mind, expel it through your mouth when you exhale. Then stand up, spread your legs a little bit wider than your shoulders. With your feet parallel, stretch your arms to the side, count to thirty, and then relax. Stretch and relax your arms in that way five times."

I planned on practicing this meditation every morning in Goa. Even though I didn't get any spiritual enlightenment by doing so, the Sufi meditation was definitely beneficial and helped me separate my mundane worries from the aim I was looking for, which was to find the drop of God that is inside every human being.

Many people lay down to get a tan or chatted in the bars in the afternoon. Most tourists were Westerners, many of them from Russia. It seemed to me that they were all leading an existence devoid of goals. They chatted, played on the beach, swam, and took pictures. Two ladies enjoyed being photographed close to a bull lying on the beach. Sometimes I asked myself if it was me who was the real outcast, someone who persisted in searching for a goal in life, while life actually has no end. All those people seemed to be devoid of spirituality, but they all had their inner lives. Some looked quite strange. I saw a man take off his swimming suit and rinse it in the sea. He remained naked for a few minutes. Nobody cared about him, and he cared about no one.

Over the days, I noticed that not everyone who spent their holiday in Goa was devoid of inner content. In the yoga class, there were youngsters who looked very learned in the spiritual field. At the break of day, the shore swarmed with people doing meditation, yoga, and other spiritual activities. Some played the flute, others the drum. Others did walking meditation, which is a kind of meditation based on watching one's own steps, while others did laughing meditation, which is obviously based on laughing. From this I inferred that no one on Earth is devoid of spirituality. Everybody has his or her inner world, but it is different from one another.

The same went for my wife. Even though we had been married for a long time, our inner landscapes differed. My wife has had the good habit of keeping a diary since her school days. She writes down everything she sees and what happens to her every day. When we compared our writings about Goa, we found that we had written and portrayed different things and situations. I had written about human behavior, while she had focused her attention on love. She had noted down the inscriptions that many lovers drew on the moist sand. There were a lot of details in her diary I hadn't noticed.

"I am sure," I said to my wife, "that if we ask each person in Goa to write their impressions, everyone will note down something different. Some will focus their attention on the sun that dives into the ocean, marking the end of the day. Others will write about the evening star that gleams a few minutes after the sun has set, or they will describe the ebbs and flows and the small fish that come near the shoreline and then dart towards the ocean. Some will focus their attention on the hang gliders that depart from the hill, or on the sky lanterns that fly across the beach at night, while others will tell of the many stray dogs on the beach that seem to be familiar with tourists. Why is there such difference in the way people see places and situations?"

"It happens because we are all different from one another," my wife answered. "There is a difference, a veil of incommunicability that separates all living creatures. Love and understanding are the bridge that makes communication and dialog possible."

As for my wife, she noticed a detail that many people, including I, would have overlooked. A man was sitting near the water's edge and playing the flute. Four stray dogs lay peacefully beside him. Apparently, they loved the sound of the flute.

"I heard," I said to my wife, "that cows in some farms are made to listen to good music, and the sound of the melodies helps them produce more milk."

"Every living creature has a soul and loves music," she added. "Even plants are sensitive to music and good words. If you say 'I love you' to a plant, it will grow better and produce more flowers and fruit."

I remember talking once about an existential subject with one of the workers at my father's company, who looked well-educated. "What is the goal of your life?" I asked.

"I have given up trying to find a goal in life; otherwise, I get lost," he answered. "I pursue small goals like planning an enjoyable vacation or saving money to buy a gift for my girlfriend. These are my little aims and have nothing to do with metaphysical speculations."

Who knows if the worker was right! As for me, I cannot live without asking myself the why of things. It is probably because of my conditioning from my philosophy teacher. I didn't excel in philosophy in high school. It appeared too abstract to my empiric mind. The teacher was not pleased with my progress at school. He was convinced that I was a very shallow student and one day threatened to fail me.

"I'll fail you, Vincenzino, unless you start to ask yourself why everything exists and happens. You have to ask yourself why the earth is round, why the moon orbits the earth, and why the planets orbit the sun. If you are on the bus, you have to ask yourself why it is moving. In other words, you have to find an answer to everything that happens."

That teacher conditioned me to such an extent that I cannot live my life as it happens. I search for the meaning and the why of every thing and situation I come across. My wife was convinced that my search for answers to the many questions that life presents was useless.

"You have to just enjoy your life, without asking what happens after death," she said. "The only people who can learn that are those who have already died. You will know the truth when you die. For the moment, confine yourself to enjoying life in the best way you can."

Goa is a place where yoga teachers thrive. Yoga schools vary according to the kind of yoga one wants to do. My wife and I enrolled in a Hata yoga school. The class lasted about two hours and started at 8:30 in the morning. After our Sufi meditation was over, we walked along the shore for a while and then moved to the yoga class, which was held on a rooftop terrace of an unpretentious building behind the beach. It didn't shine for cleanliness, but the shade of the trees and the view of the ocean compensated for the dusty floor.

The teacher was from New Delhi. He didn't look like a teacher; rather, he looked like a beggar, and his clothes were not very clean. Nevertheless, his yoga was very good. I had the impression that he believed in his work and was eager to lead the class. Over the days, I noticed that he expressed philosophical truths in simple ways while leading the class. "Everybody is different. No competition, no comparison. Do according to your comfort level. No hurry, no worry. Something is better than nothing." He repeated these words every day, as if they came from a tape recorder.

The class began with breathing exercises called *pranayama*. We then performed *asanas*, which looked like stretching exercises, but the stretching involved the entire body. According to our teacher, we had to perform the *asanas* as if they were a meditation, because they affected both body and mind.

After two hours of yoga, all the muscles of the body were tuned up due to both the breathing exercises and the stretching. I felt very relaxed after doing yoga in an environment surrounded by trees on one side and the ocean on the other. Yoga stretches out all body muscles, which are often contracted due to the sedentary lifestyle one leads or mental ailments, like anxiety which stiffen the body as a side effect.

I had a feeling that by doing meditation, yoga, and swimming in the warm waters of the Indian Ocean, my body condition was improving. I was slowly purifying my body and mind, which would take me closer to God, as Saint Francis had taught me.

While I was performing the *asanas*, I recalled a friend of mine who wanted to solve all his health problems by taking medicines. Whenever he had a slight ailment, he went to the doctor who prescribed a medication for him. Even when he felt anxious or depressed, he quenched the feeling through anxiolytic agents. He trusted his doctor blindly. His absolute faith in taking medicines made it seem as though he was taking Holy Communion.

Even though Enna is a small city, he refused to walk the short distance from his home to his workplace. As for eating, he was never short of hot and tasty food. Even though he had some health problems due to lack of motion and an unhealthy diet, his doctor would resolve the problem by prescribing him the right medicine.

Another friend of mine was fond of thermal baths and springs. He thought that by drinking spring water and taking thermal baths, his health would improve. They are probably both helpful, but without a proper lifestyle to go along with them, there is no need to go there.

Both of them died before their time.

In my opinion, the best medicine is living in contact with nature, breathing pure air, jogging in the forest, or swimming in the ocean. Also, yoga and other holistic disciplines are useful in keeping the body and mind in good health.

Every time I went to my doctor's office in Enna to ask for a medical certificate to go to the gym or to the swimming pool, I found the waiting room packed with people waiting to have prescriptions filled. If all those patients practiced a sport in the open air, the doctor's waiting room would be less crowded and the National Health Service would save a lot of money!

Sadly, I, the one who wanted to hand people the right remedy to live a long life, got a fever. Apparently, swimming and doing yoga were not enough to keep me in shape.

"It serves you right!" said my wife. "You had the self-importance to criticize your friends who didn't follow your advice for keeping well, and now your elixir of life is not working for you. You boast about knowing everything. You should be more humble. Remember your Aunt Marietta?"

"Yes, of course. I loved my dear aunt."

"Well, she lived to the venerable age of one hundred years. She was a housewife. She never did yoga or other physical activities."

"I also remember her husband," I remarked. "He was a good shooter and walked in the forest often. He was crazy about hygiene. He always washed his hands before eating, but he dried them naturally. He thought the towel might contain germs. Nevertheless, he ended his life early by killing himself."

"Remember your Aunt Agata?" continued my wife. "She was from Catania and a rich businesswoman with many servants and cooks at her service. She didn't move much, nor did she play any sports or do yoga. In the morning, her chauffeur drove her to her firm. She stayed in the control room all day long, before finally going back home where a tasty meal made by her cook was waiting for her. Well, she lived to be ninety-six and was able to manage her business until a month before she died.

"Therefore," continued my wife, "everybody has the right to lead their life according to their own wishes. Forcing people to do yoga or jogging in the open air is like condemning them to a lifestyle that doesn't suit them."

"The cases you have mentioned are just exceptions," I retorted. "Every rule has its exceptions. You cannot deny that if you maintain your car well it lasts longer. The same can be said about the human body. A good lifestyle, which is comparable to good car maintenance, makes human life last longer.

"On the other hand, only God knows when our last day comes. So, placing one's trust in a physician, or following my suggestions about eating good food, doing moderate physical exercise, and yoga, cannot solve the problem that all humans are doomed to die."

In Goa, I wanted to try Ramana Maharshi's method of meditation again. I couldn't succeed in meditating more than a few minutes in Enna, probably because I was too distracted by work worries, but here the environment was more suited to meditation, especially at sunset when there was an unusual atmosphere of peace at the beach. Many people sat on the sand to watch the sun disappear.

I sat down on the sand, closed my eyes, and while I asked myself who I was, I tried to go deep inside to see my real nature. I realized that my body had undergone many changes since I was a little boy. It had become bigger. Over time, my teeth had rotted and had been replaced with manmade ones, and my hair had thinned, but something inside me had not changed. In fact, the little child who ran in the streets of Enna and dried his nose with his hand was still me. The sensation that I had of myself then and now was still same.

There is something unchangeable inside every human being. What I wanted to know was the nature of that invisible changeless entity. Maybe only mystics and saints can know that. As a common human being, I cannot reach lofty truths. An old proverb of Enna says *Asini e carusi Diu l'aiuta* (God helps donkeys and children), which is equivalent to the Italian saying, "Fortune smiles on beginners." Who knows, maybe someday fortune will smile on me and I'll get enlightenment.

A few days later, I changed my routine. I dropped my daily meditation and replaced it with jogging on the seashore and watching nature and the people around me. In fact, when a person looks for enlightenment, there are no fixed rules. It is possible to look inside oneself, as in meditation, or outside as well. Watching the ocean, the sun, the moon, or the people around us is like watching a painting by God.

One morning I was standing in front of the ocean when I had the feeling that Jesus was suggesting a new kind of meditation to me: "Open your heart to everybody. That is the best meditation!" he seemed to say.

I tried this new meditation as the days passed, and I can say it was very powerful. I sat silently on the beach and focused my attention on opening my heart to all living beings, both friends and those unknown to me. After a while, I felt that my body and mind were being purified. I talked with my wife about this discovery.

"Yes, I agree with you," she said. "Focusing our attention on opening our heart to everybody makes us realize that God is within every person. It is no coincidence that the Indians use the word *namaste* as a greeting, which means 'the godliness inside me greets the godliness inside you.'"

"I will name this discovery 'open-heart meditation,'" I said with my eyes beaming with joy.

Ever since that day, I have been doing the open-heart meditation every night before falling asleep. I lie down with my eyes closed and imagine baby Jesus entering my heart, purifying it, and flooding it with love. Then, I imagine that I pour this love on all human beings without discriminating against anyone.

According to John the Evangelist, God is nothing but love. If this is the truth, meditating on opening one's heart to love is the only way to get closer to God and to learn something about the afterlife. Obviously, the open-heart meditation needs to be put into practice.

The Arambol beach has a different look in the morning than it does in the evening. Usually, we went to the beach at daybreak. The sun had not risen yet behind the hills, and the fishermen strained to beach their heavy boats. Sometimes, I helped some of them with that hard effort. Some people enjoyed jogging, while others did tai chi. I noticed that a great many had themselves tattooed. An old man even had a tattoo on his face, while other tattoos on his body depicted barbed wire and scenes of violence.

Each person seemed a separate world. It happened that a man who brought his chessboard to the beach invited me to play with him under the scorching sun. I didn't feel like playing chess at the time and kindly declined his invitation, but I later saw him playing with someone else.

What struck me was the solitude of many people in Arambol. I observed the solitary souls in the early morning at the beach and in the evening at the restaurant.

"I would not be able to spend my holidays alone at a beach resort," my wife said.

"Me either!" I answered.

Indeed, during my youth, it was quite unusual to see a person walking alone in the streets; a lonely person was considered mad. In the summer when I wanted to go to the beach, I was careful not to leave Enna alone. I feared that if someone from the town saw me alone, they would have pity and say, "Look at poor Vincenzino. He is alone like a madman!"

Therefore, I was never alone, and it didn't matter if my fellow traveler was smart or cheerful. The important thing was that I had a companion. One year, I went on holiday at a seaside resort with a companion who wasn't very intelligent, just so that I wasn't alone.

In Goa, I had the opportunity to see the absurdity of my previous behavior. There is a basic distinction between solitude and loneliness. The former is free choice, while the latter is a feeling usually linked with melancholy or sadness. You can be in solitude without feeling sad. Many people in Arambol were living in their freely chosen solitude, but I didn't get the feeling that they felt alone.

Walking along the beach, I saw a lady that danced before the sea, a man playing the flute, and a group of Indian young men who played cricket. As for us, we saluted the rising sun and imagined that its golden light pervaded our entire bodies, healing and purifying them.

Late in the evening, the atmosphere was completely different. The beach was crowded. It was like being at the Belvedere in Enna during the summer, where people enjoyed strolling on the crammed public walk.

Little by little, daylight gave its place to night, and every now and then the disgusting smell of marijuana wafted in the air. It happened that some drug peddlers approached to try to sell us marijuana. I was looking for natural paradise, not an artificial and transient pleasure like that given by drugs, so I refused.

It was still cold in Rishikesh. We had stayed in Arambol for ten days, so we decided to visit other places in the south of India before going north. It was said that there were many enlightened gurus and holy places in India. I wanted to visit those areas. I thought I might be able to feel the same energy that emanated from Saint Francis's tomb in the Indian holy places.

Chapter Sixteen
Puttaparthi

I wanted to meet an enlightened person, hoping he or she would give me some more insight into my spiritual path. I had heard somewhere that an exceptional guru named Sai Baba lived in the city of Puttaparthi in southern India. It was said that he was the reincarnation of a former Indian saint of the same name.

We took a night bus from Goa and arrived near the village of Hampi in the early morning. From there we took a rickshaw, which drove us into the heart of the old city. The alleyways seemed to be all the same, and if it had not been for my wife's sense of direction, I would have had difficulty finding the way to our guesthouse.

The remains of that ancient capital were spread over a wide area. What caught my attention was the large number of monkeys that lived in town and around the old temples. They were ready to snatch bags containing food away from unaware tourists. I noticed a policeman who had a long stick on his desk, which he used just to chase away the monkeys.

A river ran through the town, and in the evening, we took a seat in one of the bars along its banks just to enjoy the peace of the place.

We stayed in Hampi for two days, visiting the historical places. The day before our departure, while we were inside an ancient temple, I noticed a couple of people who seemed to be homeless close to a gate dirty with excrement. I asked them if we could get through the gate, and they answered yes. My wife didn't want to pass through that filthy gate, but she finally gave in.

To our surprise, once we had passed the gate, a sloping rocky space stretched out before us. The color of the rock verged on light pink. We walked uphill up to a small temple. When we reached the top of the slope, an incomparable sunset and a view of an extensive valley below, dotted with villages and houses, appeared before our eyes.

"Sometimes," said my wife, "we should take the narrow alley that leads to bliss, while the wide and cozy way often takes us to a dead end. If I had not passed through that filthy gate, I would not have seen this unequalled scenery."

On the way home, my wife unexpectedly came across a lady from her country. She said that she had been in a cold city in the north of India where she had attended a *Vipassana* meditation course for a month.

"How did you manage to attend a meditation course for so long? I cannot do *Vipassana* for more than ten minutes," I said.

"You have to start gradually," she answered. "For the first three days, you have to confine yourself to watching the air that passes through your nostrils and hits your upper lip. Then you have to watch your entire body from the crown of your head to your feet. Meditation starts at four thirty in the morning and ends at nine in the evening. Little by little, as you meditate you have the sensation that your mind is being purified."

"What is the sense of watching yourself for so long a time?" I asked.

"If you watch yourself, you can learn who you are. Through *Vipassana*, you observe yourself completely," said my wife.

The Greek lady was a lonely traveler. She was short with black curly hair and was bubbling over with joy. She was dying to talk with us, as if she had not seen a human being for years.

"Let me introduce myself," she said. "My name is Maria. I have been visiting India for a long time. One of my most adventurous travels was the one I took from Lumbini to Lee. Actually, Lumbini is located in Nepal, but it is very near the Indian border. It is the town where Buddha is from, and many monasteries have been built around the palace where he was supposed to have been born. From Lumbini, I moved to Varanasi. It is a holy, fantastic city, which the Ganges runs through. Of course, I bathed in that holy river."

"I thought it was very dirty," said my wife.

"Yes, it is," answered the lady, "but it is said that the *sadhus* keep the water of the river clean so that nothing happens to the devout person who lowers themselves into it.

"At Varanasi, I took a bus to Haridwar, which is another holy city, and from there another bus to Manali at the foot of the Himalayas. I then took a minibus to cross the mountain range and went to Lee, where I planned to stay for a while."

"I didn't know it was possible to cross the Himalayas by bus," said my wife.

"Actually," she replied, "there is a mountain pass from Manali to Lee. It is the highest pass in the world at fifty-five hundred meters above sea level. It is difficult to breathe at that altitude. You have to drink a lot of water. There are no toilets on the road, so the bus stops from time to time along the way.

"Our bus broke down, and we were given the option of spending the night in a marquee at an altitude of around four thousand meters or continuing our way with another bus that had a few vacant seats. I opted for continuing my journey because I couldn't endure the altitude. I was very dizzy and had the feeling that I would collapse at any moment.

"The bus travelled on a vast plateau. No roads or paths were visible, but the driver seemed to know the way very well. I never imagined such vast tablelands in the Himalayas. It was almost like a lunar landscape. The soil was dry, and needles and rocks emerged from the ground here and there—no trees, not a blade of grass. I had the feeling of having landed on another deserted planet in our solar system. Apparently, the monsoons couldn't overcome the mountain range.

Nevertheless, now and then I spotted some isolated green areas.

"How is it possible that there are only patches green with trees?" I asked a person sitting next to me. 'They are like oases in the desert. Somehow, there is water underneath the ground. The city of Lee is just an oasis. It doesn't rain there much, but the area is rich in underground water,' he answered. We reached the maximum altitude of the pass, and I felt relieved. From then on, the bus would go downhill. The worst had passed, and I gradually started breathing normally."

The Greek lady's account sounded fascinating, but it was late. We were tired and sleepy, and we had to wake up early in the morning. I told her we couldn't stay and talk any longer.

"May I know your next destination?" she asked.

"Yes, of course," my wife answered. "We're going to Puttaparthi to meet Sai Baba."

"I know him," she said. "He is a holy man, but you cannot leave India without seeing Amma."

"Who is Amma?" I asked.

"She is a holy woman, and her ashram is in Kerala, a state in the extreme south of India."

We took a bus to Bangalore, and from there another bus to Puttaparthi. As soon as we arrived in town, we headed for Sai Baba's ashram. I had never seen such a large and well-maintained ashram. Furthermore, it was the cheapest place I had visited so far. We could have a good meal on ten rupees, the equivalent of a few cents.

People said that Sai Baba was an uncommon man. He had the power to make golden rings and necklaces out of thin air. It was also said that he was able to create a special holy powder in the same way. At the entrance, a lady who said she was from Switzerland directed us to our room. She asked us not to have sex while we were staying in the ashram. Moreover, she asked me to buy a traditional Indian dress for my wife. In fact, it was not possible for ladies to stay in that holy place in casual Western clothes.

The meeting place with Sai Baba was a large hall that could hold ten thousand or more people. The meeting happened in the evening. Men and women were not allowed to stay together in the hall, so my wife took a seat on the right, while I sat down on the left side of the hall. Sai Baba was sitting in a wheelchair. I couldn't see him because I was far away, but my wife spotted him and got the feeling of seeing a very weak man.

Later, at lunch, I exchanged a few words with an Italian guy whose wife was a devotee of Sai Baba. "I've come here for twenty-five years!" he said. "I have seen Sai Baba's materializations many times. He gave my wife a golden ring, which she keeps at home in Italy."

Before leaving the ashram, my wife bought a booklet that described Sai Baba's teachings. *Food is God* was the title of the small book. The first line said, "You are what you eat." By reading that booklet, I learned how to purify my body and mind by eating natural, sound food, which obviously didn't include meat.

Chapter Seventeen

Amma

The Greek lady's words resounded in our minds: "You cannot leave India without seeing Amma. She is a holy woman!"

We were not far from Kerala. Furthermore, the journey to Amma's ashram looked alluring, because to go there we had to cross the Kerala Backwaters by boat.

We headed for the town of Alleppey, the starting point for the boats bound for the backwaters. The boat was wooden and plowed the waters very slowly. Now and then, it stopped to take aboard or land people. An Italian lady took pictures with her camera the entire way. I compared the crossing to one I had years ago when I sailed up the Mekong River in Laos on a slow boat like this. At the time, the sailing lasted two days; now it would take around seven hours.

I couldn't tell if we were sailing fresh water or seawater. In fact, sometimes the course narrowed and took the shape of a river, while right after the levees were so broad that they looked like seashores. Vegetation was green and luxuriant, but I couldn't spot any waterfowl. Shortly before arriving at our destination, the water became so vast that it was evident that we were sailing the sea.

We landed at a small wooden dock. To go to the ashram, we crossed an arched bridge built to modern standards, but it was so narrow that only pedestrians could walk on it. Amma was not in the ashram. She used to move around India, and often visited other countries as well, but this time we were lucky and were told that Amma would return in three days.

We came to this place on the advice of the Greek lady we had met in Hampi, but we didn't know anything about Amma.

"What does she do?" my wife asked a Scottish man who was having dinner next to us.

"She doesn't do anything special. She confines herself to hugging people. So, when she comes here you will be hugged by her. While she hugs, she whispers something in your ear."

"What is the meaning of her hugging?" I asked.

"She hugs you and transmits good energy and her love to you and to all beings. I could perceive her love message," answered the Scottish man.

"Did you come here just to meet Amma, or there is some other special reason?" asked my wife.

"When I am at the ashram, I go to the Ayurveda Hospital, which is nearby, to have a treatment called *panchakarma* to purify my body."

"Can we get this therapy as well while we are waiting for Amma?" asked my wife.

"Yes, you can come with me, and I'll show you the hospital, but the complete treatment takes several days. How long are you going to stay here?"

"Just three days," I answered. "After hugging Amma we will leave."

We spent three days waiting in the ashram. I noticed that schools and hospitals had sprung up around the area. Apparently, Amma had been beneficial to local people. There was also a temple where she prayed, but it was open to everybody. The guests in the ashram usually gathered there in the evening. A statue of the goddess Kali stood out from the central wall of the temple. She is the goddess of all-consuming time.

We were asked to do volunteer work while we stayed in the ashram. Therefore, for a few hours a day, we cleaned the staircases and statues at the entrance to the temple.

In the evening while I was in the temple, I took a seat and tried to practice my open-heart meditation. I closed my eyes, and for just a few minutes watched my breathing. Then, I focused my attention on my heart, imagining opening it to all human beings, even to my enemies.

"What is the difference between good and evil?" I once asked a friend of mine.

"Good is opening, while evil is the closure of your heart," he answered then.

Now I could understand his saying. Closing oneself to the world turns into acting badly. On the contrary, an open heart can only bring good to oneself and others.

Some time ago, a cousin of mine gave me the nickname "Hedgehog." In hindsight, I can say he was right on. In fact, for the greater part of my life, I had acted as if I wore an armor made of thorns to protect myself from other people and from the happenings of life. By practicing my open-heart meditation, I realized how difficult it had been for me to open my heart, which had been locked for too many years.

On the third day, Amma arrived at the ashram. I spotted her in the temple from a distance in the evening. The following day she would hug everybody.

The line was quite long, but the long-awaited moment finally arrived. First, Amma hugged my wife and then me. The hug lasted just a few seconds, because the guard that regulated the line hastened us to be quick.

"What did Amma whisper in your ear?" I asked my wife.

"She said, 'You can do, you can do!' And what about you?"

"She whispered, 'Oh my dear, oh my dear,'" I answered.

We left the ashram by bus. Our next destination was Auroville.

Chapter Eighteen
Auroville

In the minds of the founders, Auroville should have been an international city open to people from every country and all walks of life to come together and live their lives with full freedom of speech, thinking, religion, and political opinions. With the passing days, I noticed that there was no discrimination based on someone's place of origin. As for trade, there was no currency. In fact, all visitors had to purchase a special card called an *Aurocard*, by which purchasing could be made.

Auroville is near Pondicherry, which had been a French colony. The French name, Auroville, means the "city of Sri Aurobindo," who was the founder of the community along with a French lady called Mirra Alfassa, also known as the "Mother."

Sri Aurobindo invented a kind of yoga called "integral." When my wife and I visited his ashram in Pondicherry, we bought a booklet about it. But after reading it, I couldn't find a method to practice this integral yoga; in fact, I couldn't understand what it was. The book talked about the creation of a super mind. Maybe, according to Aurobindo's integral yoga, the super mind was intended to transcend materiality to be one with the universe.

When years ago I visited Tanzania, I noticed that many tourists and volunteers came from Germany. In my opinion, it was due to the fact that Tanzania, previously called Tanganyika, had been a German colony.

The same went for Auroville. Many visitors and residents were French because Pondicherry had been a French colony. I don't think this was an accident. Both the French and the Germans are still fond of their ex-colonies. Despite the proclaimed universalism, nationalism is still strong in people's minds, and many individuals are still proud of their nation's past glories.

It was possible to become a citizen of Auroville, but it took quite a long bureaucratic procedure. I don't know exactly what the residents did to make a living. I heard that they had some kind of job. Some were teachers, other farmers, and so on. A Korean lady, who became an Auroville dweller, invented a job to get by. She made and sold *kimchi*, a traditional fermented Korean health food.

There were neither temples nor churches in the area. Apparently, the founders had intended to prevent the erection of any place of worship that might discriminate against the residents on the basis of their creed. To carry out the ecumenical end, a round gilt building called the Matrimandir had been erected that encompassed all religions. People both from Auroville and from the outside were allowed to enter just to meditate. But while residents could go in anytime, non-residents needed to make a reservation.

My wife and I were admitted two days after our booking, on the condition that we watch a video about Auroville before entering the Matrimandir.

The wide, gilded dome stood on a large lawn. At the entrance to the area was a big banyan tree. It was reputed to be sacred. In the evening, people lit candles and meditated around the big tree.

We entered the building and followed a circular walkway. I didn't see any statues or religious symbols. We were told that we would see a prismatic crystal on the top floor of the Matrimandir that emanated special energy. When we at last reached the top floor, people were meditating facing the crystal. It was dark inside. I didn't see the prismatic crystal;

my wife spotted it but said she didn't feel that it emanated energy.

The city of Auroville was scattered across the countryside. The buildings were not tall, in an effort not to spoil the environment. The community centers, like the city hall, schools, swimming pools, cinema, yoga centers, and restaurants, were so scattered around that to move from one place to another, you needed a motorbike, or at least a moped. Despite the fact that I had not ridden a moped for a long time, I was forced to rent one. The roads were made of packed earth and not busy, so it was easy to move from one place to another.

We usually had our meals at the restaurant, but in the morning our breakfast was served in the guesthouse kitchen. It was a good opportunity to meet other guests and chat. We sat at the same round table with a French couple. Both of them had been married previously but had now been married to each other for twenty-five years and had one daughter. They both had other children from their previous marriages.

"What a big mess," my wife said to me later. "Children from three different unions!"

"What matters is that they love each other," I replied—and they actually did.

The husband was a good painter. He showed us some pictures of his paintings. They were amazing.

"Are they oil painted?" asked my wife.

"Unfortunately not," he said, sighing deeply.

"Why do you say unfortunately?" I asked.

"I have been painting in pastels my whole life. Over time, my body has been absorbing the pastel powder, and that has most likely been the cause of my cancer."

I grimaced with sorrow. Indeed, every time I heard the word cancer, I always diverted my attention to different topics. But this time I couldn't, because every morning we met in the kitchen to have our breakfast and sat together at the same table. A natural feeling of friendship arose between us. His wife was very talkative and witty. I noticed that Jacques would spread butter and jam on a slice of bread and hand it to his wife. He remained sitting at the round table without eating anything.

One day he solved the mystery of his fasting: "I have to fast for twenty-one days. If I don't eat anything, the carcinogenic cells die, but they will form again later. There is a very good Tibetan doctor that comes here from time to time. When he comes, he sees me."

I wanted to ask him how it was possible to fast for twenty-one days and still keep fit. In fact, except for his paleness, he seemed to be in good health and was plump. However, I refrained from saying anything that might invade his privacy.

Before we left, he organized a full-moon tea party on the roof terrace. Only six were present at the party: Jacques, his wife, two French ladies, and my wife and me. A tablecloth had been laid on the floor with cakes and beverages, while soft music radiated in the air. The food and cakes were delicious, but Jacques didn't eat anything because he still had to fast for ten more days. It was a unique party. I had never seen a person that couldn't eat food organize a party for his friends. We ate cakes and other delicacies. There was neither beer nor wine, because they don't sell alcohol in Auroville.

"How long are you going to stay in Auroville?" asked Jacques.

"One week more and we'll move to Thiruvannamalai," answered my wife.

"It is a holy place. I know that area very well!" Jacques said. "When you go to Thiruvannamalai, don't miss doing three things. First, you must climb Arunachala Mountain. It is not difficult, but you have to get up early in the morning or the sun will be scorching. You'd better go alone and leave your wife in the cave to meditate. It is an arduous climb.

"Secondly, you must take part in the Full Moon Festival. Every month on the full moon, people from many parts of India come together and walk round Arunachala Mountain.

"Third, not far from the ashram is the house of a lady with special powers. Around ten in the morning, people gather in the hall of her house. She passes amid them silently. She confines herself to passing amid the people. Now and then she stares at somebody. Even though she doesn't talk, she transmits energy. She is very powerful!"

The party went on for about three hours. We enjoyed the full-moon night, talking music, art, and spirituality. After a while, the two French ladies left and we chatted with Jacques and his wife a little longer. I have to say that it was a party I would never forget.

Next to Auroville is Sadhana Forest. The word *sadhana* means "spiritual practice." According to the founder, who was an ex-philosophy professor from Israel, the forest should be a place where people spend their time in total contact with nature, far from everything that sounds modern, like electricity, running water, and stone houses.

There were almost two hundred volunteers from all over the world in Sadhana Forest, who had come just to spend some time plunged into a primitive environment. Their task consisted of planting trees and preserving the forest from fires, which could break out due to the dryness of the area.

We arrived in the forest by bus in the afternoon. The Israeli professor gave a speech about life in the forest and said that a few families lived there. One of the visitors asked, "What about your children? Do they go to school? Who gives them an education?"

"Our children," the professor answered, "have home schooling. Then, if they want to go to school, they can, but if they don't want to go, we don't force them to have compulsory education."

The professor led us around the forest and their tiny village, which was built on pilings. The dormitories for the volunteers were just over the pilings. There was neither running water nor electricity, except in one or two pilings. They produced power by a bicycle and solar panels.

They offered us a vegan meal and showed a film about life in the forest. We also saw how mercilessly they grow chickens and pigs in developed countries, which are fed inside very narrow cages until they are killed.

In the evening, when we got off the bus, a young man gave us a flier. Once at home, we read it. The young man complained that he was unjustly expelled from Sadhana Forest. Apparently, despite human endeavors, it is not possible to create a perfect society where everybody can live happily and without conflict, even in the forest.

Before leaving Auroville, we visited an ancient city called Mamallapuram. It was not far from Pondicherry, so in the morning we went there and returned to Auroville in the late afternoon. What attracted me was Krishna's Butterball, a huge, rounded boulder that stood on a slope and looked as if it was about to roll down at any moment.

A new spiritual stage was waiting for us. It was the holy mountain called Arunachala.

Chapter Nineteen
Arunachala Mountain

The city of Thiruvannamalai is where the master, Ramana Maharshi, spent almost all his life.

One day, when he was still a teenager, he was seized by an irrational fear of death. He had the sensation of being about to die, even though he didn't suffer from any disease. From that moment on his life changed. He started meditating about his real nature. His main question was "Who am I?" After meditating for a long time, he realized that he was not his body. His real nature and identity would survive after death. In fact, only his body was subject to annihilation, while his real self wouldn't die. At the age of sixteen, when he started meditating, he moved to Thiruvannamalai, a city at the foothills of the holy mountain of Arunachala.

While my wife and I were visiting the biggest temple in Thiruvannamalai, called Arunachaleswara, we noticed an underground room where Ramana Maharshi withdrew to meditate. He remained in that small room for many days without caring about insects and rodents ravaging his body.

Later, a *sadhu* saw him and was so enchanted by Ramana Maharshi's figure that he started serving him and became his personal attendant for the rest of his life. Ramana lived inside a cave, called Virupaksha, in Arunachala for nearly seventeen years. His attendant begged for alms, cooked, and took care of him. Ramana's holiness spread all around India and foreign countries as well.

As time went on, more and more people came to see him. After seventeen years in the small cave, Ramana moved to another cave, called Skandashram, where he lived for five years. Then he moved to the ashram that had developed around his mother's tomb.

As soon as we arrived in Thiruvannamalai, we headed for Ramana's ashram with the intention of remaining there for a few days. At the front desk, a person dressed in white, who looked like a monk, accommodated us in a wide, clean room outside the ashram. As for meals, we would eat at the refectory inside the ashram. We ate three times a day. The food was delicious, but we had to eat with our hands. Cutlery was not available at all.

After three days at the ashram, I went to reception to check out and pay for our lodging, but the same person that had welcomed us three days before said, "You don't have to pay. It is free!"

It was the first time in my life that I had been given free accommodations. I considered it a gift from Ramana Maharshi.

We could move to Rishikesh soon, because it was late in February and the weather was supposed to be warmer, but we wanted to stay in Thiruvannamalai a little longer to learn more about the places where the great guru spent his life. Moreover, Jacques had given us three pieces of advice, and we wanted to follow them. Finally, we found accommodations in a guesthouse not far from the ashram.

Jacques said we should climb Arunachala Mountain. Looking up from the bottom, it seemed to be quite a challenge. The hill was a bit high. Furthermore, somebody had told us that it was dangerous to venture out in that place without a guide. It was impossible to climb the mountain in the daytime because the sun was too strong. Therefore, we had to set off when it was still dark and come down no later than nine o'clock.

Where to find a guide? Fortunately, the owner of our guesthouse knew the track well and offered to lead us. We set off at five o'clock in the morning. It was dark, but it was possible to see people in the street. Apparently, life in India never stops. There were four of us: our guide, a girl from Korea who was also staying in our guesthouse, my wife, and me.

We followed our guide in the darkness, and I asked, "Why is this mountain considered sacred?"

He answered, "The Hindu trinity is formed by three gods: Brahma the creator, Vishnu the preserver, and Shiva the destroyer. One day, a dispute arose between Brahma and Vishnu. Both of them claimed to be superior. To settle the dispute, Shiva manifested himself as an infinite column of light so dazzling that it was impossible to look at. Brahma and Vishnu prayed to Shiva to take a less dazzling form, so he took the form of Arunachala Mountain. This place is sacred to Lord Shiva and represents the element of fire."

To go to the mountain, we crossed Ramana's ashram and followed a path to Skandashram Cave. Jacques had advised that my wife wait in the cave, but she wanted to climb to the top of the mountain. So, we all walked to the top of the hill. Our guide told us to be quick because the sun would soon rise and it would be impossible to stay on the mountain.

"How high is the mountain?" I asked.

"It is eight hundred thirteen meters above sea level," our guide answered.

While we walked, the magnificent temple of Arunachaleswara appeared in the distance. "What a grand temple! It is one of the five temples associated with the five basic elements: water, air, earth, fire, and sky," he said.

From time to time, we stopped for a few minutes. The Korean girl had brought some eggs, oranges, and bananas, which she shared with all of us. Monkeys and dogs waited at a distance to eat some of our leftovers.

We got to the hilltop at daybreak. I felt as happy as a mountaineer that had climbed the highest peak in the world. The sun appeared faintly on the horizon, and I was a little bit cold. The top was exposed to the wind, but from there I saw a vast landscape that stretched to the horizon. Our guide showed us two footprints that had been impressed by Shiva. There was also a trident to symbolize that the mountain was sacred to Lord Shiva.

After we climbed down the mountain, we expected to have leg pain, but mysteriously we didn't have any, even though we were a little bit tired.

The second thing Jacques advised us to do was take part in the Full Moon Festival. There were three days to the full moon, and we didn't intend to miss the event. We stayed in Thiruvannamalai, postponing our journey to Rishikesh.

In the mornings we went to meditate in the same places where Ramana used to. Sometimes we meditated in Virupaksha Cave, sometimes in Skandashram Cave, which were not far from each other, and sometimes in Ramana's ashram. I wanted to meditate as Ramana had advised, so I sat in a cross-legged position and focused my attention on who I was. I stayed in that position for an hour, but unfortunately, I was unable to meditate for more than five continuative minutes because my mind was too distracted, and I had the tendency not to live in the present. My mind was always thinking about the past or the future. Meditation was impossible.

One day while we were hanging about on the streets near the ashram, we stumbled across the house that belonged to the lady Jacques had recommended we see. She lived in a three-story building. The ground floor was just a wide hall where visitors gathered every morning around 9:30 to wait for her arrival at ten o'clock.

My wife and I sat on the floor and waited. There was an armchair opposite us. At ten sharp, a lady with an olive complexion and wearing a sari entered the hall. Her hair was covered with a veil. She stepped slowly towards the armchair and sat down. Her features were still striking, despite that fact that she was probably over fifty.

She sat on the armchair motionless; only her eyes moved. She fixed her eyes and shifted her gaze from one person to another. Then she stood up and walked along the rug that separated her from the visitors. She kept staring at the visitors, and then stepped to the exit as slowly as she had entered.

People said they had felt some energy when she stared at them. As for us, neither my wife nor I felt anything. Nevertheless, that doesn't mean that the lady was not a powerful, enlightened person.

I have only felt energy three times so far. It had happened at Saint Francis's tomb, another time while I was visiting a lady with stigmata, named Natuzza Evolo, and a third time in the town of Calascibetta, near Enna, where a young man named Rosario, who claimed to see Our Lady, lived.

At last, the long-awaited full moon day arrived. People flocked to Thiruvannamalai all afternoon. Under the full moon, which enhanced the splendor of the contours of Arunachala Mountain, the human river seemed to flow as if it was about to burst its banks. Millions of people looked like a huge snake that sinuously slithered around the holy mountain. I couldn't believe my eyes.

The walk was fourteen kilometers. Most Indians covered the distance barefoot. A few foreigners tried to do the same, but the consequences were often unfortunate. I spotted a white man with his feet bleeding. He was forced to give up the walk.

The street was surrounded with stalls selling many kinds of goods, above all refreshments, but also Ayurvedic medicines and toys. Here and there, people lined up for free food provided inside the temples along the way. We too were invited to eat. We entered an open square close to a temple and enjoyed a wonderful free meal.

It was an experience I would never forget. I didn't want to leave Thiruvannamalai and the places where Ramana meditated, but now it was time to move on. We had to reach our main destination—Rishikesh.

From Thiruvannamalai, we went to Chennai and took a flight to Delhi. Once at the airport, we went to the Kashmiri gate and took a night bus to Rishikesh.

Chapter Twenty
Rishikesh

We arrived in Rishikesh around five in the morning. It was still dark and cold. We took a rickshaw, which directed us to a guesthouse. On the way, we spotted four or five homeless people sleeping under a small portico. Each of them was covered with a blanket; it was definitely not enough to protect them from the coldness of the night.

The rickshaw man got us a drafty room in an area of Rishikesh called Tapovan. The blanket was too thin to warm us up, but we were still grateful to God for being in a much better situation than the homeless people we had seen, who were shivering.

At daybreak we heard rolls of thunder. The sky clouded over, a strong wind blew, and the windowpanes rattled. The draft in the room flapped the curtains, and then it started raining. We suddenly missed the days spent on the beach in Arambol when we jogged happily across the seashore. Why didn't we remain in the warm south of India? I felt guilty about my wife, who felt the cold, but our spiritual quest had to go on. Being in a seemingly hostile place would be a good lesson for us.

There are two ways to live our lives. One is to be content with little, remain confined to our birthplace, and lead a peaceful life. The other is to get out of our friendly environment and venture into the unknown for the sake of knowledge and exploration. Opting for one way instead of the other doesn't depend on one's merit, but on the inner psychological makeup. As for me, if I hadn't suffered from a pathological anxiety and fear of death, I would never have started my journey around the world in search of a solution to the issue.

A Sicilian proverb says *"bon timpu e malu timpu un dura tuttu u timpu"* (neither bad weather nor good weather lasts forever). The proverb is an allegory of life, which passes through sunshine and storms. Sometimes life flows smoothly and other times stormy, but it is worth living to the fullest.

Around noon, the sky was less cloudy, and now and then the sun peeped out from behind the clouds. We took advantage of the fair weather to have a walk around the area. We spotted a stretch of the Ganges River. The water looked green and clean. It was different from what I had seen years ago in Varanasi where the riverbed was broader and the water flowed quietly. Here the channel was narrower and the river was choppy.

Rishikesh is considered a holy city. They don't sell alcohol in the shops, and you cannot find meat in the restaurants. The Ganges is a sacred river for the Hindus. At the sight of the green color covering the river like an emerald blanket, I too felt a certain air of sacredness in it.

We walked downhill along a street flanked with shops, restaurants, and temples. There were many yoga and meditation schools. We then turned onto a narrow staircase that led us to the bank of the holy river. Actually, the river didn't look as rough and narrow as it had appeared to be up high. In some stretches it was broad and calm, similar to what I had seen in Varanasi, but its water was much cleaner, and it had an olive-green hue.

We went to the bank and dipped our feet into the river. I scooped up some water with my hand to see its color; it was colorless. Apparently, the olive-green hue was the reflection of the trees in the surrounding hills.

That night I couldn't sleep well. I was seized with the fear of death once again. My wife was sleeping close to me, and I wondered if she had made a good choice in getting married to such an anxious man.

Just like my Uncle Vincenzo, I was assailed by the doubt that all the cells in our body die at the same time. Actually, there are body functions that continue after death. For instance, hair and nails keep growing. I have always been terrified of being buried when my mind is still alive and conscious even though my body is dead. However, I realized that my anxiety and continuous fear of death wouldn't help my spiritual search. Being terrified beyond measure would only confuse my ideas and mind, preventing me from living my life.

In the holy city of Rishikesh, I wanted to try my open-heart meditation again. As soon as we woke up, after having a cup of coffee and eating some bananas, we meditated for fifteen minutes. My wife did her breathing meditation, while I watched my breathing for a few minutes and then tried my open-heart technique. While I was watching my heart, imagining that it was open to everybody, I recalled a statue of Jesus I'd kept in my room since I was a baby. The statue is about one meter high. Jesus is portrayed as a master with a white robe and a red tunic and with his heart sticking out of his chest.

Not only is the heart fundamental for Christians. Buddhists also believe that the mind is located in the heart. They think that the mind is a mental continuum without beginning or end. The Buddhist "mind" may be considered the equivalent of what Christians name the soul. Obviously, when I say that the house of the mind or soul is in the heart, I don't refer to the physical heart, which can even be implanted from one person to another, but to the spiritual heart, whose house lies close to the physical heart.

While I was meditating on opening my heart to life, to people, and to every living being, I had the sensation of having a stone instead of a heart. It was as if I had my heart locked in a safe impossible to open. However, I was sure that continued meditation would open my heart to life sooner or later.

"Meditation is useless if you don't put your resolution into practice," my wife said. "In fact, you must open your heart to everybody in real life, not only in meditation."

I actually found it quite difficult to open my heart to certain people with whom I had had an argument or I didn't like, but I had to do it or my open-heart meditation would have been just nonsense.

The weather in Rishikesh changed radically the following day. The sun was shining, and it became much hotter. We walked the same street as the day before and arrived at a narrow bridge. Only pedestrians and motorbikes could use it. Monkeys stood along the handrails, hoping to get some food.

We crossed the bridge and passed to the other bank of the river, which was also full of shops and restaurants. I admired the river in all its majesty, and noticed that the olive-green color was constant, even in stretches where the banks were surrounded by houses, when the trees were far away and the sky was cloudy. Its wonderful green color remained even at twilight. Obviously, the green color depended on a phenomenon I didn't know about. There had to be something mysterious in the amazing Ganges. It could be considered sacred not only by Hindus, but by everybody. In fact, it cannot be ruled out that God, who is the same for all people, regardless of the race, becomes manifest in different ways, even in this holy river.

Cows wandered freely in the narrow streets, while donkeys and mules carried river sand, gravel, and red bricks to building sites. I hadn't seen this kind of transportation for at least seventy years, when long lines of donkeys, mules, and horses carried goods and people from the countryside into Enna.

The *satsangs* were one of the peculiar features of Rishikesh. *Satsang* is a Sanskrit word that means gathering together with a master for the truth.

We entered a hall where a satsang was to be given. At one end there was an armchair, and about a hundred people sat in the hall facing the empty chair. Then, one lady about fifty years old came in and sat on it. Before she could open her mouth, one young man in the hall raised his arm and asked to speak. He was given a microphone, and then he asked a question. After him, other people asked questions, and the lady in the armchair answered each of them. This happened for almost one hour. The questions were about how one should live life and what a person can do to self-inquire and know their real nature.

Most of the people in the hall were young. One of the young men who asked to speak caught my attention. "If I don't judge people," he asked, "how can I know which person is right for me? Obviously, in my daily life, I need to judge and weigh people and situations. Do I act correctly when I judge people?"

The master in the armchair answered without hesitation. "You will know better if you don't judge. In fact, you don't need to judge, because you can learn what to do just by using your heart."

A lady of about forty was given the microphone and then asked her question: "Every morning my mind spins with thoughts. I strive to be still, but I cannot stop the whirl of thoughts. What can I do to be still?"

"You don't need to strive to be still. What you can do is just watch your thoughts. Yes, confine yourself to watching and watching, and then you'll see that your thoughts will melt and become like water. Only then will you be still," answered the master.

The following day we went to attend another satsang. The master was a man from Jamaica. This time, the venue was not in Tapovan, but near the marketplace in Rishikesh. The hall was quite wide and could hold more than a thousand people. On the wall behind the platform, two portraits were hung— one of Ramana Maharshi and one of Papaji. Other portraits on the walls portrayed Amma, the former Sai Baba, and the Jamaican master too.

The satsang was not dissimilar from that we had attended the day before. Most of the questions and answers were on the same topics as the previous day.

When the satsang was almost at an end, the master invited the person who was questioning him to come to the platform, and then he asked, "Can you tell me something impermanent that is the same on Monday, Tuesday, Wednesday, and the days to come? According to you, there is a certain starting point or a universal, unchangeable truth? What does ultimate truth mean?"

The young man strayed from the topic and was unable to give the right answer. Then the guru addressed the audience for an answer. A lady stood up and said, "The real truth is that now I am awake, while when I sleep, I am not awake."

"That is not a universal truth," said the master. "The consciousness of being awake or asleep depends on subjective perception!"

Nobody in the hall could give the right answer.

Another satsang was given by a guru who came from a Portuguese-speaking country. From his complexion, I inferred he was Brazilian. He spoke only Portuguese; a girl sitting close to him translated his words into English. This time, the satsang didn't start with questions and answers, unlike the previous ones. The guru, who had a long white beard and a pigtail, gave a long opening speech.

"The path to self-realization," he said, "passes through the heart. There cannot be spiritual life if the person builds walls around them. I can say that spirituality is synonymous with love. A human being has to open his heart to everybody and pull down all the walls he has been building to protect himself from the outside. A spiritual search means creating harmony inside and outside oneself."

When we left the hall, my wife, even though she appreciated the goodness of the master, made a clarification. "All the three masters we have seen talk of love and of opening one's heart. If we keep attending satsangs, I am sure we'll find other gurus speaking in the same way. The most difficult thing to do is to put the opening of one's heart towards everybody into practice. In daily life, instead of opening our heart, we lock it. Whether we like it or not, we raise walls all around it to protect ourselves from life's dangers."

Despite her words, every night before falling asleep, I did my open-heart meditation. I was convinced that through meditation I would get the habit of opening my heart in real life also. Watching my heart, I could see the walls surrounding it. They were the walls I had erected during my life to protect myself from disappointments. With those walls, I avoided being hurt.

Most of the disappointments came from being refused or left by the women I liked. I often felt unbearable pain from a fallen dream. Whenever a girl said to me, "Sorry, you are not my kind of lover," or worse, "We can be just friends because you are a good boy, but I will never be your lover," my self-pride was so wounded that I had to somehow find a way to protect myself from such pain.

Every time I had to cope with a challenge like an aptitude test or a job application, I was more worried about the potential wound my heart might suffer in the case of failure than about the situation itself. Over time, the fear of failure led me to avoid situations that would create problems for me. As a result, my mind was always projecting into the future or into the past, instead of being present in real life.

There are two main kinds of visual acuity. A far-sighted person can see far away but cannot see things close; he cannot even read a line without glasses. The near-sighted person cannot see far off but is quite able to see things close. As for me, I lived in the future or in the past and was unable to live in the now. It was as if I needed glasses to live my life.

Here, in this mystic city of Rishikesh, I at long last decided to live not only in the future or in the past, but also in the present to have a complete view. Whenever I perceived that my mind wasn't living in the present, I told myself, "Put on your glasses and you will enjoy the now."

When I did my open-heart meditation, I also focused my attention on opening my heart to life and to the joys that it brings us. It may seem a banal meditation, but in my case, it was not so obvious. In fact, I was unable to live my life fully and joyfully.

There was a distant episode at the root of my tendency not to live in the present and enjoy my life. When I was eighteen years old, I got my driver's license. At that time, I was in a relationship with a girl named Giuseppina, who was from Palermo. Her father was the prefect of Enna. Although she belonged to a high-class family, her parents did not allow her to come in my car with me. It would have aroused scandal in a small city like Enna.

She was a typical Sicilian girl, with black hair and eyes and Arab features. I noticed her one day while she was crossing the gate of the prefecture. I was bewitched by her majestic gait. She looked like the most polished girl in the world. After that, whenever I saw her, my heart leapt.

I didn't know how to approach her. She didn't have many friends and had a preference for going to church. She went to the Church of San Giuseppe, which stood across from the prefecture palace, every evening. So, I started attending Mass as well. I chose a pew not far from hers, but instead of following the Mass, my mind wandered elsewhere, dreaming of an endless love with Giuseppina.

My first contact with her happened naturally. I smiled at her whenever she turned her head towards my pew in the church. Then, once the Mass was over, I waited for her outside the church and kept smiling at her—but I didn't dare make an approach. One day after Mass, we happened to be close to each other while following the stream of people heading for the exit. Being side by side, it was quite natural for me to ask her name.

"My name is Giuseppina," she answered.

"My name is Vincenzino," I said.

"What a beautiful name! It is uncommon," she said.

"Yes, it is. My parents named me that as a sign of respect for my mother's younger brother, who died before his time. Giuseppina is also a beautiful name. It is the woman's version of the name Giuseppe, who was Jesus's putative father. Now I know why you always come to the Church of San Giuseppe."

"How can you know that?"

"Because you are Giuseppina, you come to San Giuseppe Church."

She burst out laughing. Meanwhile, we arrived at the entrance to the prefecture, which was a stone's throw from the church. "See you tomorrow at the exit of the church!" she said, still smiling.

I kept watching her until she disappeared beyond the forecourt of the palace. At that moment, I was the happiest person in the world.

In the passing days, we saw each other over and over again. Our strolls became longer. We didn't confine our walks to just going from the church to the prefecture. We sometimes walked Via Roma or the Belvedere, or to the Castle of Lombardia, and we even walked in the park that surrounds the tower of Frederick the Second.

After a year of walking in the streets of Enna, I tried to convince her to get into my car. Actually, I used my father's car. However, all my endeavors failed. She was unshakable.

"If we were in a great city like Palermo," she said, "I would. But in this small city, I cannot get in your car because my father would find out. I don't feel like disobeying him. If he knew I was in the car with you, he would be very disappointed." I loved her so much that I respected her decision.

Later, her father was transferred to Palermo to become the city prefect. It was a great blow to me, but we exchanged letters and talked quite often on the phone. An old song says that being away is like the wind that puts out small flames and sets blaze to big fires. My love for her was a really big fire, and I couldn't stay away from her for long.

One day, I asked my father permission to go to Palermo with his car. At first, he was reluctant, but he knew I was going to meet Giuseppina, a girl of high rank, and finally consented.

"Don't drive fast!" he said. "Palermo is a big city. Be careful at intersections!"

"Don't worry, Father. I am a good driver."

It took three hours to drive from Enna to Palermo. I arrived half an hour early at the Piazza Politeama, the place where we had fixed the appointment. At noon sharp, Giuseppina appeared in the distance. She wore a black skirt and a red silk blouse. She looked like a fairy. We drank an orange juice at a refreshment booth, and then she suggested we take a walk on Via Libertà.

"You promised," I said, "that when we were in Palermo you would get in my car. Do you remember?"

"Yes, I do, but I have a terrible fear that my father will find out."

"Don't worry! Palermo is a big city and your father will never know."

"Okay, I'll do as you ask, but we had better go to Monte Pellegrino, so nobody can see us and report back to my father."

To go to Monte Pellegrino, I drove towards Mondello and took the panoramic road that leads to the top of the mountain. The road was full of sharp U-bends.

"I feel dizzy if I look down," Giuseppina said.

At the end of the winding road, we arrived at a square. From there, a flight of steps led to the Sanctuary of Santa Rosalia, also called the *Santuzza*, who is the patron saint of Palermo.

It is said that in 1624, when the plague was causing many deaths in Palermo, Rosalia appeared to a shooter and led him to the cave on Mount Pellegrino, where her bones could be found. Then she asked him to take her bones to Palermo to be carried in procession along the streets. The hunter did what Santa Rosalia wished and, after her remains were carried in procession three times, the plague ended. From then on, Santa Rosalia has been the patron saint of Palermo.

The sanctuary was inside the cave where Santa Rosalia's remains were found. Entering the cave, I was enchanted by the silent atmosphere. The German writer Wolfgang Goethe, who visited the place, described Monte Pellegrino as "the most beautiful promontory in the world."

Not far from the entrance to the cave were some votive offerings from people who had been granted a blessing. Going forward, my attention was drawn to the drops coming from the top of the cave. They were canalized on thin silvery metal sheets to a basin and were used to fill the holy water stoup at the entrance. I don't know why, but I had the feeling that the dripping water was teardrops, as if that holy cave were shedding tears for me.

At the end of the cave was a marble statue portraying the Immaculate Conception. I genuflected and said a prayer to Our Lady. Unfortunately, Giuseppina and I couldn't escape our fate! Before long, a thunderbolt would fall on us.

While I was praying, I recalled one of my mother's poems I read when I found Vincenzo's diary:

LIFE

We were sitting on our stone staircase.
"What is life?" I asked my siblings.
"Life is breathing. Even trees breathe," replied Biagio.
"Life is a tiny bird on a small branch.
Unexpectedly the sprig snaps,
And the little bird flies away," were Vincenzo's words.
"Life is sometimes a beautiful dream,
Other times a nightmare," said Carolina.
"Life is a wonderful drawing in the sand of the sea,

But it is governed by fate!
Therefore, the drawer knows in advance
When the tide will erase it," I concluded.

After we left the sanctuary, I drove off the road, looking for a secluded place. I found a slope from where we saw the beach of Mondello and the sea that stretched to the horizon. While we were admiring that amazing scenery, our eyes met, and as if by magic our lips also met. We closed our eyes and kept kissing each other as if the world had disappeared and only we remained on the surface of the earth.

We were so enraptured that we didn't notice that the car was slowly moving towards the precipice. In fact, to get closer to her, I had unwittingly slipped the gear into neutral. Moreover, the hand brake was not in perfect working order. As soon as the car hit a big rock, I realized what was going to happen, but now it was too late, because the car had gained speed and it was impossible to keep it under control. The ground was too uneven and steep. I applied the foot brake, but the car kept skidding.

"Get out of the car!" I cried out.

I opened the door and got out, while Giuseppina was not quick enough to do the same. Inevitably, the car fell from the cliff nearly three meters high. From paradise, I fell into hell. Giuseppina lost her life, while I kept living with that tragic event engraved in my heart and mind.

Fifty years had passed since then, and now while I was in Rishikesh, I again tried to open the doors of my heart that I had kept locked for half a century. I wanted to smile again at life.

During my open-heart meditation, I could see my heart as if it were a little mouse shut inside a mousetrap. It had been imprisoned for too long, but now I wanted to let it free to go with the flow and joys of life, as it was fifty years ago before that appalling, fatal accident.

Sometimes, I thought my desire to start living a normal life again was just ridiculous. In fact, I was now seventy years old and had exhausted the greatest part of my life. It was too late now. It was as if I wanted to rekindle the fire on burnt wood. However, something is better than nothing, and life is worth being lived all the way.

By practicing the open-heart meditation that Jesus taught me when I walked along the shoreline at Arambol Beach, I saw nature in a different way. Now, the Ganges, the green hills, the moon, and all people seemed to smile at me.

"I am convinced," I said to my wife, "that God is within everything and in every creature. We should open our hearts to everybody. The only way to know God is through his creatures. If we open our hearts to all beings, we'll see God inside them."

"I don't think so. According to you, God is also inside a serial killer? Or a robber? Or a rapist? If God were inside those despicable beings, they would not act in such a bad way," she said.

"No one has ever been able to open his heart to all human beings as Jesus did. Jesus's love was unconditional and all-encompassing. He never discriminated on the basis of one's actions. He loved all human beings without distinction, even his executioners.

"If Jesus loved everybody, criminals included, it means that also serial killers, robbers, and rapists have God inside them. We cannot judge anybody, for we don't know the ultimate truth about things, people, and phenomena. In fact, reality can be different from appearance. We don't have the right to separate the good from the evil, because we don't know either of them. I can only say that criminals also suffer because of their ignorance and distorted minds. Behind wickedness there are delusions, which are wrong representations of life and of human relationships," I replied.

While I was meditating on opening my heart to life, another question arose in my mind—how to live life. In fact, there are many ways of living. On this point, a conversation I had a long time ago with a politician friend of mine came to my mind. His career in politics had been so successful that in just a few years he was elected mayor of his city.

"In life, you can be either a tractor or be towed, either a leader or a follower, a proactive or a submissive person. As for me, I have chosen to be a tractor—that is, a leader.

"There are two main characters acting on the stage of the play of life. Those who take the initiative and those who are subjected to others' initiatives. Only the former make history, as the latter just follow other people's will. If you want to go on in your life, be a leader!"

At that time, I was puzzled by my friend's words, and I am still not convinced of the soundness of his thesis. By meditating on opening my heart to everybody, I have realized that it is a trifle to be a leader or a follower, a winner or a loser. What matters is a pure heart open to life, and then you will naturally achieve your position and role in society. By living with a spirit of service, you will find out that there are neither leaders nor followers, because everyone is subject to the first principle of serving and being in communion with others. I am aware that my idea can be considered utopian, but what matters is how I behave, not what others think of me or of my ideas. I want to live with a spirit of service. Others can do what they like.

Our stay in the mystic city of Rishikesh was coming to an end. Before leaving, we went to see the River Ganges one more time. For two days, the water had turned yellowish because it had rained much in the mountains and the flood had raised mud from the riverbed, but now the olive-green water was again as shining as ever.

We went to the bank and sat on a rock. From that position, we could admire the suspension bridge that connected the two opposite banks of the river. In some stretches, the river was flanked with black cliffs and green hills. If I had been a painter, I would have set up an easel and painted that unique scenery.

We were admiring the river when a little girl came close to us. She wore a torn gown, but her black eyes showed liveliness. She wanted to sell us a little round-shaped boat made of dry leaves with flowers, a tiny candle, and an incense stick inside.

"What is this?" my wife asked.

"It is a *diya*."

"What is it for?"

The little girl, despite her young age, looked like an expert seller. "The diya," she said, "is made just to make wishes. You light the candle and entrust the diya to the River Ganges."

"Okay, you convinced me. I'll buy it," I said.

The little girl lit the candle and the incense stick and put the diya on the river. Then she dipped her little hand into the water and waved it to drive the diya towards the river's current.

"Now you can express your wish!" she said before going off, skipping gaily.

The diya floated, driven by the current. We followed our small boat and made our wishes. As soon as I closed my eyes, I saw my car somersaulting in the air fifty years ago on Mount Pellegrino before falling straight down into the crag. I opened my eyes for an instant and watched the diya disappear in the distance. The small candle was still lit.

"Deliver my wishes, little boat! May I meet Giuseppina someday in another life to express my regret for what happened that day. May we all be born again in a new star or a new planet rich in spirituality, or a new earth free from diseases, old age, and death; a new earth where people don't live mechanically but are aware of whatever they do; a new earth free from ignorance and error, where people don't turn to suicide to resolve their unbearable sufferings; a new world without violence, free from the poor, beggars, the homeless, maladjusted people, and social malaise."

I would have continued my wish list, but all day would not have been enough to finish it. Before reopening my eyes, my thought went to my disabled friends and a friend of mine who was suffering from a congenital disease called thalassemia. To be kept alive, he needed regular blood transfusions. I expressed the wish that congenital diseases would be eradicated someday, as well as the physical disabilities like those that struck my British and Italian friends for whom I volunteered on several occasions.

The diya loaded with my wishes had gone far off, and along with it my dreamed new earth had faded away. Harsh reality was another thing. We said goodbye to the holy River Ganges and the mystic city of Rishikesh.

Chapter Twenty-One
The Marian Sanctuaries

My natural desire to meet the supernatural and allay my fear of death has, over time, been leading me to the places where it was said the Virgin Mary had appeared to human beings.

Of course, I am not the only one interested in the life-after-death topic. I heard that a billionaire once offered a million-dollar prize to anyone who provided incontrovertible evidence that the soul survives the death of the body. He also created a working group of scientists and theologians to do research on the afterlife.

I also heard that there is a haunted castle in Scotland where visitors eager to have extrasensory experiences can spend the night to meet the ghosts in the castle.

There are also people who resort to mediums and shamans. During seances, they evoke spirits and are even able to talk with the souls of the dead.

As for me, I have always been skeptical about paranormal experiences as a way to learn whether the soul is immortal or not.

In the past, I walked the path of the intellect to know the ultimate truth about life after death. I researched this topic by reading hundreds of books about enlightenment, meditation, religion, Holy Scriptures, and so on. I don't want to say that my work was useless. Not at all! Learning is better than ignorance, but it is not enough to get closer to God, because the spiritual path can only be covered by the soul and not by the intellect. Furthermore, the way to the immaterial world passes through the miracle and the wonder which are beyond the intellect. How can you prove a miracle with your empiric mind? Only the heart can perceive and understand the miracle. Therefore, I have been following the same path where my heart led me. It took me to the tomb of my spiritual guide, Saint Francis of Assisi, to India, to Australia, to Africa, to other countries, and also to the Marian sanctuaries.

A constant of the Marian sanctuaries I have visited is that Our Lady has always appeared to children or to humble people. I have also realized that the apparitions of Our Lady are the apparitions of God Himself. Who can say with absolute certainty that God has masculine features? There is no doubt that the miracle Our Lady performed in Fatima, seen by thousands of people, came from God Himself. Who can move and spin the sun like a top if not God?

The idea of God as a woman can be found in ancient civilization from the Paleolithic on and even in my hometown of Enna, where Demeter was considered the Mother Goddess. No pagan god was above her.

Among the apparitions of the Virgin Mary, that in Medjugorje, a town in Bosnia and Herzegovina, is not considered authentic by the Catholic Church, but millions of pilgrims from all over the world, including Catholic priests, flock to the charming town of Medjugorje every year. I too have visited that holy place. Following the voice of my heart, I walked up to Podbrdo Hill, the impervious place where the Virgin Mary appeared to a few boys and girls, and to Krizevac Mountain, a hill about five hundred meters high on the top of which a monumental cross stands. I was struck by the atmosphere of peace and sacredness that hovered in those places.

The Marian Sanctuary of Civitavecchia, near Rome, Italy, is somehow connected to that of Medjugorje. I visited it on the way back from Assisi.

In 1994, the parish priest of the Church of Saint Augustine in Civitavecchia visited Medjugorje and bought a statuette of

Our Lady. Arriving in Italy, the priest gave the statuette as a gift to the Gregori family, who placed it in a niche in their garden.

One day, five-year-old Jessica noticed that tears of blood were streaming down the little statue's face. She informed her father, who phoned the parish priest, Pablo Martin. The news of the tears of the Madonna spread quickly, so much so that, to avoid crowds of onlookers flocking to the garden of Gregori house, the statuette was moved to the Church of Saint Augustine. It shed blood fourteen times and was even seized by the prosecutor. The results of the chemical analysis on the tears showed that they contained male blood. Nowadays, the small statue of Our Lady is exhibited for the veneration of the faithful in the Church of Saint Augustine.

In Medjugorje, I met a priest from Tanzania named Olivarius. He wore a long shirt typical of his country embossed with the image of Our Lady of Fatima and the three little shepherds. He told me about an important Marian sanctuary in Rwanda, the only one in Africa. He said that the Virgin Mary appeared many times between November 1981 and December 1983 in a place called Kibeho, in Rwanda.

The surprising thing is that both in ex-Yugoslavia and in Rwanda, horrific massacres occurred a few years after the apparitions of Our Lady. In my opinion, this confirms the authenticity of the apparitions.

While I am talking about Marian sanctuaries, I cannot help but mention the "miraculous medal."

One day, I went to St Francis's Church in Enna, where the Franciscan friar, while celebrating Mass, told us the story of Saint Catherine Labouré.

The friar said, "Catherine was born into a well-to-do family in 1806. Since she was a little girl, Saint Vincent De Paul had appeared to her in a dream."

In 1830, Saint Catherine became a novice in the hospice of Daughters of Charity, the religious order founded by Saint Vincent De Paul. One night, a young boy woke up Catherine and asked her to follow him to the chapel. She followed the boy, the doors of the chapel burst open, and the church suddenly lit up. The Virgin Mary was sitting on a chair and asked Catherine to come closer.

At the end of that year, Catherine met Our Lady again. This time, the Virgin Mary was standing on a globe and ordered that a commemorative medal of the apparition be struck: "the miraculous medal."

The Franciscan friar handed out some medals to the congregation to be given to those in need. I got three medals.

Later, I gave one medal to a man from Manchester named Robert, who was about forty and was blind and in a wheelchair. Every now and then, he stood up, but not for long. When he did, he looked like a rugby player. I had a feeling he must have been a champion before he got sick. In any case, he was a great gentleman. Although an atheist, he accepted the miraculous medal I gave him and put it inside his wallet.

As for the second medal, I gave, or rather exchanged it for another medal of the Virgin Mary with a young man of about twenty from Liverpool named Stephen, who suffered from epileptic fits. I still keep his precious medal in my wallet.

I entrusted the third medal to my wife, who said she would give it to a person in need.

When I went to Paris, I visited the chapel where the apparitions happened. I wanted to see the incorrupt body of Saint Catherine, but it was not possible because Mass was said continuously in the chapel and I couldn't get close enough to the sarcophagus.

Even though I couldn't see the body of Saint Catherine, I felt very peaceful while visiting the chapel. Furthermore, I learned something about Saint Vincent De Paul and his Sisters of Charity.

Now, let's have a look, one by one, at some other Marian sanctuaries where my heart has been leading me throughout my life.

Syracuse

The first experience I had regarding the apparitions of Our Lady happened in Syracuse a long time ago. I didn't go there of my own will, for I was just twelve years old. Nevertheless, as if it were yesterday, I remember when my family went to Syracuse to see a plaster plaque of Our Blessed Lady weeping.

In 1953, a bride and a groom were presented with a plaster plaque portraying the Immaculate Heart of Mary. The newlyweds were very poor and, since they had no house of their own, went to live with the husband's parents for some time. They hung the plaque of the Virgin Mary they had received on the wall above the headboard of their double bed.

The wife, Antonia, had a difficult pregnancy and suffered from convulsions and blurred vision. One day, after a seizure and a bout of temporary blindness, Antonia opened her eyes and saw that the plaster plaque portraying the Virgin Mary was weeping. When she called out to her relatives and told them that tears ran down the face of Our Lady, nobody believed her. But later, everyone saw that the bust of the Madonna was really in tears.

Tears kept flowing from Mary's eyes for a few days and were seen by all who visited Antonia's house. Filmed sequences of the plaque showed the phenomenon. The tears were collected and sent to laboratory to be analyzed. The tests showed that they were human tears. After that, the Catholic Church declared the lacrimation a miracle.

I remember that when we arrived in Syracuse and parked our car at the end of the square adjacent to the house where the miracle had happened, there were so many people in the square and around the house that it was impossible for us to move on. As I wanted to see what was going on, my father, who was taller than average, picked me up so that I could see the happenings.

I saw a line of detached one-story houses on the opposite side of the square and people standing and looking at one of those houses. Suddenly, I heard a man's voice that sounded like a stammer.

"What happened?" I asked my father. "Why is that person stammering?"

"That man has been cured miraculously. He couldn't walk, but now he has left his wheelchair and crutches and walks well. Seen from here, he looks very happy. He is somehow trying to give vent to his joy through the gibberish you have just heard," my father replied.

When I returned to the same place many years later, the square and the low houses didn't exist anymore. In their place was a large pyramid-shaped church. The plaster plaque portraying the Weeping Madonna of Syracuse had been moved inside the new church to be exposed to the believers.

Lourdes

The cult of the Virgin of Lourdes is followed by many in Enna, and every year in May a train loaded with pilgrims, volunteers, and seriously ill people travels to Lourdes. It is called the "White Train."

Lourdes is a place for pilgrimages for Catholics from all over the world, and every year around five million visit the cave where the apparitions happened.

On February 11, 1858, Our Lady appeared to a little girl named Bernadette Soubirous in a cave called Massabielle, in Lourdes, France. The apparitions occurred for five months and were initially seen with skepticism by the Catholic Church, but when the apparition revealed herself to be the Immaculate Conception, all doubts were removed, because the little girl Bernadette could never come up with a deep theological concept like that of the Immaculate Conception of the Virgin Mary, a dogma that was proclaimed by Pope Pius IX on December 8, 1854.

The journey from Enna to Lourdes takes forty-eight hours, because the White Train stops continuously to give precedence to regular trains. A volunteer's main task is serving meals in the train and pushing wheelchairs once arriving in Lourdes. Only the most experienced ones look after those with serious disabilities.

One year after Giuseppina's death, I still acted like an automaton, and a dark fog separated me from the rest of the world. The police had investigated the accident for a few months, but I was eventually acquitted. My mother was very worried about me. She had no idea what to do and confined herself to praying for me. Moreover, every week she went to the Convent of Saint Marc to ask the cloistered nuns to pray for me. She hoped that all those prayers would sooner or later rid me of my heavy depression.

"What about going to Lourdes?" she said one day.

I was so depressed that I didn't have the strength and will to answer her, but she insisted. "Do you want to go to Lourdes on the White Train? It leaves from Enna in ten days. It is a good opportunity to take your mind off your mistaken idea that you are guilty of Giuseppina's death. It was an accident indeed. It wasn't your fault!"

"I don't want to go," I replied curtly.

"But it is a good opportunity to help the sick!" my mother said.

I actually considered myself a social waste, but the thought that I could be helpful to somebody in need made me feel less despicable. Moreover, I couldn't remain in a state of inactivity forever. I had stayed at home like a prisoner for a year, but sooner or later I had to come down from my ivory tower.

"Okay, I'll go," I said, and a feeble ray of hope revived in my heart. Perhaps someday I would return to live as a normal human being.

After twelve months spent in my room reading books, magazines, and listening to the radio, my eyes were not accustomed to daylight. My mother had arranged everything for my journey, including packing my luggage and providing my volunteer uniform, which was brown, while the ladies wore white skirts, white stockings, blue cloaks, and veils similar to those worn by nuns.

My parents came to see me off at the station and entrusted me to the priest who was the spiritual guide of the pilgrimage. He was from a town near Enna, Valguarnera Caropepe. Father Guido was a red-haired man who, despite the reformation of the Second Vatican Council that had given priests the freedom of dressing, still wore a cassock.

The train was very old, and two special cars dating back to the Second World War had been arranged to accommodate disabled people on stretchers. The two cars still bore the huge red crosses from the war. We didn't have any hoist, so we had to lift the stretchers into the cars by hand. It wasn't a hard a task because we had many volunteers to do the work.

We were finishing lifting stretchers when I saw a stretcher on wheels coming from the side entrance to the station. On it was a young man who had to weigh nearly two hundred kilos. I couldn't imagine how we were going to get him on the train. It took six of us to lift the stretcher. My arms and legs were still weak after a year of inaction, but through our joint efforts, we finally set him on the train.

It was the late afternoon when the train finally left the station. The sun was setting beyond the mountains, and in a few hours, we would serve dinner to the pilgrims and invalids. Meanwhile, I went to my compartment and watched the green countryside and the wheat waving under the breeze through the window. My eyes were looking outside, but my mind still saw the car plunging down into the ravine with its human load. Apparently, going out of my house had changed nothing. I was as absentminded and depressed as I was when secluded in my room. The environment had changed, but my heart was still shut to life.

Before entering the ferry from Messina to mainland Italy, the train stopped many times to take on more sick people, pilgrims, and volunteers. We were four volunteers in our compartment, but from time to time, Father Guido came and sat down to chat with us.

When the train left the station in Catania, we started serving dinner. The train was very long, and each volunteer was given the task of serving a certain car. I was told to serve dinner in the car with the most seriously ill.

I was doing just that when I heard someone call out my name. I turned back, thinking another volunteer from Enna was calling me, but I didn't see anybody.

"Vincenzino! Vincenzino!" the voice kept calling.

I stopped serving and saw that it was the fat young man we had lifted on the car that was calling me. "How do you know my name?" I asked.

"It is written on your badge!" he answered.

I was so absentminded that I hadn't paid attention to the badge on my uniform. "What is your name?" I asked.

"My name is Carmelo, and I want to thank you for the great effort you made in lifting me. As you see, my body is all out of proportion. My weight keeps increasing more and more, and I can only move my head, eyes, and lips. The whole rest of my body is paralyzed like dead flesh. I can see that you are not at all serene, but believe me, your adverse fortune is nothing compared to mine."

Tears streamed down his big cheeks. "Can you see the moon and the stars out of the window?" he asked.

I bent my head, and Carmelo also slowly turned his head to watch the full moon. "Ask the moon and the stars if it is right that my body lies on a stretcher from my birth to my death while my mind is clear and realizes the uselessness of my life."

His words dumbfounded me. I had thought that only my problems existed and other people were immune from trouble. After Giuseppina's death, I had isolated myself in my room, thinking I was the most unlucky person in the world. But now, Carmelo was opening my eyes to real life; his condition was far worse than mine!

"Tell me," continued Carmelo, "why there are half-men like me? I have done nothing to deserve such an adverse fate. Do you think my harrowing life derives from God or from a different malicious being? I am completely useless. While you may be helpful to others, Vincenzino, I am just human waste who is kept alive by a moral and criminal code that doesn't allow society to kill the heap of flesh I am."

It was as if I was catapulted into life again. After a long time of seclusion, now in front of me was someone who was talking to me and wanted me to answer him, but I actually didn't know what to say. I looked around to see if the meals had all been served and noticed that the other volunteers had done the work in my place. On the other hand, Carmelo had been fed in advance by a qualified nurse.

As for the second of his questions, my answer sprang from my heart naturally. "You are not a useless person, Carmelo. Thanks to you, I am coming back to life. I have been living like a vegetable for a year, except for speaking with my mother in monosyllables. Talking with you has been as if a thunderbolt has fallen on me. You have shocked me! I can see and watch you, while I saw no one before, so immersed in my thoughts as I was."

"What happened to you?"

"It was an old love story that ended tragically, but now I can see that there are people like you who have no hope to live a normal life, while I am in a better condition. You have been like a mirror for me. Through you, I have looked inside myself and realized the uselessness of continuing to torture myself."

"What about my first question?"

During my year of insulation, I read many books and magazines. One of the most significant was the Book of Job in the Bible.

"Do you know the story of Job, Carmelo?"

"I heard something about him. Job was renowned because of his patience, right?"

"Job was a rich and pious man," I answered, "who later lost all his riches, his children, and even his body became purulent. 'What have I done to deserve this bad luck?' Job asked God one day. The answer was that man cannot know what God's plans for us are. Therefore, Carmelo, accept your situation and do your best to live your life fully, even under such bad condition. Cheer up, Carmelo! *Duppu acchianata c'è a scinnuta* (after the climb there is the descent).

"There is another life after death, Carmelo. 'I do not promise you happiness in this world, but in the life to come,' Our Lady said one day to Saint Bernadette. Your suffering today will be your joy tomorrow, Carmelo. Try and have faith in yourself and in God! Life never ends. We are immortal! I am sure that someday you'll live in a bright star. You will be an angel of light surrounded by other angels, with no need for your material body. You will hover in the air like a multicolored bird and dance to the melodious music of angelic choirs. You will meet our master Jesus and talk with him.

"Therefore, Carmelo, hold out to the end of your life and have faith in God, an immense source of love that will not forsake you. Who knows, perhaps you will be able to meet Jesus even in this life, for nothing is impossible for God!"

I told Carmelo the story of the tragic accident on Mount Pellegrino where Giuseppina lost her life. He listened to me patiently and then fell asleep. I kissed him in the forehead and went back to my compartment.

The forty-eight hours spent on the train seemed never-ending, but the other volunteers in our compartment were cheerful. From time to time, Father Guido also joined us to say the rosary. When we arrived at the station in Lourdes, we had to offload the baggage and take the invalids to the hospitals. Finally, we volunteers went to the hotel.

My task was to carry the invalids from one place to another. The wheelchairs in Lourdes had a handle in the front, while a few disabled people had their own personal wheelchairs that could be pushed.

Every day, in the morning and in the afternoon, the disabled in their wheelchairs were lined up in the hospital courtyard, and the volunteers took them wherever they wished to go. They usually wanted to go to the Massabielle Cave to pray before the statues of Our Lady and Saint Bernadette, or to the baths which stood in the place where Saint Bernadette found a spring by digging in the ground with her hands. This water was supposed to be miraculous, and several miracles had actually been recorded and corroborated by the Catholic Church. Those who wanted to have a bath were just dipped into the water for a few seconds. They got dressed while they were still wet, but the water had the properties of drying immediately, so towels were not needed.

There were frequent Masses both in the cave and in the churches and basilicas. In the late afternoon, the sick and disabled were usually lined up in the vast square in front of the basilica, and Holy Communion was given to them.

One afternoon while I was in the square looking after a sick old man, I lost my faith. I had the feeling that God was just a human creation. I saw the earth and the universe as matter without spirit, and no God who could vivify them. It was a real paradox that I came to Lourdes to strengthen my faith in God and in life, but instead I turned into an atheist. I remained in this condition as a disbeliever for several months, but with the passing time, I felt that my life was completely empty without Jesus. After the terrible accident with Giuseppina, my only anchor was Jesus. Therefore, my atheism didn't last long, and for the rest of my life Jesus has been my only safe harbor.

During my stay in Lourdes, I wanted to do my very best to serve the invalids I looked after. One afternoon I took a sick lady from the hospital courtyard. She was around sixty years old and dressed in black.

"Where would you like me to take you?" I asked.

"I want to go shopping!" she answered.

In Lourdes, there are so many shops that sell holy images, rosary beads, small statues, and every kind of holy item, that sometimes I had the impression that big business gravitated around the cult of Our Lady.

The sick lady wanted to buy a small golden medal, so we went around many shops to find the item she liked. After two hours of shopping, she found the one she wanted. Afterwards, she wanted me to take her to the top of the hill, for she wanted to cover the Stations of the Cross. At last, after a long afternoon of carrying her here and there, I took her back to the hospital.

As soon as we arrived at the hospital courtyard, the sick lady got up from the wheelchair and walked at a brisk pace. I looked at her with a slight annoyance. Why had she asked me to carry her around when she was able to walk by herself? But suddenly the lady started crying out, "It is a miracle! A miracle! I couldn't walk before. That volunteer can testify to it," she said, pointing to me.

A few people gathered around me. "Is it true?" one of them asked.

"What?"

"It was really a miracle?" he insisted.

"I don't know," I answered. "I can only say that the lady was already sitting in the wheelchair when I took her out to the shops. I then took her to the hill where the Stations of the Cross are, but I cannot say whether she was able to walk before I met her or not."

"Okay, thank you," said the man who had questioned me, and soon the small crowd of onlookers dispersed.

The following day at lunchtime, I heard from the other volunteers of a miracle that had happened in Lourdes. I didn't ask what kind of miracle they were talking about. It possibly referred to the lady that had regained her ability to walk. At the time, I had fallen into my feelings of atheism, so I wasn't interested in the subject.

Many years went by, and that episode seemed to have fallen into oblivion, but one day it came to mind for some reason. I wondered why that sick lady would have deceived me, pretending to have been miraculously cured when she was already in good health. What was the point?

That afternoon in Lourdes was still vivid in my mind. I relived seeing the lady dressed in black sitting in the wheelchair waiting for a volunteer. When I arrived at the hospital, as soon as I saw her, I headed for her and grasped the handle of the wheelchair without uttering a word. Once we were in the street, I asked her where to go. We then went shopping and finally to the hill. At last, I took her back to the hospital.

I decided that there had to be a rational explanation. Maybe the old lady was lazy and didn't want to walk by herself.

Perhaps she took advantage of me to stroll around Lourdes while sitting comfortably in the wheelchair. Nevertheless, my conjecture collided with the fact that the lady had been admitted to the hospital in Lourdes.

If my memory serves me right, there were two hospitals for sick people at that time in Lourdes, one bigger and one smaller. Neither of them admitted patients that were not disabled. There had to be medical records certifying her disability. Being wise after the event, at that time I was very shallow. I should have investigated the matter in depth. However, if she is still in my mind after so many years, perhaps something supernatural really did happen that afternoon in Lourdes.

La Salette

The Carmelite monks of Sicily and of Veneto organized a pilgrimage to Lisieux, a small city in the north of France where the Carmelite nun, Saint Therese of the Child Jesus, had lived in a convent. The pilgrimage started from Verona, a city in the north of Italy, where the group coming from Sicily joined the other from Veneto.

I could never imagine going on a pilgrimage to the north of France, and I hadn't even heard of Saint Therese of the Child Jesus. It was a girl named Margherita, who attended Saint Joseph Church in Enna, who suggested that I take part in the pilgrimage with her. Despite her young age, she had a degree in classic literature and taught ancient Greek at Enna's high school.

"It is not just a pilgrimage. It is also a sightseeing tour. We will visit Paris, a few castles by the Loire River, and Versailles," she said to me.

I had fallen in love with her, and the chance to go on a trip together thrilled me. So, I accepted with enthusiasm. Unfortunately, people's minds and hearts are changeable, and a few days before the start of the trip she told me that she had changed her mind and wouldn't come. What to do? I could cancel my booking, but I didn't, despite the fact that traveling with a group of people I didn't know didn't thrill me at all.

At that time, I was afraid of traveling by airplane, and that was not my only phobia. I also feared being isolated from other people. What would I do alone on the trip? All the other participants knew one another, while I didn't know anyone. I resigned myself to being alone for the duration of the trip, but I felt very ill at ease.

After I arrived at the train station in Verona, I walked to the meeting place, which was not far away. A girl was waiting there for the rest of the group. As soon as I saw her, I seized the opportunity not to be alone.

"My name is Vincenzino. What is your name?"

"My name is Lucia," she answered. She was tall and lean and had shadows under her eyes.

"Do you want to sit together on the bus?" I asked.

She looked at me with her broad eyes full of surprise. Certainty she would have preferred saying no, but she was too polite to refuse my request. "Okay," she answered, "you can sit next to me."

I was relieved because I had solved my problem of being alone, but over time I realized that I had behaved stupidly. In fact, I had compelled that well-mannered girl to stay with me while she might have preferred to travel with her friends whose company was more enjoyable than mine. I had treated her not as a human being but as a tool to solve my problem.

The trip leader was a Carmelite monk from northern Italy. His name was Father Leo, and he was a very learned person who knew Saint Therese's life to perfection. He gladdened our trip on the bus by telling biblical stories and, above all, talking about Saint Therese.

"Saint Therese of the Child Jesus was declared a Doctor of the Church by Pope John Paul II. She is the youngest person, and the third woman, to be so honored in the history of the Catholic Church. She died from tuberculosis when she was just twenty-four years old," Father Leo said.

"What did she do to be declared a Doctor of the Church?" asked one of the pilgrims.

"She pointed out the 'Little Way' to humans. It does not take vast learning to know God, but it does take humility and simplicity of heart," answered Father Leo.

We had just visited the Palace of Versailles, and on the bus, Father Leo kept telling the humble life story of Saint Therese. As for me, I couldn't help comparing a nobleman's life in the Palace of Versailles to life in a convent. They were two opposite ways of living. I concluded that everyone follows his or her own path according to their destiny and tendencies, but in the end, paradise has its gates open to all, because God is inside every human being.

What made an impression on me was when Father Leo told us the story of Saint Therese's miraculous recovery.

"At the end of 1882, Saint Therese was seized by a persistent headache that lasted until Easter of the following year. She was just nine years old. Afterwards, she got worse, and the doctor diagnosed a serious rare disease, unusual for a little girl. She was bound to die, but one day while she was praying before a statue portraying Our Lady, she saw the Virgin Mary smiling at her. Suddenly, big tears welled in the little girl's eyes. From then on, she started recovering, and five years later she entered the Carmelite convent as a cloistered nun."

"How is it possible," I asked Father Leo, "for a teenager to be allowed to take the vows?"

"You are right to ask this question," he answered, "but Saint Therese got a dispensation from the bishop. Indeed, canon law is not as strict as civil law, thanks to the institution of dispensation. Obviously, if the bishop allowed Saint Therese to enter the convent at a very young age, he did so after due consideration."

On the way back, when we were near the sanctuary of La Salette, I took a seat next to another pilgrim. At that moment, I saw Lucia laughing for the first time. She was sitting next to a nun, with whom she was at ease. As for me, I had overcome my stupid fear of being alone.

Father Leo told us the story of the apparition of Our Lady of La Salette. "One hundred fifty years ago, La Salette was a small village in Southern France. There were less than one thousand people living there. One day, two children who had been minding the cows on Mount Sous-Les Baisses came back to the village and reported that they had seen a weeping beautiful lady.

"According to the children's account, the apparition, who spoke their dialect, was weeping because people didn't respect

God anymore. The lady gave the children a few messages, which were all based on her desire for human hearts to convert to God."

Our bus took us up to the top of the mount where the apparition had happened. At that moment, thin mist alternated with clear sky. I had a feeling that the whole area was enveloped in mystery, as if Our Lady had left the imprint of her apparition on the mountain.

When I returned home from the pilgrimage, I saw Margherita with another man. I thought maybe they were just friends, but unfortunately, they were already engaged, and six months later they got married.

I lost Margherita, but I gained much more. In fact, the pilgrimage to Lisieux and La Salette strengthened my personality. I felt stronger and less picky. Apparently, the teachings of Saint Therese about keeping a simple and pure heart had worked.

Fatima

I learned about Our Lady of Fatima for the first time when I was about sixteen. At the time, the crowned statue of the Virgin of Fatima was carried in procession throughout Italy. It arrived in Enna by helicopter and was then taken to the monastery of Montesalvo, where it remained for a few hours. I followed the statue all the way from the playground where the helicopter had landed to the monastery and vice versa.

The following day at school, I talked about Our Lady of Fatima with my schoolmates, who didn't seem as enthusiastic as I was about the coming of the statue.

"Have you ever heard about the three secrets of Fatima?" asked Carlo, one of my schoolmates. He was a priest's nephew. His uncle, besides being a priest, was also a teacher of Latin at our school.

"No, I haven't. I don't even know anything about Our Lady of Fatima. I just followed the statue because I felt like it," I answered.

"Okay, I'll tell you what happened on May 13, 1917, in Portugal. That day, the Virgin Mary appeared to three children named Lucia, Francisco, and Giacinta, in a place called Cova da Iria, in Portugal, and asked them to come back to the same place on the thirteenth of each month for five consecutive months at the same time.

"The civil and religious authorities didn't believe the three young shepherds, and even Lucia's mother accused her daughter of telling lies. On August thirteenth, the police kept in jail and grilled the three children to make them confess that they hadn't told the truth, but the little seers were unshakable and kept their side of the story. Of course, they couldn't go to Cova da Iria that day because they were in jail, but Our Lady appeared again to them on August nineteenth, and this time she promised that on October thirteenth, which would be the day of the last apparition, she would give evidence of the authenticity of the apparition so that everybody would believe them.

"On the appointed day, people from all over Portugal came to Cova da Iria to be present at the miraculous event that had been predicted by Our Lady. There were believers and non-believers there, as well as civil and religious authorities and some anticlerical journalists.

"It was a rainy day. After noon, it stopped raining and a cloud enveloped the three children. Our Lady asked Lucia to build a chapel in that place and announced that the war would be over soon. The miracle happened all of a sudden. The sun started twirling in the sky. It was visible to the naked eye. It seemed that it was falling down toward the crowd. Finally, it halted before going up again in the sky."

I listened to Carlo with my mouth wide open. I was really mesmerized by his account, but my mind was turned to the secrets. "What about the secrets?" I asked.

"Oh, they are terrible! You should know that the third secret of Fatima has not been revealed yet. It was given to the pope by one of the three children to whom the Virgin Mary had appeared. In fact, of the three young shepherds, two died very young, while the third, Lucia, is still living."

"Do you know the contents of the first two secrets?" I asked.

"Yes. In the first secret, Lucia, Giacinta, and Francisco were shown hell. In the second secret, Our Lady said that after the First World War, another world conflict would burst forth that would be worse than the previous one. Furthermore, the Virgin Mary said that someday Russia would be converted and the world would enjoy a time of peace."

"Does your uncle the priest know anything about the third secret?" I asked.

"No, he doesn't. Nobody knows it except the pope. In my opinion," said Carlo, "there must be something catastrophic in the message of Our Lady. Otherwise, the pope would have revealed it. Perhaps, the message refers to the end of the world."

At Carlo's words, a shudder of fear ran throughout my body, because I linked the end of the world to the end of my life.

More than fifty years had gone by since my conversation with Carlo. Meanwhile, the third secret, which had been kept in the Vatican archives for fifty-six years, was revealed by Pope John Paul II, who said that the secret was related to him.

The text of the third secret was also reported in our local newspaper on June 27, 2000. I read the article, cut it out, and put it into the drawer of my bedside table, where I still keep it. The article tells the secret and contains a theological comment by Cardinal Joseph Ratzinger, who later would become pope. Not one catastrophic prediction was contained in the third secret. The real meaning of the message, according to Vatican, was that one can change his or her destiny through prayer and penance.

I had believed that every human being has his or her destiny already assigned and cannot do anything to change it. Now the third secret of Fatima was turning my way of thinking upside down. On the other hand, it is unthinkable that God, who is the giver of life and the creator of all things, is not able to change a person's fate.

Here is the unabridged text of the third secret:

After the two parts which I have already explained, at the left of Our Lady and a little above, we saw an Angel with a flaming sword in his left hand; flashing, it gave out flames that looked as though they would set the world on fire; but they died out in contact with the splendor that Our Lady radiated towards him from her right hand: pointing to the earth with his right hand, the Angel cried out in a loud voice: 'Penance, Penance, Penance!' And we saw in an immense light that is God: 'something similar to how people appear in a mirror when they pass in front of it' a Bishop dressed in

White 'we had the impression that it was the Holy Father.'
Other Bishops, Priests, men and women Religious going up a
steep mountain, at the top of which there was a big Cross of
rough-hewn trunks as of a cork-tree with the bark; before
reaching there the Holy Father passed through a big city
half in ruins and half trembling with halting step, afflicted
with pain and sorrow, he prayed for the souls of the corpses
he met on his way; having reached the top of the mountain,
on his knees at the foot of the big Cross he was killed by a
group of soldiers who fired bullets and arrows at him, and in
the same way there died one after another the other
Bishops, Priests, men and women Religious, and various lay
people of different ranks and positions. Beneath the two
arms of the Cross there were two Angels each with a crystal
aspersorium in his hand, in which they gathered up the
blood of the Martyrs and with it sprinkled the souls that
were making their way to God.

    Tuy, January 3, 1944

My wife and I were flying from Rome to Lisbon when I told her, who is not a believer, what happened on May 13, 1981, at Saint Peter's Square in Rome.

"It was a peaceful afternoon at Saint Peter's Square when Pope John Paul II was passing through the crowd. Suddenly, a Turkish man, who was a professional killer, fired two bullets at the pope. The pope was taken to the hospital unconscious and was about to die while the attempted assassin tried to run away, but he was blocked by a nun named Sister Lucia. Don't you think these are singular coincidences?"

"What coincidences?" asked my wife.

"The first coincidence is the date of the event. Both the first apparition to the shepherd children and the attempt on the pope's life happened on the same day, May thirteenth. Furthermore, the person that caught the killer was called Lucia, like the young shepherdess of Fatima."

"They are astonishing coincidences indeed. Did the pope survive?"

"Yes, he survived and had no doubt that it had been Our Lady who had deflected the bullets, which otherwise would have been fatal. The pope was bound to die, and the prophecy contained in the third secret of Fatima would have been carried out if not for the intercession of the Virgin Mary. Hence, the future and prophecies can be changed if it is God's will."

We landed at the airport in Lisbon and remained in the city for a few days before going to Fatima. While in Portugal, we visited Cabo da Roca, which is the extreme western tip of Europe. It is the place where the land ends and the ocean begins. Watching the immense ocean from the top of the headland, I revived the dreams of the great navigators of the past who left the safety of the land to sail the unknown. Seen from an altitude of 140 meters above sea level, the ocean gave me a sense of immensity and infinity. It was like watching the firmament from above rather than from below.

We arrived at Fatima in the early afternoon and found accommodations in a very good hotel near the sanctuary. A few steps further was a square wider than I had ever seen, and at the opposite end was the sanctuary of Our Lady of Fatima. What impressed me was the view of the tombs of the three shepherd children; two were close to each other, while Francisco's was detached. Near the sanctuary is a museum where the crown of Our Lady is kept. Set in the crown is the bullet that crossed Pope John Paul II's body without damaging vital organs. Not far from the square there was a small train that took tourists to the houses where the little shepherds had lived and to the hillock where the angel had appeared to them.

We left Fatima bound for another holy place called Santiago de Compostela in Spain.

Banneux

One day my wife said, "There's another important sanctuary you have not seen yet. It is in Banneux, Belgium."

I really didn't know about Our Lady of Banneux, even though I was always looking for holy places. "We should go there," I said. "And we'll take the opportunity to visit Belgium, which is a small country, but rich in history and traditions."

When we arrived in Brussels, we found accommodations near downtown. What left me speechless was the view of the Grand Place, which is an architectural jewel. We visited the tourist attractions in Brussels and then moved to Banneux by bus. It is a village near the city of Liege.

Mariette was the first-born child of seven children. She went to school and to catechism, but she didn't make much progress because she didn't have enough time to devote to study; she had to help her mother in the daily chores. On the evening of January 15, 1933, she was looking out of the window, waiting for her brother who had not yet come home, when she saw a young, beautiful, shining lady in the garden.

"Mom!" she called. "I see a lady in the garden. She is the Holy Virgin."

The Virgin Mary appeared to Mariette eight times. Our Lady called herself the "Virgin of the Poor." During the second apparition, the Virgin Mary led Mariette to a spring and said that it should be reserved for Herself and for all nations. As it had happened in other places where the Holy Mother had appeared, she also recommended praying and asked that a chapel be built there.

When we arrived in Banneux, the bus stopped next to a square. At the end of the square there was a street that led to the sanctuary. The atmosphere in Banneux was different from the other Marian sanctuaries I had visited before. It was much simpler and without many shops. We walked towards the chapel and found a water basin on the right, which was where little Mariette had dipped her hands. We too dipped our hands and drank some of the water.

After visiting the chapel, we walked through the woods that bound the water basin. While we were walking, I realized why Our Lady had called herself the Virgin of the Poor. We well-to-do people tend to underestimate the issue of poverty. It is one of the most serious social problems indeed! Here, amid the woods of Banneux, in my mind I saw all the jobless, poor Sicilians that had migrated to Belgium to work in the coal mines after the end of the Second World War. Many of them died trapped underground, while those who survived contracted an illness called silicosis, which was a progressive disease caused by the inhalation of dust in mines. My mind went to the immigrants that try to reach the Sicilian coast packed in precarious boats which sometimes capsize, causing the deaths of hundreds of people whose only fault is being poor and seeking a better place to live.

I recalled a butcher in Enna who had a large family. My father used to go to his shop to buy lamb at Easter. Over time, many butcher shops sprang up in Enna, so that butcher couldn't match the competition and became poor. He took on debts to feed his family, hoping he would be able to pay them, but things didn't go well. He fell into despair and couldn't find a way out. One night he left his home and told his wife that he had to cut a few lambs' throats, but things went differently. He pulled down the shutters in his shop, and instead of cutting lambs' throats, he cut his own. The following day, his blood still leaked through the chink of the shutter, flowing into the street.

There are many tragedies caused by poverty that we don't know. Sometimes, even when we are aware of this issue, we ignore it instead of doing something to try to overcome the scourge of poverty.

How many conflicts are sparked off by poverty! Indigence gives rise to social malaise, and then to a Mafia, terrorism, and war. It is not by chance that terrorists and members of the Mafia are recruited from the poorest classes.

We left Banneux and headed for Amsterdam. My wife wanted to visit the Van Gogh Museum, which contains an ample collection of his paintings. He was a genius, but also a very unlucky man who suffered from mental disorders. He was found dead at the age of thirty-seven from a gunshot wound that he likely fired himself.

Our Lady of Guadalupe

My search for God led me first to Australia and then to Mexico. I wanted to learn whether religion was just an invention by priests or it was an innate idea. If a newborn baby is taken away from their mother and grows up alone without meeting anyone that can teach them religion, will they ever develop the idea of God? I wanted to study ancient civilizations that had had no contact with people from foreign countries to see if they had ever practiced a form of religion.

To study the native Australians, I flew to the city of Darwin in northern Australia, as I knew that many Aborigines lived in that part of the country. My aim was to live for a while in an Aboriginal village, but it was not as easy as I had supposed. In fact, I needed special permission from the Australian government to stay with the natives. I remained in Darwin for a few days, hesitant about what to do.

One day while I was walking in the street, a young man gave me a flier that advertised his religion. We chatted for a while, and he then invited me to his church, which was Christian. I went there, and I have to say that I was at ease, but they asked me to be baptized with them. I couldn't do that, because if I had accepted, I would have had to renounce my Catholic faith, which I had no intention of doing. Therefore, I kindly declined and we parted ways.

I saw some Aboriginal natives in the streets, but they looked as though they were pariahs. Most of them were homeless and beggars. I asked one of them, who looked a little bit less impoverished, what his religion was.

"Christian!" he answered, to my surprise.

"Don't you have a traditional religion?"

"Nowadays, most of us are Christian. There are some of us who practice strange rites, but it is not right to follow them."

I remained in Australia for a week and learned, by talking with a member of a group of Aboriginal dancers, that the

Aborigines have an old, traditional religion that is completely original.

"We believe in a spiritual force," he said, "that permeates everything: trees, creeks, mountains, and so on. There was a primordial era before the formation of the world. We call this 'dreamtime.' The world was undifferentiated and populated by gigantic creatures that left the footprints of their passage, which are the mountains, rivers, trees, and so on. Therefore, for us nature is sacred. Dreaming is fundamental for us, because through dreaming we can communicate with spirits."

I left Australia firmly convinced of the originality of their traditional religion. Now it was time to move on in my spiritual quest.

I wanted to gather information on the Mayan culture and religion. Until the discovery of America, the Mayans had been isolated from the other continents. Because of that, their religion, cults, and rites had to be unique. I flew from Catania to Cancun and found accommodations with a host family in the city of Merida in Yucatan, the area where the Mayan civilization had thrived.

Fortunately, the same family also lodged a lady from Texas named Melanie, who was a Spanish teacher and knew the Mexican culture. She was at least ten centimeters taller than me. Her father was from Portugal and her mother from Ukraine, but she was born in the United States. As soon as she knew I was interested in the Mayan religion, she led me to an archaeological site called Uxmal, where there was a wide pyramid.

"Pyramids," she said, "have a religious meaning. Let's go up to the top through the staircase and I'll show you why."

We climbed the steep staircase and reached the top of the pyramid where there was a little temple.

"The pyramid," she said, "symbolizes the mountain, and as you know, according to many traditions, the gods live on the top of the mountains. Think of Mount Olympus, which was the house of the Greek gods. Think of Mount Sinai where God appeared to Moses, or Mount Tabor where Jesus's transfiguration happened.

"The weak spot of the Mayan religion," she continued, "is the many human sacrifices they performed to placate their gods."

"The Mayans were not the only ones who made human sacrifices," I said. "Many civilizations did the same. Even the Greeks, who were very civilized people, made human sacrifices. Agamemnon sacrificed his daughter, Iphigenia, to the goddess Artemis to placate her, who didn't allow the Achaean fleet to sail to Troy. The Druids performed human sacrifices as well."

"Yes, you are right, but the Mayans' cruelty was unique." she replied. "They sacrificed children and prisoners of war. A missionary friar described human sacrifices that he witnessed in detail. According to his report, the victim had been kept in prison without food for a few days so that he couldn't offer resistance. Then he was brought to the temple and held down by four men. A man got close to the victim with a sharp flint in his hand. With great expertise, he suddenly made an incision in the chest and pulled out the victim's heart with his hand. Then he put the heart, which was still throbbing, on a tray and handed it to the priest, who smeared the statues of the gods with the blood that was dripping from the heart."

"The cruelties practiced by the Catholic Church were no less appalling," I countered.

"Did Catholics sacrifice their victims by ripping their heart out?"

"If you come to Rome someday, I'll show you the statue of the philosopher Giordano Bruno, who was burnt alive by the Catholics. That kind of death is cruel as well."

"Yes, I agree," she answered. "Wickedness is innate in the human heart, regardless of country or race. But now, let's forget human sacrifices for a while and go swim."

"Swim? Where? We are a long way from the sea, and there are no swimming pools in this archaeological site."

"We can go to a *cenote*!" she answered.

"What is a cenote?"

"Cenotes are sinkholes, but some of them are quite wide; so, swimming is possible. You can find those kinds of wells only in Mexico, due to the softness and porosity of the limestone. In ancient times, the Mayans performed rituals in the cenotes, for they believed that the sinkholes were a meeting point between the worlds of humans and gods. Archaeologists have found human skeletons in the cenotes."

We visited a few cenotes that day. Some were wide, and it was possible to enjoy swimming, while others were smaller but no less amazing. In one of them, we had to step down three upright ladders before reaching the water. It was a thrilling experience!

The next day, Melanie took me to another archaeological site called Chichen Itza. The area, which was once a large, thriving city, was vast. There was a pyramid with a temple on the top as well. We saw a building that looked like an observatory. There was also an area called the Great Ball Court, which according to Melanie was the widest in Mesoamerica.

"Have you ever visited the sanctuary of Our Lady of Guadalupe?" I asked.

"No, I haven't. It is in Mexico City. I am leaving in two days, so unfortunately I cannot take you there."

"It doesn't matter. I'll go there by myself," I said. I couldn't leave Mexico without visiting one of the most venerated Marian sanctuaries.

I arranged a flight from Merida. Once I arrived in Mexico City, I took the subway and got off the train after a few minutes and walked along a street that led to the basilica of the Virgin of Guadalupe. The place where the basilica stands is called La Villa de Guadalupe.

It was early in the morning, but the street already swarmed with people and food vendors. After ten minutes of walking, I arrived at the side entrance of the basilica. There was a large square before the main church. Actually, there were a few churches in the area besides the basilica that housed the original cloak on which the image of Our Lady was imprinted. The place where the basilica now stands was a holy place long before the Spanish conquered Mexico. It is called the Hill of Tepeyac. At the site there was a temple devoted to the mother goddess called Tonantzin. Later, the Spanish destroyed the temple and built a nearby chapel. But the destruction of the temple couldn't prevent the natives from pouring into the site.

Ten years after the Spanish conquered Mexico, a local peasant named Juan Diego, who had recently converted to Christianity, had a vision said to be Our Lady in the same area, who asked for a chapel to be built in the place. Diego reported what Our Lady had requested to the Franciscan bishop, but his account left the bishop doubtful. In fact, he required proof to corroborate what the native had reported.

Juan Diego went back to the hill and asked Our Lady to give him proof that she was really the Virgin Mary. This time, Our Lady asked Juan Diego to pluck some flowers and take them to the bishop. This would prove the truthfulness of the vision.

He did as Our Lady had required; he picked some roses and wrapped them with his cloak. Then he hastened away to the bishop. When he was in the presence of the prelate, he unfolded his cloak. The roses fell onto the floor, while the image of the Virgin Mary was shining on the cloak. From then on, Juan Diego's cloak was guarded with care by the Franciscan friars, and a chapel was built in the place of the apparition.

People from all over Mexico rallied to the chapel to worship the shrine, and it is reported that many miracles occurred. Nevertheless, the natives kept calling Our Lady by the name of

Tonantzin, the ancient mother goddess revered by the native population. This gave rise to the doubts of the Franciscan friars, who were convinced that the veneration of the holy image was a pagan cult.

Something similar also happened in Enna. In fact, Our Lady, who is the patron saint of Enna, replaced the ancient cult of Demeter, who was the town's mother goddess. The celebration in honor of Our Lady happens on July second every year, the same time when the old pagan cult of Demeter was celebrated. People of Enna today still invoke Kore, Demeter's daughter.

In my opinion, the name you give to God is not important; what matters is the spiritual feeling that radiates from the worshipper. So, you can name God Allah, Brahma, Vishnu, or Shiva without losing the purity of your heart. On the other hand, Jesus and the Virgin Mary are beyond time, for they existed before time, long before coming into human history. They also existed in the pagan era and were worshipped differently.

The Virgin Mary appeared to Juan Diego in the form of a crossbreed maiden and in the same place where the Spanish had destroyed the temple dedicated to the goddess Tonantzin. That means that nobody is allowed to destroy others' temples, even if they are considered pagan. In fact, religion and spirituality are not related to a particular cult. Over the years, people have given various names to God and worshipped Him in different ways, but it doesn't entitle anybody to resort to violence to make one religion prevail over another.

As for the holy image imprinted on Juan Diego's cloak, it was kept for some time by the Franciscan friars until it passed under the custody of the diocesan priests. With the passing of time, possibly in good faith, the original image was retouched in some spots. For instance, the crescent on which the Virgin Mary stands was painted with silver. Apparently, nowadays the retouches have discolored naturally, while the original image is still unaltered.

Pilgrims and visitors flocked into the square in front of the new basilica. I saw people, who from their olive complexion seemed to be natives or crossbreeds, carrying litters full of flowers. Some of them laid the litters on the floor and staged devotional songs and dances. I have to say that few times in my life have I seen such beautiful scenery. After having danced and sung, the pilgrims went into the basilica with their litters covered with flowers. I followed them and entered the basilica from one of the gates. It was a round church with an altar opposite the many rows of pews, and the holy image of the Virgin Mary was above it.

I sat on one of the pews and watched the shrine from a distance. Meanwhile, other groups continued to arrive in the basilica and headed for the back of the altar. I followed them and arrived at a moving walkway below the shrine. I admired the holy image for a few seconds while the walkaway moved. Then I went out. I spent all day at the Villa de Guadalupe and visited the churches and buildings scattered in the area.

The old basilica housed Juan Diego's cloak until 1974. A museum stood not far from the small old chapel erected on the same spot where the apparition happened. There were many exhibits in the museum. I lingered in a room full of paintings that portrayed the Virgin of Guadalupe. The painters had tried to make a copy of the original image, but none of them had been able to reproduce it perfectly. I then stood in front of a photograph that was an exact copy of the original and had been approved by the ecclesiastic organs. While I was admiring the copy, I heard a voice behind me.

"Who knows what the number eight symbolizes?" asked a man who was leading a group and had the air of being a professor.

Nobody in his group answered his question. "The number eight symbolizes the infinite," I answered.

"Exactly!" said the professor. "Now look at Mary's pink robe. There are eight four-leaf clovers on it."

Yes, I thought, *the Virgin Mary is infinite, beyond space and time. She always has been and always will be. It means that she was on the Hill of Tepeyac long before the Spanish came to Mexico, even though she was worshipped under a different name.*

I left Mexico City and returned to Merida, where I stayed for a few days. Then, I returned to Enna.

Chapter Twenty-Two
The Forum

Once I finished acting the most salient episodes of my life, our director, Paolo, went on stage.

"Now is the time for our debate," he said, addressing the audience. "Usually, when we go to the theater or to the cinema, or when we watch a TV forum, we are passive onlookers. I recognize that mass media, movies, and theatrical performances are a good source of information. In particular, theater has a cathartic function, for it purifies our mind and soul, but I want the members of the audience to be part of the play in my theater, not just passive onlookers. For this reason, whenever I direct a play, there is always a debate at the end. Therefore, if anyone in the theater room wants to say something, they can stand up and speak loudly."

A few minutes of absolute silence followed. It seemed that the play had left the members of the audience indifferent, but someone sitting in the last row raised his arm and asked for permission to speak. Paolo nodded to him.

I knew that man. He had been my first playmate. His father, Michele Macaluso, had run a shoe repair workshop in a room that my father had rented out to him. He was known as the packsaddle repairer, because besides repairing shoes, he also fixed packsaddles for donkeys and mules. He was a stout man, despite the fact that he led a sedentary life, and always wore a cap. In fact, I had never seen him without one. His mustache was so thick that you couldn't see his lips.

There was just an inner door to separate his workplace from my home. I used to cross that door and talk with him. He was kind to me, despite the lawsuit he had against my father, who had given him notice to vacate. On one of the walls of the room stood a large portrait of a mustachioed man. On the opposite wall were pinned smaller posters that portrayed people holding red flags.

"Who is that man?" I asked one day when I opened the door.

"You don't know him? He is the most powerful man in the world. His name is Joseph Stalin. He is my idol."

"The Americans are much more powerful," I replied. "They have the atomic bomb, which can wipe out your Stalin at any moment."

"The Soviet Union has nuclear weapons as well. Furthermore, Stalin's scientists have invented a lethal ray that can bring down enemy jet aircraft. One day, communism will also triumph in Italy, and social injustice will come to an end. Everybody will be given a house and a land to cultivate. There will no longer be private property, because everything will belong to the State."

I was just a child and couldn't understand politics, but his words and enthusiasm enchanted me. So, whenever I could, I went to his workshop and listened to him.

"When the working class takes power in Italy, the churches will be confiscated and converted into public offices," he said one day.

"There are no churches in communist countries?" I asked.

"Not many, as Stalin has converted most of them into swimming pools, gyms, and public offices. A few churches have been razed to the ground, like the Cathedral of Christ the Savior in Moscow. Stalin will build the Palace of the Soviets on that site, which will be the tallest building in the world!"

Undoubtedly, that shoe repairer was an ardent communist, but also a good person. After he was evicted and I couldn't meet him anymore, I appreciated his good heart, because despite the lawsuit against my father, he never mentioned it whenever I chatted with him, nor did he speak badly of my father.

When he died, the priest denied permission for his body to be taken into the church. At that time, communists were excommunicated and excluded from the sacraments. He couldn't receive Holy Communion, Extreme Unction, or a Catholic funeral. It came as a great blow to his family members, because his wife and children were Catholic. His body was taken stealthily from his home to the graveyard. Only a few relatives, comrades, and family members were present at his burial.

Now, in the small Church of Santa Croce, his son Gino was questioning me. His frame was similar to his father's. He also wore a mustache and a cap. He stood up and started off his speech by attacking my research on the afterlife.

"I want to know what you have discovered after traveling across the world for so long. You have just wasted your money, or more accurately, the money your grandfather left to you. You had better give alms instead of inquiring into life after death. There is nothing after death! You are just a stupid man!"

Hearing his fiery words, I flushed with embarrassment. I wanted to interrupt him, but Paolo shook his finger.

Then Gino went on with his tirade. "Religion is just the fruit of alienation. It is not God that creates man; it is man that creates God! Therefore, God as an independent reality doesn't exist. In the course of history, the priestly class has always enjoyed privileges. Many priests are billionaires, and the Vatican is the richest state in the world. Over the years, civil power has been allied with ecclesiastic power. During Fascism, the Catholic Church, instead of fighting dictatorship, supported it. And now, even in our little Enna, the party in power is just the Christians, while our glorious Communist Party is relegated to being the opposition. I want to know what politics and religion have to share!"

There were a few members of the audience who belonged to the Christian Party. They quivered with rage, grumbled, and wanted to intervene, but Paolo managed to calm the audience down. There were also a few priests who knew that it was not true that the Catholic Church had backed Nazi-Fascism and raised their arm to intervene, but Paolo also asked them to hold on a few minutes.

"Thank you for your contribution to the discussion, Gino," Paolo said. "I have appreciated your speech, because it has pointed out a few real issues. As for me, I believe in God just by faith. My faith is not blind but reasoned and based on the Holy Scriptures. I cannot imagine that those who wrote the Holy Scriptures were gullible. Certainly, the Evangelists gathered accurate information before writing their Gospels. Matthew, Mark, Luke, and John actually reported that Jesus died and was resurrected, and this is proof that we human beings are made not just of material flesh, but also of some kind of energy different from the body, which is subject to deterioration. However, this is just my opinion.

"Now, before going on, let Vincenzino answer Gino's questions."

"Thank you," I said, turning to Paolo who, waving his hand, reminded me not to argue. "Every now and then I have the sensation of having lived a previous life in an Eastern country. In the winter, when I get out of bed in the morning, I go to the bathroom to wash my face with warm water. In that moment, I feel as if I have done a similar action in another life between the eighteenth and nineteenth centuries while I was in a hotel or guesthouse room in a country, which might be Russia. I see myself dressed in the clothes in fashion at that time. Russia has always had a special attraction for me."

"There is no other life!" interrupted Gino, raising his voice and getting worked up. "Many religions," he continued, "believe in reincarnation, but this is a groundless assumption. Can you give me proof that we are reincarnated into another body after our death?"

His question bewildered me, and I didn't know what to answer, then I answered Gino with another question. "Do you think we come from nothingness at the time of our birth?"

"Don't be ridiculous, Vincenzino! We come from the zygote, which is the organism resulting from the union of your mother's egg and your father's sperm. Both egg and sperm have their own energy and DNA that transmits the hereditary characteristics from your parents to you. There is no soul, no previous life! When we die, our energy comes to an end, and we disappear into the same thin air from where we came."

Gino's words were so crude that they made the saliva dry up in my mouth. I was seized by the doubt that he might be right. Actually, believing in life after death could be considered an escape from reality. I didn't know what to answer. Then I pulled myself together and tried to digress.

"Before answering your question, Gino, I want you to listen to my travel to Moscow, which is the capital of what once was the Soviet Union, of which you are so nostalgic."

"Okay. Tell me about your trip to Moscow. I am all ears and eager to learn something more that I don't already know about Russian culture," said Gino with a sneer and cool irony.

Chapter Twenty-Three

Moscow

Some time ago, I got close to the Buddhist religion, specifically to a branch of it that made reference to the teachings of a great monk who lived in the north of India around the tenth century AD. A Tibetan monk, who belonged to this Buddhist branch, wanted to export these traditional teachings to Western countries, and for that purpose he created a center in Southern Ireland.

From that tiny seed, in the span of twenty-five years, the center had grown to become eight hundred scattered throughout the world. A real surprising growth! The Tibetan Buddhist monk had not established a center in Russia yet, but he had made contact with a Muscovite who wanted to spread Buddhism in his country.

I had already visited Buddhist centers in Ireland and in America, and now I was eager to get in touch with that Russian man. What attracted me to Russia was not only my passion for travel and the desire to spy out new countries, but also my want to collect data to understand whether religions are just opium for the people or if they are genuine.

I succeeded in getting the name and address of the Russian man that was training to become a Buddhist teacher, and I immediately sent him a letter manifesting my wish to visit his city for a month between December and January. I received his answer nearly immediately.

You are welcome to Russia! My name is Igor. Attached, I send you the Cyrillic alphabet. The knowledge of Cyrillic characters will be particularly useful to you, as in Moscow we don't have signs written in Latin letters. You can come to Moscow anytime, whenever you wish. You will be my guest. You don't have to pay anything for your accommodations.

Thank you, but I don't want to impose on your kindness," I replied. "I would be glad if you could find a small apartment for me where I can stay for a month. Please let me know what I need to do to get a visa from the Russian Embassy."

He sent me a formal invitation to go to Russia. I then went to the Russian Consulate in Palermo and got my visa easily.

A few days before my departure, I received another letter from Igor:

Dear Vincenzino,

I got good accommodations for you. During your stay in Moscow, you will live in an apartment that belongs to a friend of mine. The apartment is very comfortable and is located in a Soviet-style building. From there you will enjoy an amazing view of Moscow.

I arrived at the airport in Moscow at five o'clock in the morning. Igor was waiting for me at the exit. He was a man about fifty years old, as tall as me. His hair was darker than mine, and his dark eyes gave him a look of wildness. Our meeting was warm. I got into his car, and he drove me to the apartment I had rented. It was located near Sheremescaya Street, on the fourteenth floor of a building the stamp of which was markedly communist. The entrance, elevators, and rooms had a Spartan air.

In the evening, Igor picked me up, and we went to visit a friend of his named Arkion. "Once Arkion was a great violinist," Igor said. "He underwent a surgical procedure on his left hand and can no longer play his violin well. Now he is meeting with many difficulties in his life."

"What does he do to make a living?" I asked.

"From time to time, someone calls him to play in a band. He also gives a few violin lessons. He is a good teacher indeed!"

All three of us then moved to another area of Moscow to meet one of Arkion's friends. She was a French woman named Caroline and who had lived in Moscow for fifteen years. The building where she lived was quite old, but her apartment had recently been remodeled. The wooden parquet floor was scattered with toys for her three pets that lived with her: two cats and a small dog, named Julienne.

"Julienne belongs to that breed of dogs best loved by Tsarina Caterina," Caroline said. "Over time, the size of the breed has been reduced. Julienne is smaller than my cats, but he is very smart and sensitive. He looks like a human being."

We took a seat in the living room. Several musical instruments were hung on the walls. Some of them were rare and typical of Russia. Arkion took something similar to a mandolin in his hands.

"This is not an Italian mandolin," he said. "This is Russian! It is less convex than the Italian one."

There was another instrument similar to a harmonium, but it had a crank on one end and a small keyboard in the middle.

Now and then, Arkion stroked Julienne and played with him or tried some other instrument. Igor and Caroline chatted in Russian.

"We're talking about Cossack music," said Caroline, turning to me.

"I adore Cossacks!" said Igor. "They have traditions, myths, and chants that go back to the dim and distant past. Their music is very deep, and their traditions are uncontaminated. Their task is to protect the Russian borders. You can even find Cossacks in Vladivostok! At the time of the Bolshevik Revolution, half of them sided with the tsar. Over time, many Cossacks have been killed off because they didn't want to give up their traditions."

Before we parted, she and I exchanged telephone numbers. Then she drew a map that I could use to reach her house without getting lost.

The next day, I set off from my apartment and, using my map, easily located her apartment. We only stayed a few minutes at her home, just long enough to drink a cup of tea. Then we walked to her friend's house. It was a painter's studio; two painters shared the same room.

That evening, only one of the painters was in the room. His name was Oleg. He had a flowing reddish beard, was blue-eyed, and not very tall. Overall, he gave the impression of being a man who wants to live his life without having problems or straining himself to get ahead. The room was cluttered with colored tubes and paintbrushes. We sat around a small table.

After a few minutes, a lady taller than Oleg appeared. She was his wife and a painter as well. She cleared away the brushes and paint colors and laid two trays down on the table. On one she had put some salmon and another kind of fish that was a lake fish typical of Russia. On the other tray she'd put a cabbage, a vegetable pie, some bread, pistachios, and chocolate candies.

Another French lady, with her Russian husband and an Orthodox priest, joined us. Oleg showed everybody his paintings. One of them portrayed some people who were busy in a kitchen.

"We are three families that live in the same house and share the kitchen. In Russia, it is normal for families to live together. Is it the same in Italy?"

"I don't think so," I answered.

Meanwhile, the Orthodox priest reminded Caroline to come to church on Christmas Eve. "We'll go together!" Caroline said, turning to me.

"I think Christmas has gone," I said. "Today is January third."

"Orthodox Christmas happens on a different day. In Russia, we celebrate Christmas on January seventh, exactly nine months after the Archangel Gabriel told Mary that she would conceive Jesus. It is the most important holiday in Russia."

I thought it strange that while Communism wanted to suppress religion, Christmas was the most important holiday in Russia. Apparently, Karl Marx failed in trying to convince people that religion is just opium for the masses.

Caroline and I went to a large Orthodox church on Christmas Eve. I noticed that there were no pews. There were just a few benches around the walls for people with disabilities.

The Mass lasted about three hours, and the congregation stood the entire time. Orthodox rites are completely different than those in the Latin church. When the Mass was over, the priest invited Caroline and me to have dinner at his home. Starting on November 27, the members of the Orthodox Church had been fasting for forty days, and now it was the time to break the long period of fasting.

The priest's house was close by the church, and a table had been set for a few intimate friends. Caroline was one of the priest's closest friends. We ate every kind of food throughout the night: meat, cakes, salad, fruit, and above all we drank a lot of vodka. It was an unforgettable night.

Meanwhile, I got used to living in Moscow and decided to visit the monuments and places of that fantastic city by myself. By taking the subway, which was not far from my apartment, I got off near Red Square. It was a place that I had seen many times on TV during the Soviet Union's parades.

I entered the square by passing through an archway. On the opposite side, I saw the breathtaking view of Saint Basil's Cathedral. It had been built by order of Tsar Ivan Vasilyevich, also known as Ivan the Terrible, to commemorate the conquest of Kazan and Astrakhan. It is the symbol of Russian art and culture. Legend says that when the Ivan the Terrible saw the masterpiece, he was so impressed with its beauty that he ordered that the architects who had designed it be blinded so that they could not build something similar again.

The entire Kremlin area is full of masterpieces. Even the walls and towers of the Kremlin are works of art. Not far from there is the Cathedral of Christ the Savior, which is the tallest Orthodox church in the world. It stands by the bank of the Moskva River. It was rebuilt after the fall of the Berlin Wall. It had been razed to the ground by Stalin, who had planned to build the Palace of the Soviets on its site.

Stalin couldn't carry out his plan, and now the Cathedral of Christ the Savior stands to signify that it is impossible to suppress religion, which is rooted in the human heart.

Chapter Twenty-Four
The Ending of the Play

The atmosphere in Santa Croce Church warmed up. Now there were two opposing parties: the spiritualists and the materialists.

A young man from the spiritualist party raised his hand and asked to speak. Paolo nodded yes and invited him to introduce himself. He was a player on Enna's rugby team. He was curly-haired, about two meters tall, and as sturdy as a tree trunk. As soon as he stood up, the girls in the audience turned towards him, mesmerized by his figure.

"My name is Giuliano, and I have something to say about the subject matter."

"You are allowed to talk as long as you like!" said Paolo.

"Whenever I want to discover something new and never unveiled before, I picture a man lost in the desert. He is thirsty and wanders the dunes under a scorching and merciless sun. He needs some water to survive and hopes to find an oasis to quench his thirst. Suddenly, he sees a pond in the distance. He quickens his pace to get to the oasis as soon as possible, but once he gets close, the oasis disappears because it was just a mirage and not real water.

"He sees more mirages as he continues walking. What to do? He is tempted to give up and surrender to his ill luck, but he is a man of faith. He has faith in good luck and is sure that sooner or later he will find real water. He walks and walks, dune after dune, until finally he finds a real oasis. His faith has saved him."

That young man in his twenties, besides being a handsome boy, was endowed with intelligence as well. In spite of his young age, he'd expressed ideas worthy of a theologian.

"What is the meaning of what you said?" asked one of the materialists who wanted to contradict him.

"The meaning," answered the rugby player, "is that everything is a projection of our inner being. If we really want to achieve an end, we must have faith in ourselves and in God. Without faith, you will be a loser. As for the question if there is life after death, there are two possible answers: either be an agnostic or act as a person of faith. The latter, as happened to the man who wandered across the desert, has the real possibility to find the oasis, which is God."

After the young man finished talking, I had the impression that the conversation was about to become a political argument, which I wanted to prevent. In fact, the theme of the forum was about life after death; politics had nothing to do with the issue. However, Paolo was the director, and it belonged to him to steer the direction of the debate.

A member of the Christian Party turned to Gino. "The communists have been persecuting the opponents of the regime and sending them to concentration camps in Siberia. Only Christians have shown tolerance through the years."

"That is not true!" answered a member of the left-wing party. "Christians have been persecutors as well. After Emperor Constantine liberalized their religion, Christians became intolerant of pagans. They persecuted the heathens and killed them. The classic example of pagan persecution is Hypatia, a Greek scientist in Egypt who was killed by Christian monks."

"That episode belongs to the distant past. We don't know how things really happened," answered one of the Christians.

"I can mention more recent instances of intolerance from the Catholics," retorted a member of the Socialist Party. "They persecuted the heretics, whose only fault was thinking differently from the Catholic Orthodoxy. They were burnt at the stake and even tortured to wring confessions out of them."

"Nowadays," said a priest who was sitting in the audience, "the Catholic Church is tolerant and deeply respectful of religious freedom. What matters is the now, not the past. Yes, the Catholic Church has made some mistakes in the course of its long history, but that doesn't mean that it is not a sound institution."

The discussion went on for hours. The main political parties in Enna argued about things that had nothing to do with the theme of our play.

Gino raised his arm and asked to talk. "I want to know," he said, turning to me, "what is your opinion, Vincenzino? You have been researching for all your life. What have you found? Tell me something about the hereafter."

"I cannot give you the answer, Gino, because I don't know how to respond. Maybe saints, yogis, or mystics know the truth, but not me," I said.

The mayor of Enna was in the audience and asked to show the new city plans. He got on stage, followed by a few city planners.

"As you can see from the relief map," said the mayor, "many churches are doomed to be demolished. Actually, we have sixty-four churches in Enna, but a good half of them are useless because there are no priests to take care of them. Therefore, they will be razed. Where there were churches, new squares, greens, and broad streets will be built. I will turn Enna into a modern city!"

I turned to the mayor, dumbfounded. Apparently, there was not much difference between what had been done by Stalin in Soviet Union and our rulers. I looked at the map and couldn't spot the Church of Santa Croce.

"What about our church?" I asked in a feeble voice.

"It will be demolished!" answered the mayor in a harsh tone.

The news gave rise to grumbling in the audience and in the actors, but there was nothing to do to save our small church. A resolution for demolition had been taken by the city council. A new, large street would be built where our glorious old tiny Church of Santa Croce once stood.

The loss of our cultural heritage is the toll that must be paid for progress, I thought.

As soon as Paolo heard the mayor's words, his face turned pale. He had spent most of his life taking care of the Church of Santa Croce, and now the news that it would be razed distressed him as if he had lost a member of his family.

Four more actors should have performed after me, but Paolo didn't have the strength to go on with the play. He came on stage, his eyes misty, and couldn't contain his emotion, but he found the strength to address the audience.

"I thank you all for attending our play. After Vincenzino, a few more actors should have gone on, but the news that our meeting place will be wiped out doesn't give me enough strength to keep directing the play."

Little by little, the members of the audience left. They all had a hangdog look. An usher put out the candles that had formed the number eight. The two musicians got up and left the stage, carrying their instruments. The actors also headed for the exit. Paolo left the church last and closed the front gate behind him.

I don't know how it happened, but I didn't have enough strength to get out, and they left me inside the church. They'd forgotten about me! I remained alone in the darkness. I had the feeling of being paralyzed.

How was it possible that the scenery changed all of a sudden? Up to a few minutes ago, I was acting on stage, and the church was full of light and the atmosphere cheerful. Now everything had disappeared: the church, the stage, the actors, our director, the audience, and the candle-lit number eight that symbolized the infinite in Paolo's mind. Everything was over!

I suddenly thought that the change from life to death is sudden and unexpected—but I had discovered nothing about the hereafter.

I could not see anything in the darkness. I heard hammering outside. I had the impression that someone was sealing the front door from the outside. I wanted to cry and tell the hammerer that I was still alive and inside the church, but nobody could hear my voice. The church had turned into a coffin for me. I could not breathe or see anything. For a moment, I was seized by the terror that the materialists might be right: there is nothing after death!

Then I recalled the rugby player's speech. The only way for me to survive was through my faith.

Though I was sinking down, I continued to hold out to the last. I was sure that the infinite universal love energy which permeates all living beings on Earth would not forsake me.

"Always remember, Vincenzino, that the universe is ruled by an immense source of love, which cherishes even the tiniest creatures. You must conform to it in your life!" Sebastiano once told me while we were admiring the starry sky from the terrace of our house in Pollicarini.

Yes, I have to trust the universal love energy which is so powerful that it can get my soul out of this goddamn coffin. And now I can realize that my soul always guided my life in the right direction like a lantern in the dark night, I thought.

By having this faith, I saw a faint glimmer of light coming from the street door. It was not a mirage! It was a real trail of light. I followed it to see what would happen.

We'd like to know if you enjoyed the book. Please consider leaving a review on the platform from which you purchased the book

Lightning Source UK Ltd.
Milton Keynes UK
UKHW010643210421
382364UK00001B/21